MW01154411

Travelin' Man

The Intrigue and Adventures of Spence Harrington

TRAVELIN' MAN

The Intrigue and Adventures of Spence Harrington

LOUHON TUCKER

authorHOUSE®

AuthorHouse™
1663 Liberty Drive
Bloomington, IN 47403
www.authorhouse.com

Travelin' Man is a work of fiction. All of the names, characters, places, events, and incidents portrayed in this novel are either the product of the author's creation and imagination or are used fictitiously. Any resemblance to actual persons, living or dead, business establishment, organizations, places or locales is entirely coincidental.

Published by AuthorHouse, First Edition, May 2019

ISBN: 978-1-5462-6527-6 (sc)
ISBN: 978-1-5462-6526-9 (hc)
ISBN: 978-1-5462-6525-2 (e)

Library of Congress Control Number: 2018912611

Print information available on the last page.

This book is printed on acid-free paper.

Dedicated to those forever young in spirit
and yearning for the next adventure.

May you always follow your dreams!

Travelin' Man

The Intrigue and Adventures of Spence Harrington

CHAPTER 1

Zurich, Switzerland
Three Months Earlier

Yan Feng, a stealthy informant, carefully made his way along the streets of the old section of Zurich, past the nightclubs and restaurants and past the ladies of the night with their enticing offers. No offer could distract him from the wealth he was about to receive. He was less than six blocks away from the meeting he had arranged with the American agents.

The exchange was to occur at an American-style restaurant located a block east of the Bahnhofstrasse, Zurich's famous upscale and lively shopping street. Feng had visited the restaurant a week earlier to scout out the location. The restaurant was noisy and boisterous, a perfect place for the meeting. He had returned again, late one evening after closing hours, to finalize the mechanics for the careful transfer of the highly sensitive information now in his possession—financial information of such a nature that in the wrong hands it could undermine world economies and potentially lead to the overthrow of certain governments friendly to the United States. How he had obtained the documents was not important. The fact he possessed the documents, and the fact that no one other than the American agents knew the information was missing, was all that mattered.

As he walked along the streets through the occasional dark shadows of the late evening, he was gripped with fear as he became aware that he was being followed. Now, however, the distance was short, and the restaurant was in sight, less than half a block away. He could hear the American music as one of the departing guests exited the front entrance.

But just as he increased his pace, he felt a terrible pain in his back. It took him a moment to realize he had been shot.

He could hear footsteps closing in the distance. He knew he was beginning to lose consciousness, but help was just inside the restaurant. He knew he must reach the restaurant, or the fruits of his efforts and his life would be lost. Forcing his body forward, he made it just inside the restaurant and then collapsed.

The US Treasury agents and their Swiss counterparts raced to his prone body to provide assistance. As the lead American agent bent down near the body, Feng mustered the last of his strength to pull the agent close. He whispered to the agent ever so softly and then died.

CHAPTER 2

The American agents had been told the general nature of the documents but not the specifics or the detailed plans contained within. The documents must be located. It was in the national interest of both the United States and two of its key allies to obtain the documents.

However, a week had now passed since the death of the informant in Zurich, and the best and most creative minds from the secret service agencies of at least three countries had been stymied. No one had been able to decipher the dying informant's whispered last words.

Having exhausted all available internal resources, the director of the US Treasury Department began to again search for options. He then recalled having been successful in another seemingly unsolvable case when he had utilized the off-book services of a shadow resource.

Through carefully guarded channels, he contacted and solicited the assistance of Spencer Harrington. The director knew the uniqueness of the challenge, not to mention the fact that the best minds in two of the best-resourced agencies in the world had not been able to interpret the dying words, would pique Harrington's interest.

"Spencer, this is Garrin Bischoff. We need your help."

"Director, it has been some time. How can I be of service?"

Bischoff quickly summarized the situation. "Our agents had arranged to purchase some extremely valuable stolen documents. The meet was to have occurred in an American-style restaurant in Zurich. However, the informant was shot by an unknown assailant, staggered into the restaurant, and died before he could disclose the location of the documents. In his last moments, he whispered what our agent understood to be, *'Du lang,'* paused, and with his final breath said, *'Lang du,'* and then he died."

"I would guess that you have been unable to decipher the meaning of *'Du lang,' 'Lang du,'*" Harrington offered.

"That's right. We thought the wording might be some Chinese dialect, Vietnamese, or perhaps some Far Eastern language, but no luck. We have had the world's top linguists, code-breaking cryptologists, language translation experts, and computer permutation specialists working to solve the meaning of the words, but it has continued to elude them."

Harrington thought for a moment. Indeed, it was a challenge worthy of his time and that of his organization. "I'll help if I can," he responded. "My standard fee will apply."

"Same as last time?" the director asked.

"Yes, the equivalent of $10 million US, payable in Swiss francs." A sizable fee, no question, for a short, concentrated effort with no guarantee of success. But Spencer had recognized early on that placing a high value on his services added to his mystique and to the perspective that he could provide unique solutions for unique problems.

"Done!" replied the director.

"I'll catch a flight tonight for Zurich. Can you provide access to the restaurant for me tomorrow and to the work that has been performed to date?" Harrington asked.

"Consider it done. But I need whatever you can come up with within forty-eight hours."

"Not much time."

"I know, but I waited too long to bring you in on this. It's the best I can do," the director said.

Spencer Harrington arrived in Zurich the next morning and immediately went to the restaurant. After checking out the location, he met with the US Treasury agents in charge of the case and reviewed the files and work that had been performed by the various specialists trying to crack the meaning of *"Du lang," "Lang du."*

He was as puzzled and stumped as were the experts. He telephoned Ginger Martin, his very bright, spirited, and trusted assistant, and related the case to her. He knew her curiosity and competitiveness would create a high level of interest by her in the case. He respected her insights and judgment and knew that she might be helpful in finding an answer to the puzzle.

After detailing the situation, he summarized his observations. "Ginger, it certainly would seem to be almost unsolvable. But as we both know, a dying man would want the clue he was leaving to be one that could be solved. So it is solvable."

He paused and then inquired, "What could we have missed? Any thoughts?"

"Sometimes, the most likely answer is the most simple," she replied. "Walk me again through the information."

Harrington obliged her and carefully made a point to include everything from his notes. Ginger then asked two questions, which Spence quickly answered.

"You know this could be so relatively simple that a four-year-old could solve," Ginger observed.

Spence, somewhat agitated that Ginger could think that the solution could be so simple, was reminded of the great line from the 1933 movie *Duck Soup,* starring the Marx Brothers. One of the characters says, "It's so simple a four-year-old could figure it out." The lead character, frustrated, then says, "Well, then go find me a four-year-old." With the classic movie line in mind, Spence responded, "So go find me a four-year-old! I'm stumped!"

Ginger laughed. "That may not be necessary. I think I have the answer."

She then explained to Spence her reasoning and logic.

He replied, "I'll be dammed. I think you may have it! It's sure worth a try."

CHAPTER 3

It was a day later, and Spencer Harrington was on the telephone with the director. "Harrington, I am amazed again. Using the information you provided, our agents have recovered the stolen documents intact."

"Glad to be of help, Director," Harrington replied.

"Where do want your payment directed?" the director asked.

Harrington provided the wire transfer instructions and was about to end the conversation when the director said, "So tell me, just how did you figure out the meaning of *'Du lang,' 'Lang du'?"*

"Trade secrets." Spence responded with no intent to explain or suggest to the director how relatively easy it had been to crack the message.

"Come on Spencer, for ten million dollars, at least I should get a peek at how you could solve this enigma when the world's greatest criminal agencies were stumped."

Spence knew extremely well the value of expertise, experience, common sense and specialized skills and the unique abilities he and his team had developed and refined. As much as he wanted to demonstrate how his team, that being Ginger, had outsmarted the accumulated skills of the international agencies assigned to the case, Spence was not about, in anyway, to devalue the solution that had been provided to the US Treasury. There had been no objection to pay his price this time, but if they knew how quickly Ginger had deciphered the coded message, they might not be quite as eager to pay such a price the next time they or some other group needed the unique assistance of Spence and his team.

"For another ten million," Spence laughingly started to say before being cut-off by the director. "Spence, you know there is no way. I will just have to continue to be amazed at your abilities to provide answers. We got value for the price we paid—thanks again!"

An hour or so after the conversation with the director of the US Treasury, Spence received a telephone call from Ginger. "The Swiss francs have been received. I assume the Feds are happy?"

"They are ecstatic!" he replied.

"So did you tell them how it was solved?" she asked. Knowing Spencer, a kindred soul, she was highly certain of what he would say.

"No, although the director, as you might guess, was hell-bent for leather to find out." Spencer laughed. "If we were to tell him, there would be less mystique attributed to us!"

"I agree," Ginger said as she broke out in her spirited laughter.

A few days later, upon return to his home office in Vermont, Spencer and Ginger recalled the success with the Zurich puzzle. "Remind me of your two questions again," he said with a tease in his voice.

"Well, since you insist!" Ginger teased, having waited with great anticipation for the opportunity for further acknowledgment and appreciation.

She began. "Let's see. You had said that the restaurant where the meeting was to occur was at an American-style restaurant." She paused, savoring the opportunity to relish in the knowledge of the not-too-distant solution to the puzzle. "And then I first asked, 'What was on the menu?'

"Yes, and I said, 'It was an *American Graffiti* sort of place. The menu consisted of hamburgers, fries, chocolate malts, and that sort of thing. A 1960s theme.'"

"Right," Ginger said. "And then my second question followed. 'Was there a jukebox in the restaurant?'"

"I recall thinking, '*So why do you care if there was a jukebox*?' But as soon as you explained the importance of the jukebox, I suspected that you had solved the puzzle. And you sure had. You rascal!"

She could tell he was really glad for her. But come to think of it, she thought, *He was probably also pleased with that bundle of Swiss francs.'* But she also sensed—no, she knew—that losing to her would do nothing but cause his competitiveness to be even more formidable. She smiled to herself.

"Well, you do get some of the credit," Ginger said, tossing a backhanded compliment. "You said that a dying man would want the clue to be simple to understand. My guess was that the experts and specialists, as they tend to do, just overanalyzed the clue."

"A tip of the hat, nevertheless." Spencer said in respect, and then laughed. "Of course, it didn't hurt that you love '60s music!"

"Yeah, and I probably benefited by not seeing the words and just hearing over the telephone from you the phonetic pronunciation," she added, and then further explained, "With the word '*do lang*' bouncing around in my head and then the fact that there was a jukebox in the restaurant, the next thought that came into my mind was the lyrics from the 1960s hit '*He's so fine*' by the Chiffons: '*do-lang, do-lang, do-lang; do-lang, do-lang, He's so fine* ..."

"What a mind!" Spence said in jest.

"So, I considered the clue again, '*do-lang, lang do*' and eureka! I had it. Play the do-lang song on the jukebox CD backwards!"

"And sure enough," Spencer interjected, "there was a secret message imbedded on that particular CD, that when played backward provided the instructions to the location of the stolen documents." He paused and with admiration said, "Ingenious!"

"Me or the puzzle!?" Ginger said with a sly smile.

"You continue to amaze me!" Spence quietly observed.

"Why is that?" Ginger smiled and questioned as she fished for an expansion of his compliment.

"Well, I had no idea that you were such an aficionado of 60's music," he said with his eyebrows raised and a mock expression of admiration.

"I read a lot." Ginger playfully responded, knowing that her standard answer to such questions would probably not suffice with Spence in this instance.

"No, really," he went on. "How did you so quickly pick up on the do lang, do lang lyrics?"

Ginger paused as if about ready to reveal some behind the curtains deep secret and then began laughing. "Ok, if you promise not to laugh too hard!"

"I promise!" Spence said half-assuring in an attempt to convince her that any secrets were safe with him.

"Promises made, promises kept! She responded with the reminder.

Spence nodded acknowledgment as he smiled.

"Ok, I once knew this guy who loved music from the 50's, 60's and 70's. He even created a game which he called "pop classics" and the players would guess the name of a song and the artist as quickly as possible when the song was played on the radio—something like when Dick Clark had the name that tune on American Bandstand." Ginger paused, "I played the game often."

"I see." Spence said as he half-believingly smiled, "there must be more to this."

"No, other than this guy was someone who I first would never have guessed was into malt shop music. But, it turns out he was a cool guy with wide-ranging interests coupled with an ingrained, highly competitive nature. I loved the competitive contests as we engaged in the pop classics games and with each game, I became more and more knowledgeable with the music of that era."

Spence couldn't resist. "What happened to the guy?

Ginger just smiled with a twinkle in her eye, as if to say 'I'll tell you more—sometime—and then said, "we stay in touch."

Guessing that he would not learn more at the moment or probably anytime soon, Spence finished the original compliment and commented, "Well, hats off to the fellow because all of your time playing pop classics certainly served you well in this case!"

The twinkle remained in Ginger's eyes as she smiled with fond recollections of the past, "Yes, time well-spent!"

As Spence's thoughts began to turn to other matters, he turned back to Ginger, "I'm not completely sure I believe your story, but what I do know is that you cracked the case! Congratulations again! Job well done."

As Spence and Ginger sat around the crackling fireplace in Spence's Vermont office, which provided a stunning view of graceful Lake Champlain and the Adirondack Mountains beyond to the west, Spence raised his glass of wine and ever so lightly touched Ginger's glass of gin and tonic. "To us. May there be many more puzzles and challenges to solve and adventures to experience."

As he lowered his glass, he was reminded of the definition of adventure: "adventure ... a bold unusually risky undertaking; hazardous action of uncertain outcome." He thought to himself, '*that's what makes life so interesting.*'

Spence Harrington was in the business of international crime-solving adventures—the more dangerous and more mysterious, the more interesting and engaging. He had created and had at his disposal vast specialized and well-placed resources. But, one of his greatest resources was the highly-skilled and totally dedicated individuals he had recruited to join with him in his work, with the feisty Ginger Martin being his most-trusted sidekick. Together, they thrived on solving crimes and mysteries that were said to be, or at least prior to their involvement had been, unsolvable.

Before the desperate telephone call from the US Treasure Department regarding the Zurich "situation", Spence and Ginger had most recently very successfully untangled a web that led to a treasure and artifacts that had been long-buried deep below the sea oats covered sand dunes along the Florida coast.

And, that's where they now found themselves. In search of the next challenging, international crime to solve.

Chapter 4

In the background, Spencer Harrington could hear the music from the early sixties song "Travelin' Man," by Ricky Nelson, and, again, the words and the music took him back to the warm summer days as a teenager lying on the grass and clover hillside of his parents' lawn in southern Indiana dreaming of what it might be like to travel to interesting and exotic locations throughout the world. He could again almost feel the warmth of the summer sun of those days filtering through the leaves of the large maple tree, and he could almost smell the fresh and sweet fragrant aroma of the newly cut clover in the field across the gravel road. Those were warm, wonderful days in rural America. They were times that contained recollections he would, in the then distant years, come to treasure.

What a wonderful and exciting life of adventures he had experienced since those carefree days in the early sixties growing up in the rural Indiana countryside with the streams and rolling hills and woods. With a deep fondness and a longing to be able to return to those times, he would often recall those seemingly endless days of playing baseball, working in his uncle's grocery store on Saturdays, and during the summers of his high school years, building friendships that would last a lifetime and learning values that would serve him well in the years ahead.

His friends called him Spence. It was times like this, as he reflected on his past growing up in the innocence of a small

Indiana town, that Spence was amazed at the path his life had taken. As was normally the case, he began to recall some of the many adventures he had experienced (most of those he could share and discuss with only his few trusted confidants). He would recall the exotic locations that he had come to know (far distant places that he could only imagine in those summer daydreams when he was a teenager), the unique individuals he had encountered, the lifestyle he had achieved, the quiet access to power with global reaches and, of course, the intriguing mysteries he had unraveled. He suspected—no, he knew—that his childhood friends and school classmates would marvel at his life if he were to be able to tell them—*if only he could!*

CHAPTER 5

Secluded Estate Overlooking Lake Champlain
Burlington, Vermont Area

The Present

Nestled along the eastern shore of Lake Champlain in northern Vermont is the city of Burlington (more a large town than a city and certainly with the feel of a warm, friendly town) with a population of approximately forty thousand during the summer when the University of Vermont is out of session. During the fall and winter and early spring, with classes in session, the population of the city and immediate surrounding area increases to about fifty-five thousand. Burlington, some would say, and certainly those who love the area (Spence being one of those), is a throwback to those days in America when times were less stressful, and life was more about spending time with friends and enjoying the wonders and the beauty of thc outdoors and realizing the opportunities for outdoor activities that the natural surroundings of an area such as Burlington provides.

Burlington is a postcard location with a beautiful backdrop of majestic Lake Champlain and the Adirondack Mountains to the west and the Green Mountains to the east. In the spring and fall, the heavy wooded areas with the deep forest greens and the wide-variety of meadow flowers is stunningly beautiful. In late fall with the first snow and with the following snowfalls, the area provides an abundance of winter activity opportunities.

Equally appealing to Spence was the independent spirit of the people of Burlington and the surrounding areas of Vermont. A spirit that was reminiscent of the environment his parents had provided that had nurtured and built the foundation of values for Spence as he grew up in Indiana.

Spence felt from his first visit to the Burlington area that, in fact, the Vermont state motto of "Freedom and Unity," and the New Hampshire state motto of "Live Free or Die," with the freedom and independent spirit that the sayings implied, were very descriptive of this part of northern New England.

Spence sensed a yearning for northern New England and often wondered whether this yearning might have been the result of his "early" days spent in New Hampshire. His parents, who were from Indiana, had spent several months living in Manchester while his father was in the armed forces before having been assigned to London. When his father left for the assignment in London, his mother (pregnant with Spence) returned to Indiana, where Spence was born. Shortly after his birth, his mother returned to Manchester with Spence where they spent the next year before returning to Indiana.

Looking out to the west from the windows of his office, located just a few blocks from the University of Vermont, in one of the residential areas on the heavily wooded hillsides overlooking downtown Burlington, there was the scenic Adirondack Mountains of upstate New York some ten miles across the lake. In addition to the natural beauty of the sparkling waters of Lake Champlain, the surrounding lush green mountains, the deep blue summer skies, the white, deep carpets of snow in the winter, and the almost unlimited opportunities for outdoor activities was the fact that Burlington was small enough to provide the relaxed setting that Spence valued when he wanted/needed to get away. But, also Burlington was large enough to provide most of the amenities of modern life and large enough to allow for an individual to be an anonymous entity.

Even today in this post 9-11 world, if you developed the appropriate facade and blended into the background, no one would think to question your real identity, and this was the same in Burlington. It was this last factor that Spence not only appreciated but it was a consideration that was of paramount importance.

The picturesque beauty and relative isolation of Burlington provided an ideal location for Spence. Burlington is separated to the west by Lake Champlain and the mountains of New York, to the north by the sparsely populated lakes and rolling hills region of northern Vermont—a two-hour-plus drive to Montreal—and to the south and east by several hours' drive through the Green Mountains of Vermont.

Spence had first become aware of Burlington some twenty years or so ago when he had researched the area after pondering a pint of Ben and Jerry's ice cream as he devoured the contents; he could not now, with the passage of so many years, recall with certainty, but he had reason to believe that the ice cream was probably "Chunky Monkey," since chocolate was far and away his favorite. He had been looking for a place to base his operations and had thought about and looked into many locations. However, for one reason or another, no place had either met his requirements or had appealed to him.

When he noticed that Ben and Jerry's was located in Burlington, and the marketing on the box of the ice cream packaging had read "made only from the milk of cows from Vermont," something piqued his curiosity as he thought, *What did old Ben and Jerry know about Burlington that caused them to make it their home, and why were they so proud of the area?* He was going to find out, and he was good, very good, at finding out. These investigative skills had provided him with a lifestyle beyond the dreams of most.

With his head lightly cushioned on the pillow of the lounge chair on the deck of his summer home on the wooded hillside overlooking the lake, and his arms and legs, tanned from the past month of outdoor activities and sailing on the lake, gently absorbing the rays of the sun filtering through the leaves of the nearby maple trees, he was again reminded how much he really loved these times when he could appreciate just doing nothing. Occasionally he shifted his head slightly on the pillow to avoid the brightness of the sun as its rays periodically found a new direction through the branches of the tree. A short distance through the trees and down the grassy slope was the lake. Spence could hear the rhythm of the waves lapping against the shore.

Off to the left and down the hill through the pine trees, some fifty yards away, was the boathouse that housed not only his sailboat but also an armored high-powered speedboat. Spence was hopeful that he would never need to use the speedboat for purposes other than pleasure, but experience had taught him many years ago that there was real truth in the philosophy of "better safe than sorry." The boathouse was approximately one hundred yards back from the lake on a hidden narrow inlet that jutted into Spence's property. Even the closest observer from the lake would not notice that the inlet existed. The entrance to the inlet had been well disguised with live bushes and trees that were growing on two large eight-foot-wide wooden, deep, pontoon planters that served as doors. The doors were electronically controlled and could be quickly opened and closed to allow his boat to pass undetected. Since Spence owned all of the property along the natural inlet, and since large leafy trees provided an umbrella over the waters of the inlet, the inlet was quite hidden from view. Even in the winter, with the deep snow cover that normally blanketed this area of northern Vermont, the passage from the lake, as well as the house and boathouse, was well hidden.

The property was actually located on Shelburne Point in Shelburne, a village located just a few miles south of Burlington. Shelburne is the home of the Vermont Teddy Bear Company and also the home of the wonderful Shelburne Farms and the beautiful turn-of-the-century Shelburne Inn, which majestically overlooks Lake Champlain. Shelburne Point is a finger of wooded land that juts out into Lake Champlain. The "Point" contains a number of extremely private estates and secluded properties with stunning views of the lake and of the Adirondack Mountains in the distance on the New York side of the lake. The scenic and highly secluded location was ideal for Spencer Harrington.

Chapter 6

It was a beautiful, bright day, and the waters of Lake Champlain glistened from the midafternoon sun and reflected the various green shades of the surrounding pine forests that hugged the shoreline. As Spencer Harrington stretched on the lounge chair, he could not help but wonder where his next opportunity for adventure would lead. He also recalled the many events and adventures that had brought him to this point in his life. As he lazily watched, through a break in the trees, a sailboat maneuver off in the distance, he was interrupted by the sounds of Ginger and McGinnis. What a pair they were. They were two of his most trusted confidants and friends.

He had known McGinnis for a much shorter time than Ginger. Nevertheless, McGinnis was an equal with Ginger—one of the handful of confidants whose counsel and judgment he trusted and loyalty he treasured. McGinnis was a fun-loving two-year-old English sheepdog. Ginger had given McGinnis to Spence when the dog was just a black and white furry puppy.

And then there was Ginger. What would he do without her?

How best to describe Ginger?

First and foremost, she was not just his executive assistant. She was his trusted friend. Ginger understood and shared his zest for life. She also brought logical constraint in a professional, convincing manner when circumstances required a counterbalance to his unrealistic enthusiasm. Normally, those circumstances arose when Spence allowed his emotions for a project and his appetite for challenge to outweigh the risks associated with the project. Ginger was also a wonderful judge of character and of people. She had protected Spence on several occasions from moving forward with relationships that may have not been in his best interest.

They were a team, and Spence knew, without reservations, that Ginger would always protect their mutual best interests. She shared, and even more importantly, reflected, his integrity and his consideration for others; she also had that uncanny knack of healthy skepticism.

Ginger was thirty-six—a young thirty-six. Her pleasant light-green eyes, sandy almost reddish come-hither hair, lean and appealing facial features with a few light freckles, and her trim five-foot-four-inch frame projected an enduring sense of cheerfulness and energy. Her features caused most of those who came into contact with her to think she was several years younger than her real age. At the same time, her friendly and engaging personality but confident and firm manner signaled that she was not someone to be taken lightly.

The way her firm, proportional breasts seemed to accessorize her blouses certainly did nothing to detract from her appeal.

She had a spirit for adventure, and Spence suspected that in her youth she'd probably been part tomboy and part girl next door—the girl everyone chased but no one had yet caught. Ginger was one of those women with spirit who could be one of the guys but also someone most guys dreamed, at one time or another, of spending time with romantically.

Ginger was one of those women who could leave you wondering what it would be like for her to be attracted to you and what it might be like if she was yours. A pleasant—but quickly passing thought—from time to time for Spence also, but he had too great a respect for her to even let any "what if" thoughts confuse their relationship. He could not let the great relationship they shared change the bond between them. That's not to say that Spence did not enjoy those days when Ginger wore a slightly more revealing blouse. In fact, as he thought about it, he looked forward to those days.

Ginger had grown up in Peggy's Cove, Nova Scotia. Peggy's Cove is a lobster and fishing village an hour or so drive south of Halifax on the North Atlantic coast. There is a strong independent nature to the people of the area and a great appreciation for the natural beauty of the rocky coastline and the scenic landscapes that surround this area of Nova Scotia.

After graduating from the University of Connecticut with a degree in international business and a degree in political science, Ginger was recruited to the London office of Chase Bank, where she had the fortunate opportunity to spend several years specializing in the area of country sector economic forecasting. In this role, she was able to travel extensively on an international basis and developed strong relationships with her counterparts in the bank's offices in various countries around the world. The opportunities and experiences were a dream come true for a young woman from a small town in Nova Scotia who had never left the Halifax area until she left for her freshman year in college.

As the high quality of her work, her insights, quick wit, and strength of character began to be noticed within the higher levels of the bank, she began to receive opportunities for very interesting assignments. With the extensive international knowledge she gained, she also became a very valuable commodity within the bank, and, as a result, her desires for assignment to particular areas of the world were usually quickly granted.

In addition to her time in London, she spent time on assignment (normally a year or so in duration) in Zurich, Singapore, Oslo, and Milan. No one outside the very highest levels of Scotland Yard knew that, because of her cross-border travels and her engaging personality and desire for adventure, she had been recruited to provide secret services throughout the world for the highest levels within Scotland Yard. Her position as an international banker provided an excellent cover.

After her time in Milan, she left the bank and moved to Burlington, where she taught multicurrency risk management and international business courses at the University of Vermont. Teaching provided an opportunity for her to try to forget the love she had lost in Milan, a love that came along once in a lifetime and that never could be completely forgotten. Teaching also gave her the time in Vermont to enjoy and embrace her passion for downhill skiing that had developed during her time in Switzerland and Norway.

It was during one of her skiing weekends in the mountains of Vermont that she met Spence. They had found themselves together on the same chairlift. Although the ride up the mountain had been relatively brief, Ginger and Spence seemed to click from the first moment. The ride had been filled with laughter. So much so that they had challenged each other to see who could be the fastest to reach the midway point down the mountain. They were both surprised to find that the race was a dead-heat, and both quickly respected and admired the competitive spirit of the other.

They found that they both were alone with no other plans or commitments other than their desire to enjoy an invigorating weekend of skiing. Spence had suggested that they ski together for the morning and then have lunch together. Ginger was at first hesitant, having become comfortable, with the passage of time, with being alone. The peaceful, snowy, romantic mountain, unfortunately, gave rise to her thoughts of the love she once, but no longer, had. However, the offer from this handsome new acquaintance was very inviting. She accepted Spence's invitation and found Spence's company not only enjoyable but refreshing.

They had skied to a restaurant not far from the resort, where they were both staying, just as heavy snow had begun to fall. Their table was in front of a crackling fireplace. Because it was likely, due to the weather, that they would not be able to ski the rest of the day, and because they were very much enjoying each other's company, they spent a long relaxing lunch together. In fact, they spent the rest of the weekend together, and they had been together ever since.

The bond that Spence and Ginger shared was based on mutual trust, respect, and an appreciation for each other's depth of character, sense of humor, and spirit for adventure. They had never been lovers, but they shared a deep love and admiration for each other and were protective of each other. Although they were mutually attracted to each other, deep within each was a fear that if they ever let their passions emerge, they would put at risk the wonderful working relationship that had developed. What they were doing was challenging but also very rewarding and great fun. They could not put at risk what they had created.

Spence was fortunate—very fortunate—to have Ginger. He knew that without Ginger his confidence in their international organization would be significantly impaired. As Spence watched the sailboat in the distance, he heard Ginger call out.

"Spence, McGinnis and I are going to walk into town to pick up a few things. Anything we can get for you?"

Spence thought for a moment and called back, "If you happen to pass Gudrun's Bakery, and if they still have any of those Swiss creampuffs, you might pick up a couple."

As the pleasing chatter from Ginger and McGinnis faded into the distance, and they headed off on their adventure, Spence was left alone on this peaceful afternoon. He was surrounded by the clear waters and beautiful woods of Northern Vermont. His thoughts drifted back again to those experiences and opportunities, the outcomes of which had provided for a luxurious lifestyle, and which had formed his interesting, adventuresome, and sometimes dangerous but highly intriguing life.

CHAPTER 7

Some three years earlier, Spence had had the opportunity to have dinner in Chicago with Tucker Wolcott, a friend and business associate who on occasion had been very helpful and who always could be counted on to obtain and provide information on a very discreet basis. In addition, Tucker could be trusted, and he provided valuable insights that Spence had benefited from over the years.

Tucker was one of the several trusted and highly respected, well-placed professionals that Spence had included in his informal network of resources around the world. Tucker Wolcott was president of the highly regarded midmarket, rapidly growing, international investment banking firm of Wolcott & Hamilton Partners LP, located on the northern end of the "Magnificent Mile" in Chicago.

Spence always enjoyed the opportunities, although intentionally quite infrequent, to visit with Tucker for several reasons. First, Spence truly liked Tucker and found his honesty, humor, candor, and absence of political agenda refreshing. Tucker had a unique ability to quickly assess and respond to the information needs presented by Spence. Tucker's ability to tap sources throughout the world and access critical and highly classified information, his quiet but very competitive nature (quite similar to that of Spence), his reserved humor but quick wit that could surprise you at the most unexpected times and certainly surprise those who did not know him (much like a fox in a henhouse), and his sharp mind had intrigued Spence from the first time they had met many years ago.

Second, Tucker Wolcott had an extremely comfortable and interesting home, which Spence was thankful to be allowed to call home on those occasions when he had visited Chicago in recent years. Located on exclusive East Lake Shore Drive (a somewhat secluded area in the heart of the "Gold Coast" of Chicago), Tucker owned the entire fourth floor of a turn-of-the-century residential brownstone building on the tree-lined street overlooking Chicago's famed Oak Street Beach on Lake Michigan. Tucker Wolcott's home was one of the places dotted around the world where Spence could fade away and relax with limited risk he would be found.

East Lake Shore Drive and this quiet, small area of Chicago just to the east of Michigan Avenue (one of the great shopping streets of the world rivaling Orchard Road in Singapore, Oxford Street, and the Knightsbridge area in London, and the famous Bahnhofstrasse in Zurich) reminded Spence of the quiet, wealthy areas of perhaps Switzerland, Australia, or Germany. When Spence thought of the East Lake Shore Drive area and the building where Tucker Wolcott lived, he thought of the Las Vegas motto of recent years: "What happens in Las Vegas, stays in Las Vegas." While not directly applicable, he had the feeling that this area of Chicago was "old money," and everyone's privacy was highly respected.

Lake Shore Drive runs along Lake Michigan and is a major Chicago motorway. However, East Lake Shore Drive is a quiet street with trees bordering both sides. The street is no more than eight or so blocks long and runs east from the storied Drake Hotel on north Michigan Avenue. In less than a two-block walk from Tucker's building, you could be at the Cape Cod Room on the second floor of the Drake Hotel, or you could be headed south on Michigan Avenue to the many other world-class restaurants, hotels, and shopping opportunities.

The Cape Cod Room was a place that Spence thoroughly enjoyed. As the name suggested, the restaurant focused on seafood and had some of the better chowders that he had come across. The Cape Cod Room overlooks Michigan Avenue to the west and Lake Michigan to the north and northeast. The room has dark mahogany paneling with a feeling of richness. Each table is covered with red-and-white-checkered tablecloths, and on each table is a lamp that throws off a warm, golden soft glow. In the entry areas, the walls are covered with the pictures of celebrities from the movies, television, and music, and pictures of political leaders from many parts of the world. The fine food coupled with the wonderful views and the autonomy and privacy that the restaurant provides had just been another reason for Spence to look forward to accepting Tucker Wolcott's standing invitation to spend time at his home.

The snow had begun to fall lightly midway during dinner, and now, as Spence and Tucker left the Cape Rod Room and headed out of the Drake Hotel, they both marveled at the beauty of the falling snow in this bustling city. It was mid-December, and the Christmas lights and decorations sparkled as Spence gazed down the Magnificent Mile south on Michigan Avenue. Growing up in southern Indiana, Spence had loved those times when there had been snow. But those times did not come all that often, and when they did, the snow tended not to last. He had remembered seeing pictures in grade school of the deep and beautiful snow in Switzerland and had dreamed of some day spending time there—just one of the many dreams that had been realized several times over.

It had misted for a short time that evening in Chicago before the temperature had fallen sharply and quickly. As the rain turned to snow, the gently falling but quickly accumulating snow began to cling to everything it touched. As Spence looked about, the scene was somewhat reminiscent of downtown Zurich or perhaps Lucerne during winter with the snow, the multicolored lights, and the people scurrying about from shop to shop.

Tucker knew Spence well enough to be able to tell that Spence was not ready to take the short walk back to Tucker's building.

"Spence, what do you say we take a few minutes and get into the Christmas spirit. Let's walk a few blocks down Michigan Avenue, maybe down to Marshall Fields at Water Tower Place—it's no more than about three blocks south." Marshall Field's was now part of the Macy's empire, but Tucker, like many Chicagoans with great fondness for Marshall Fields, just could not reconcile or accept the change to the Macy's name for this great and longtime Chicago icon.

"Tucker, that would be great. In fact, if you have some time and do not mind, I need to look for a couple of Christmas gifts."

Wolcott laughed and gently needled Spence. "Spence, I thought you must have people who took care of all of that for you!"

Spence laughed. "Well, there are always some things you just have to do yourself."

"Ah ha," Wolcott said, knowing not to push too hard into Spence's professional or personal life but still knowing he was on safe ground, he found the opportunity to needle a bit further. "A couple two or three young ladies, I suspect."

Spence just smiled as they continued walking. In a short time, they reached the entrance to Water Tower Place and Marshall Fields.

Water Tower Place is a multistory shopping mecca in the heart of Chicago's North Michigan Avenue shopping district and provides a wide-ranging selection of high-end, sometimes hard to find, and quite expensive items from around the world. A busy place most of the time, but especially so during the Christmas season as shoppers multiply and families and couples enjoy the beautiful decorations of the season as they ride the glass elevators and escalators, all the time peering out at the excitement that abounds throughout this beautiful building.

As they entered Water Tower Place, Wolcott pointed to the Macy's logo. "Spence, I know things are meant to change, and I embrace change. The changes and movements in the financial markets have provided us both, I would guess, with a strong financial base."

Tucker paused and then continued.

"However, the Marshall Fields name had been a part of Chicago for approximately 150 years, and Marshall Fields has reflected the independent personality of Chicago. With the name change to Macy's, we Chicagoans have lost not only a good friend but also one of the anchors we had clinged to since our childhood days when we marveled at all of the wonders at the flagship store at State and Washington in downtown Chicago."

Spence could see the sadness on Tucker's face as Tucker contemplated the loss of this friend to generations of Chicagoans.

"Well, Spence, let's get you headed toward an outstanding shopping experience. Someday you will be able to say to your grandchildren that you were at one of the great Chicago institutions—which shortly will be no more!"

Tucker provided Spence with general directions and then headed off as he said, "Spence, take your time. I will grab a cup of coffee and find a seat at the Starbuck's on the third floor."

Spence knew what he wanted and welcomed the privacy.

"Tucker, thanks. I should not be long."

Looking for a Christmas gift for Ginger was always a challenge for Spence. For some reason, he seemed to always have less of a problem in deciding on the gifts for her counterparts in France and Australia. He was never sure why.

Spence found the Water Tower Place store directory and headed off in the direction of the store that he had in mind. He quickly found the store. After being shown a number of items, he selected the one that he had envisioned for some time. He had the item wrapped with festive Christmas paper.

He quickly headed off to find Tucker, but he did stop to look around. He realized that Tucker had in fact understated the degree of excitement and the volume of beautiful decorations that

Water Tower Place had to offer. As he watched the multitude of people scurrying about, he was reminded of how oblivious these people were to the dangerous activities that were being schemed throughout the world—activities that might someday affect their lives and disrupt their world. Without the efforts of Spence and perhaps others like him—hopefully, others like him—the day would arrive sooner not later.

Spence found Tucker peacefully enjoying the last of his coffee. They headed for the escalator and took it to the ground floor. As they left Water Tower Place and headed north on Michigan Avenue, they picked up the pace as the snow was becoming heavier, and the wind was whipping around in quick bursts. They reached the Drake Hotel and turned east on East Lake Shore Drive. Within minutes they reached Tucker's building.

Upon entering the building and passing through the unseen RFD screening, they walked to the paneled hallway that hid the entry to the elevator. Tucker pushed the proper sequence on the checkered wooden panel, and the door opened. The elevator was interesting in that it included a padded bench so that you could sit rather than stand while riding. The interior was dark mahogany paneling with mirrors covering the upper portions of the two side walls. The door of the elevator opened, and Tucker and Spence were facing the entryway to Tucker's home. Tucker inserted a security code, and they entered.

Spence had copied some of the features of Tucker's home in his own residences. For instance, the walk-in dual custom-made coolers in the kitchen with heavy oak windows and doors, which had reminded Spence of the cooler in his uncle's store in Indiana where he had worked during the summers of his high school years, had been made an integral part of two of Spence's homes.

"Spence, let's relax and have something that will warm us up from the weather outside."

Tucker led the way into the library/den—a favorite room for Spence. To the right as he entered through the large, heavy, wooden double-doors was a fireplace framed by stone. The floors were of highly polished wood but generously covered with beautiful carpets with pleasing color tones. The room contained a number of very comfortable leather chairs and a large leather couch. Facing the street and looking down on Oak Street Beach were beautiful paneled windows. On the table near one of the windows was a long brass telescope that, on an occasion during one summer visit, Spence had used to catch a glimpse of the attractive young ladies enjoying sunbathing on Oak Street Beach on the shore of Lake Michigan across the street in downtown Chicago. How could you not love this city?

This visit to Chicago was purely social and was a chance to enjoy time with a friend. A friend who Spence knew suspected that there was much more behind his periodic information requests but did not pry into Spence's activities or his whereabouts during the extended periods between their visits, nor did Tucker ever question the reason for the information from Spence.

This had been a particularly enjoyable evening, and they both had enjoyed the soft warmth of their drinks as they relaxed in the deep leather chairs near the fireplace as the flames danced and crackled. They spent the last hour or so exchanging thoughts and views on a wide range of matters of current interest—it would have been interesting and enlightening for most to have been able to listen in to the conversations of these two individuals who had access to the world's financial and political leaders. The conclusion might have been drawn that there is in fact a handful of individuals, known to Spence and Tucker, who either have the ability to influence the lives of ordinary folks or who certainly are striving to achieve such influence.

After having somewhat exhausted their discussions, Tucker looked at the soft glow from the fireplace.

"Spence, I don't think I mentioned that our oldest daughter and her husband and daughter just returned from having spent a year in southern France."

Although well traveled, Spence was not all that familiar with France.

"Tucker, my only times in France have been quick trips to Paris, and although I always intend to spend some free time and get acquainted with the French culture, I have never done so. How did your daughter and her family find their experience?"

"Spence, it's great to have them back, and I know they are glad to be home, but I think we may have lost their hearts to France! They spent the year in Aix-En-Provence in the southern part of the country—a marvelous area with almost indescribable beauty that can provide a haven from the pressures and demands of modern civilization."

"My wife and I had the opportunity to spend a week visiting with our daughter and her family and to see some of the countryside. Spence, if you ever have the chance to get to the southern part of France and have the time to truly enjoy and absorb the experience, you should not miss doing so!"

Tucker finished his drink, wished Spence a good evening and headed off to bed. Spence remained behind as he watched the twinkle of the lights from the expensive high-rise apartment and condominium buildings in the distance to the north along the lake. He enjoyed the beauty and the peacefulness of the late evening but was mindful that out there in the darkness were individuals bent on destroying this environment of safety and comfort.

CHAPTER 8

Several months after having visited with Tucker Wolcott in Chicago, a business investment opportunity had taken Spence to Monte Carlo. The small independent principality of Monaco is located between the southern Mediterranean coast of France and Italy and boasts one of the highest per capita incomes of any place in the world outside of the Mideast.

Spence had successfully completed his business meetings in Monte Carlo earlier than expected and still had a couple of days before he was scheduled to leave. He was about to telephone the pilots and move his return flight up when he was reminded of the encouragement and recommendation of Tucker Wolcott to visit the southern part of France. It was mid-June, and the weather was absolutely gorgeous. As usual, Ginger had things well under control, and he could afford to be frivolous and do some sightseeing. If nothing else, he would not have to defend to Tucker why he had been so relatively close to southern France and not followed Tucker's suggestion to visit.

Later that morning, Spence telephoned Ginger and asked that she arrange for a sporty BMW convertible rental car be delivered to the Grand Casino Hotel where he was staying. Sporty cars in the parking area of the Grand Casino was an understatement. The area around this opulent hotel was always populated with Bentley's, Morgan's and other top-of-the-line world-class luxury automobiles. Think back to the James Bond movie *Goldeneye* when Bond was in Monte Carlo, and this was the place.

Spence left the Grand Casino and drove to the west taking in the breathtaking views of the Mediterranean coast from the road that wanders high along the cliffs. He drove through Cannes and along the famous beaches of the French Riviera through St. Raphael and St. Tropez and continued on, enjoying the beauty of the drive. When he reached the town of Cassis, some ninety kilometers or so before Marseille, he turned north and headed toward Aix-en-Provence and the heart of Provence.

Aix-en-Provence (pronounced *x*) is a city with a population of approximately 150,000 located in the mountainous country of Provence of southern France. Provence is bordered to the north by the French and Italian Alps and to the south (perhaps half an hour drive) by the Mediterranean coast and the western edge of the French Riviera. As you approach Provence, there is a magical moment when you leave the north of France behind. Cypress trees and red-tile roofs appear, and you begin to catch the scent of wild thyme and lavender. In Provence, the influence of the Phoenicians, the Greeks, and the Romans is still evident, having left traces untouched through the millennia. The Greeks introduced to the area the grape and the olive, and both have had vital roles in the Provencal economy through the centuries.

Nowhere else in Europe and rarely in the Western world can you experience antiquity with such intimacy—its exoticism and its purity, external and alive. But beyond this link to civilizations of the past, Provence is a region that reverberates through all of your senses. Van Gogh's palette comes to life in a landscape of golden hues and crystal blue skies beneath fields of vivid lavender, thyme, rosemary, and fields of bright yellow sunflowers providing the undeniable picture of Provence.

Journey through the countryside of Provence and through the vestiges of ancient Roman settlements, medieval hilltop villages, and miles of vibrant green vineyards. Stroll through the outdoor markets with the barrels of plump olives, mounds of rich and colorful spices, thick wedges of cheese, fishes and other seafood from the nearby Mediterranean, the wonderful wines, the crusty long paper-wrapped breads, fruits and vegetables of all descriptions, and, of course, the beautiful flowers. The Mediterranean spirit fills the air with warmth and an unhurried pace.

And then there is the Provencal cuisine, which is so distinctive from the rest of France and the rest of French cooking. A Mediterranean influence brings the local dishes alive with hot spices; seafood, olives, and olive oil are the spirit of the recipes. Spend any time at all in Provence, and you will experience and long remember pastis (a sweet, anise—licorvice flavored aperitif served best cold), aioli (a potent garlic spread served on crispy hot toast), bouillabaisse (the region's most famous and most delicious seafood dish), crème brulee (a favorite in Provence), olive and anchovy tapenade (spreads served on toast), and, of course, as with most of France, no meal would be complete without the wonderful local cheese and wine.

In this setting is the city of Aix-en-Provence—a city of art and a city of light and activity. The center of Aix is the "medieval old town" ringed by a circle of boulevards and squares. Cours Mirabeau is the center and the heart of Aix. The Cours Mirabeau is a beautiful double tree-lined avenue side lined with wonderful terrace cafes, bookshops, shops, and markets with cheeses, wines, and flowers. Large plane trees overhang the length of this wide pedestrian avenue providing daylong shade on warm summer days.

If you sit at only one French sidewalk café outside of Paris, it should be here on the Cours Mirebeau where the air is warm and the surroundings so unique, and where the sidewalk comes alive. The south side of the avenue is lined with seventeenth and eighteenth century four- and five-story buildings that now house banks, law firms, and other professional organizations. The Cours

Mireabeau has some of the finest fountains in France, and then there are the open-air markets with the fresh produce and foods from the region. The days in this region are bright with gentle breezes, and velvet evening air makes for peaceful times relaxing at the outdoor cafes or sitting on the patios absorbing the beauty of the evening skies.

A short drive to the south is the Mediterranean and the picturesque resorts, beaches, and the harbor of Cassis.

After just a few hours in the region of Provence, Spence knew he would return. This area would serve nicely as his European hideaway.

Over several visits and spanning several months, Spence had looked at numerous homes and converted farmhouses. The visits had been time-consuming but great fun. Each visit was more enjoyable than the last, and each visit to Aix-en-Provence and its surrounding areas with the sights, smells, sounds (or rather the peaceful quietness and quaintness) further nurtured his growing appreciation for the area and his desire to be able to spend time here on his own terms—at his own place. Aix-en-Provence was also just about the right size for Spence. The city and surrounding area was large enough to provide the autonomy that Spence required and large enough to provide the amenities that were desirable but small enough to avoid the problems that normally came with a large population center.

It had been hard to describe, but he had a clear picture of what he wanted. After much searching, he had found a wonderful property set peacefully on four hectares (approximately ten acres) amid vineyards and orchards at the end of a winding, peaceful, tree-lined lane. The property was on a flat section of land dotted with trees and surrounded by forests that ran down the sloping hillsides. It was a quiet secluded site in the hills of Provence overlooking the historic and elegant city of Aix-en-Provence to the west and southwest. The view to the east was dominated in the distance by the majestic Mount St. Victoire.

The grounds of the property consisted of a main house and a four-room cottage (which housed the caretaker and his wife) and was a short walk through one of the two gardens to the main house. Spence had named the main house and the property "Villa Rose" in honor of his mother and her love for flowers. His mother would have surely loved this beautiful location.

The fragrant perfumes of lavender, thyme, and rosemary gently floating through the breeze; the cool waters of the crystal clear pool and the sounds of the cicadas and the chirping of the birds from the nearby orchards together with the taste of the locally grown melons and the indescribable cheeses, sausages, warm breads, and wine regaled all of his senses.

The main house (as well as the cottage) was made of stone and had been a seventeenth century two-story farmhouse but had been fully renovated over the ensuing many years, and except for the lack of air conditioning (hardly any of the residences in Provence had air conditioning because generally it was not necessary, and to have closed windows would have been to shut out nature and all of the beautiful sounds, smells, and tastes that permeate the area), the main house had all of the features and appliances of the most modern of homes. The stone walls and the wooden beams throughout kept the interior cool during the summer, and the fireplace in the central living room area kept the main house cozy during the winter—although the winters were relatively mild being so close to the Mediterranean.

The house had two bedrooms with adjoining bathrooms and a reading room and exercise room on the second level. The first level included the main living room, a modern kitchen with the latest subzero refrigerator and a Wolfe stove and oven, (which Ginger had arranged to have installed), and a small room through a set of french doors that provided a view of the mountains. Spence had really come to enjoy this room. He could sit with his morning coffee and review email traffic. The house also included a library, and behind the library was a room that Spence had cleverly designed and created. The room was hidden away and only accessible through one of the floor to ceiling bookshelves. This well-protected room housed certain highly confidential files, vast amounts of various foreign currency, and other essential items. The room also housed communication scramblers and other security equipment such as diversion routers so that any email or other electronic communications to and from Villa Rose could not be traced to the origin.

In addition to the fireplace with a stone mantle, the living room had a high ceiling with wooden beams and french doors on one side opening onto a stone terrace with a sun awning supported by wooden beams and stone. The stone surrounding one side of the terrace was covered by ivy. The terrace provided stunning panoramic views and a wonderful place to have lunch or dinner. A stone walk led away from the main house through a small garden of pink hollyhocks to an in-ground swimming pool. The pool was surrounded by a small grass lawn. Just beyond the lawn, the pool area was protected by pine trees and leafy shade trees along the top of the steep cliff.

There were plots of various sizes of lavender, sunflowers, and rosemary within sight of the main house. On the upper hillside were two small orchards and a vineyard together with numerous olive trees.

Throughout the house, the walls were tastefully decorated with Provencal-style fabrics with bright, colorful yellows, greens, and blues. The walls were dotted with watercolor landscapes of the Provence region, and throughout the house were imaginative arrangements of locally picked wildflowers.

Some two hundred yards to the south of the main house, Spence had arranged to have a small two-story stone building constructed using aged stone from the area. The building blended in with the existing main house and with the caretaker's cottage. The building was surrounded on three sides by trees. The one side of the house without trees provided a beautiful view of the distant mountains.

A reinforced concrete lighted tunnel led from this building to a room that had been constructed below the main house. Communication lines (voice, data, and video) had been installed in the tunnel linking this building with the main house. In addition, a room had been constructed beneath the building with access from the tunnel. The room housed redundant online communication and computer equipment similar to the equipment in the room behind the library in the main house. Built into the roof of the new building was reception and signaling equipment that provided wireless communication capability for Villa Rose.

The building consisted of five rooms. There was a kitchen that included a sitting area large enough to accommodate eight for breakfast or lunch. Although when designing and considering the purposes of the building, neither Spence nor Ginger ever anticipated there would ever be more than two or perhaps three at the building at any one time. However, appearance and perception was very important. In addition to the kitchen area, there were two relatively small but nicely equipped offices that appeared more like a comfortable library or den. The second floor contained a nicely furnished bedroom, bathroom, and reading room.

In a fashion somewhat similar to the manner in which the hidden room had been constructed behind the library in the main house, the second floor of the new building had been designed in such a way as to provide an optical illusion. Behind a panel in the bedroom, on the second floor, was a hidden stairway down to the tunnel. There was also a hidden entry to the stairway from each of the offices on the first floor. The stairway was carpeted, and the walls had been soundproofed so that once in the passageway, no one from within the building could hear or detect movement down the stairs.

The stairs led to a basement storage room. At the far end of the storage room were two well-disguised doors that provided entry to the tunnels. Should anyone discover the hidden stairway, it would take some time to conclude that the stairway lead to anything other than a basement storage room—hopefully, they would view this stairway as just another unique seventeenth or eighteenth century architectural design quirk. Clearly, the cleverly planned stairway and tunnel system had been designed to provide both a safe room and to create more options for escape if ever necessary.

One door opened to the tunnel leading to the main house. The second door opened to a tunnel that ran to an underground garage about a quarter of a mile away at the edge of the Villa Rose property. The garage housed two heavily fortified but otherwise standard-appearing cars. Just to the outside was a hillside that faced a paved back road that led away from the Aix-en-Provence area. The door of the garage had been disguised to take on the appearance of the hillside. Once the door was opened, which was easy to accomplish, a car could be driven a short distance through the pine-needle-covered floor of the woods and onto the back road and to safety.

The construction of the building and the tunnel system had taken many months and longer than normal since Spence had brought in, at different times, two different Swiss construction crews and one German construction firm in order to ensure that no one from the area knew what was in place and that none of the construction firms had an understanding of the complete layout.

The new building was referred to as the "office." Given Spence's professional background and apparent activities, it was logical to expect that he would be associated with an office and, in fact, require administrative support.

Spence enjoyed walking the path that ran from the edge of the Villa Rose property through the woods and down the hillsides to a small street that led into the old section of "Aix" as the city of Aix-en-Provence was affectionately called. His daily journeys would take him in various directions along the narrow winding sixteenth, seventeenth, and eighteenth century cobble-stone streets past the many shops. He seemed to always stop at one of the many small shops to pick up one of the long crusty breads, a bottle of wine, or perhaps a quart of milk and some cheese. If you had the time, and he did, Aix provided endless opportunities to explore and to appreciate life.

Chapter 9

Not only had Spence fallen in love with and acquired Villa Rose, but he was continually thankful for finding Peggy, and there was no doubt that Peggy was a real find.

He could clearly recall the day he had first met Peggy Mounier. It was midmorning and one of those early fall days when Aix-en-Provence was alive with the sights and smells of Provence. Spence had arrived at the law offices of Amhurst to personally sign the closing documents for the purchase of Villa Rose and, hopefully soon, to be the base for his European activities. As he entered the Ashurst offices, through the heavy wooden doors with the brightly polished brass doorknobs and handles, on the south side of the street midway down the tree-lined Cours Mirabeau Boulevard, he noticed a feeling of quiet elegance that might be expected of a French law firm.

His friend from Chicago, Tucker Wolcott, had recommended this firm and had vouched for their expertise, professionalism, and discretion. Tucker had made the introduction and arranged for Spence to meet with and to receive the personal attention and assistance of Jacques LaMarre, the firm's managing partner.

Spence entered the building and quietly walked the short distance down the lushly carpeted narrow entry hallway that led to the receptionist area. The receptionist was a young lady in her midtwenties with dark hair and beautiful dark eyes, sharp attractive facial features, and a pleasing smile. She sat behind an elegant elevated dark wooden desk. There was a three-foot wooden partition topped with a railing running to the walls on each side of the entryway behind her. Clearly, no one was intended to enter the Ashurst offices unless they had a prior appointment and unless first cleared by the receptionist.

Hoping that the receptionist understood English since Spence had little grasp of the French language—although that was about to change—Spence approached the receptionist.

"Hello. My name is Spencer Harrington, and I have an appointment with Monsieur LaMarre."

Without waiting for a response, Spence continued. "I am a little early for our appointment and will be pleased to wait until Monsieur LaMarre is available."

"Oui, Monsieur Harrington" she began in French and then quickly switched to English.

Spence was immediately disappointed that he did not speak French. Her demeanor and the romantic flow of the words suggested a friendly and inviting personality.

"Mr. Harrington, I will let Monsieur LaMarre's assistant know you have arrived."

She then led him to a tastefully decorated and furnished small conference room adjacent to the reception area. "May I get you anything, Mr. Harrington?" she inquired.

Spence thought for a moment but declined. "No, thank you. I will be fine."

The receptionist turned to leave. As she was beginning to close the door, she turned to Spence.

"Should you change your mind, Mr. Harrington, of if we can make your wait, which should not be long, more comfortable in anyway, please just ring me by touching the button on the table." Spence notice a small polished wooden box on the table with a green button in the center,

Some ten minutes or so had passed, and Spence was enjoying the soft background instrumental music of what he suspected was a French melody when there was a gentle knock as the door opened.

Spence was immediately shaken from his peaceful relaxation by the appearance in the doorway of a strikingly beautiful dark-haired young woman. Spence guessed she was in her early thirties. She quickly walked the few steps toward Spence extending her hand as she began to introduce herself.

"Hello, my name is Peggy Mounier. Monsieur LaMarre has asked me to meet with you and to ensure that our firm meets your needs in all respects. Monsieur LaMarre has asked that I extend to you his most sincere apology for not being able to meet with you. He has been in meetings at the firm's office in Paris the last two days, and the surprise transit strike late last night has made it impossible for him to return in time to meet with you."

Without verbally responding, Spence nodded his understanding and acceptance.

Ms. Mounier continued. "I hope you do not mind meeting with me."

Spence thought *I do not mind one bit*! It was clear that she was not only quite beautiful but very intelligent with an engaging personality.

As with all things French—especially administrative and legal matters—the closing procedures were cumbersome and time-consuming. At a juncture in the proceedings and at a point that Spence guessed was midway, or at least he certainly hoped that they were at least half done, Ms. Mounier requested of the seller's representative that the meeting be adjourned for perhaps ten minutes so that anyone who would like could adjourn to the bathroom. With only Spence and the very attractive Ms. Mounier now left in the room, Ms. Mounier turned to Spence.

"Monsieur Harrington, I thought you might like a break. Everything is going well, and we should be completed in another twenty to thirty minutes" (this was after some forty minutes had been consumed already).

She smiled for the first time since the meeting had begun, although Spence had noticed that from time to time during the meeting she had turned his way with a twinkle in her eye as if to say, "Don't worry. Your interests are being well taken care of—trust me."

"I should have warned you that completing the closing procedures for the purchase of a property in France, especially when the purchaser is not a French citizen, can take longer than may seem normal. But, again, let me assure you that everything is going well."

Spence nodded and smiled.

Spence had not been able to understand the conversations, although on what perhaps were the more important points, Ms. Mounier had taken the time to explain to him in English the nature of the document he was being asked to sign or the subject being discussed. He had been impressed with her assertive but nonthreatening approach and the confident manner in which she was managing not only the meeting but also the seller's representative.

The meeting had, in fact, taken longer than Spence would have liked and longer than he had anticipated, but he was becoming more and more intrigued with Ms. Mounier and was beginning to think how disappointed he would be when the meeting did end and he and Ms. Mounier would go their separate ways.

Almost to what seemed to be on the second, when the ten minutes ended, Ms. Mounier called the seller's representative back into the room and moved forward with the final phases of the closing procedures. After some additional twenty minutes or so of signing and exchanging various documents and affidavits, Ms. Mounier stood and excitedly announced "Voilà" (There you go).

She then turned to the seller's representative as she handed him the bank check for the purchase of the property "*Merci beaucoup*!" (Thank you very much) for your patience and assistance. If we are finished, my assistant will be pleased to see you out." She then gently hit the call button located near the end of the table, and within a few moments her assistant entered the room. After Ms. Mounier and Spence had shaken his hand and wished him well, Ms. Mounier's assistant escorted the seller out of the conference room.

Ms. Mounier turned to Spence with a smile. "Well, Mr. Harrington, you are now a French land baron!" She then laughed.

Spence had been wrong before on matters such as this but not often. It sure seemed to him that she had also found him interesting if not attractive.

Spence extended his hand. "Mademoiselle Mounier, thank you so much for handling this matter in such a professional and efficient manner on my behalf. I look forward to an opportunity to see you sometime in the future."

"Mr. Harrington, the future may be more immediate if you are willing. Given the hour …," it was now almost twelve thirty in the afternoon, "it would be my pleasure if you would join me for lunch. There are some wonderful outdoor cafes up and down the Cours Mirabeau."

Spence thought for a moment before responding. The politics of life are strange. Here he had been thinking how best to invite her to lunch and assessing the odds of her saying yes and considering how he would counter when she most likely would politely decline. Now, with her having extended the invitation, he was in a much more flexible position with many more options in how he might play the politics of the situation. He could decline and always wonder and regret the opportunity lost. Or he could accept and follow his instincts; had he thought further, he would have recalled that his instincts had served him well.

"Mademoiselle Mounier, it would be my pleasure to join you for lunch. I am in your hands!"

Peggy Mounier led as they left the Ashurst offices. They walked into the bright sunlight of a beautiful early fall afternoon and onto the Cours Mirabeau. They walked about a block or so and then crossed the wide avenue to 53 Cours Mirabeau and the café Les Deux Gargons where they were graciously greeted by the equivalent of a maitre d'.

As they were led to an outdoor terrace table sheltered by the shade of one of the many trees and with a wonderful view of the bustling activity of the avenue, Mademoiselle Mounier turned to Spence.

"Monsieur Harrington, you are in for a treat."

Spence smiled and quickly attempted to determine if she was serious or somewhat of a tease. He suspected she was serious, but his instincts were telling him that this was a lady with spirit and spunk and one very confident lady. She was also a woman who clearly must know the influence her sensuality must have on men. Was she testing or teasing him now, or was she merely building the anticipation for a unique lunch?

Spence intentionally delayed any response. One, for the first time in a long time he was somewhat at a loss for words. Second, and more importantly, he was hoping that she would clarify her comment and that he would not guess wrong and say something that would seriously impair the possibility of getting to know her better.

As they walked, she commented, "The Les Deux Gargons is one of the best outdoor cafes this side of Paris."

Spence could not help but notice her hair as it brushed against her forehead from a light breeze that made its way through the terrace.

In the background, Spence could hear the light street music of a French melody. It was one of those rare days (well, not so rare in this part of southern France) when the weather was pleasing to the soul—perhaps in the low seventies with little humidity, clear bright blue skies with a few white puffy clouds, and a sense of spirit in the air. The leaves from the overhanging branches of the nearby trees sparkled from the bright sunshine, and shadows danced about the tables from the ever-present but hardly noticeable breeze. The avenue was alive with activity, and the café terrace provided a vantage point from which to have a leisurely lunch and observe the residents of Aix as they went about their lives.

Spence nodded as he acknowledged the wonderful aromas that were floating along with the breeze from the direction of the restaurant.

"Mademoiselle, you are teasing my senses!"

Her eyes seemed to twinkle, and with a warm and a slight devilishly smile she countered.

"But Monsieur Harrington, that is what we French do best!"

They both shared laughter as the waiter approached with menus.

Spence thought for a brief moment. Was there a relaxed camaraderie and an environment of trust developing, or was she like so many others he had met along the years in his business dealings—an ultimate professional with only an objective of working to create and nurture a business relationship from which to gain access to additional business or perhaps valuable networking contacts?

Spence understood the game and was not troubled if this was her objective. He did not view relationship building, even including the pampering (such as lunch at a very nice outdoor café) that sometimes is a key component or at least a component that some think is necessary as "being used" but rather a necessary component of business. Although it was most likely the case that she was entirely engaged in and focused on developing a professional relationship that would be of possible benefit in the future, Spence hoped this was not the motive being played out this early afternoon, as he was really beginning to like and become intrigued with Mademoiselle Mounier.

The weather was almost perfect. One of those days when the temperature was neutral, very comfortable and relaxing, and the air had a fresh clean feeling.

The waiter stood for a few moments without inquiring about a drink order. In France and especially in the southern part of France, it was a natural part of living to have wine with dinner and usually also with lunch. It was almost a given that they would have requested a nice glass or bottle of wine and to have inquired would have been an insult. The waiter was patient.

Spence looked at Mademoiselle Mounier and inquired, "Would you like to join me in sharing a bottle of wine?" She smiled and nodded her approval.

"I thought a nice local wine would be nice, but I will probably need your assistance with the waiter. What do you like or recommend?"

She smiled and turned to the waiter. A period of rapid and animated French between Mademoiselle Mounier and the waiter then ensued. Spence could not comprehend all that was being said, but the exchange was very amicable, and the waiter seemed to be pleased with the result.

The waiter nodded and quickly turned and began briskly walking toward the entrance to the restaurant—his starched white apron gently flapping with his hurried footsteps.

As the waiter left, Mademoiselle Mounier tuned to Spence and laughed, "He seemed pleased with the selection. I hope the selection meets your pleasure!"

Spence smiled. "I am still in your hands. Remember!" They both laughed.

"I chose a very nice rosé, somewhat dry and fruity and a wonderful wine for summer."

Peggy paused for a moment and then continued.

"As part of our services, I also provide Provence orientation guidance." She laughed.

"Did you know that approximately 80 percent of the wine from the Provence area is rosé?"

Spence laughed and said, "And here I thought your expertise was just limited to the areas of the law!"

Spence, in a more serious tone, said, "I apologize for not asking you when we left your office. If you are pressed for time, we can order quickly."

Mademoiselle Mounier responded, "Oh no. I am fine with time this afternoon. Quite seriously, I was not certain how long the closing might take. I had set aside most of the day just to be safe. So this is a pleasant interlude."

Spence was relieved but at the same time was quickly processing the comment and her body language.

He was thinking, *Was her desire to have lunch with me because she thought she would enjoy my company, or was lunch a nice way to fill in part of her free afternoon*?' It was a question to which he was looking forward to soon receiving an answer.

She went on. "And to rush lunch in southern France at any time but on such a beautiful summer day would be inexcusable!"

She smiled and quickly continued. "But I am famished."

She picked up the menus and handed one of them to Spence. "Taking care of your interests today required a lot of energy!"

Spence thought, *There is clearly something different about this young woman. Something intriguing. Setting aside her natural beauty, which is accentuated by the well-defined features of her face, her dark hair and deep brown eyes, and the attractiveness of her trim but ample body, she is not French.*

She sure looked like she could have stepped out of a French travel poster. Her appearance, her mannerisms, and her skill with the French language was impressive. (Although he was much more conversant with the French language than he wanted anyone to know, he would readily admit that he was not in a position to judge which part of France she was from). And then it dawned on him. It was her sense of humor and sense of free spirit. She was different. But why?

Spence gave the appearance of confidently looking through the menu, but, in reality, he was unable to decipher many of the items. He had the feeling that the items he could not understand on the menu were probably what he would have enjoyed most. As they say in France. "*C'est la vie*," or, "So is life."

As he was pondering his lunch decision, Mademoiselle Mounier looked up from her menu and said, "Monsieur Harrington, may I make a suggestion for lunch?"

"Mademoiselle Mounier, I would welcome your recommendation, But only if you call me Spence."

She smiled. "Yes, but only if you call me Peggy."

"Mademoiselle, you are a fine negotiator!"

She laughed. "Yes, but it is still Peggy."

Spence returned the laughter and then said, "Well, Peggy, let's hear the recommendation."

With an alluring sweet and yet firm voice, she replied, "You will not hurt my feelings if you do not agree with the recommendation. But this restaurant has excellent mussels, and the asparagus is still in season. A somewhat light lunch. But the manner in which they serve the mussels is outstanding, and the asparagus is very tender with a very light hollandaise sauce. Perhaps some local berries and cream for dessert."

Spence was looking for something light on the menu, and Peggy's thoughts were right in line with what he might have selected (if he could have understood the remaining items on the menu). Just as importantly, her recommendation was what he might have envisioned as just the right lunch for the occasion and for the locale.

"Peggy, you have piqued my interest and curiosity. Your recommendation sounds good to me. In fact, it sounds very good."

Spence looked again at her and said, "Thinking of mussels, I have heard of Leon's in Paris. I understand that the various locations specialize in mussels and the frites, and are also quite good. I will make a point to try Leon's the next time I am in Paris."

Peggy replied, "Yes, the Leon's cafes are quite good and are fun places when you want a rather quick meal. They do know mussels."

The waiter arrived with two glasses and the bottle of wine. He opened the bottle and handed the cork to Spence and then poured a small amount from the bottle into one of the glasses. Spence ignored the cork but took a sip from the glass. He looked across the table. "Peggy, this is outstanding, but what do you think?"

She smiled, not so much from having been given the opportunity to express her opinion but by the sound of her first name. It was rare in a business or quasi-business setting to use first names in France. She was pleased.

She nodded her agreement and turned to the waiter. "*Merci beaucoup*."

The waiter poured the wine into each of their glasses to the halfway point and handed a glass to both Spence and Peggy.

As the waiter left, Spence raised his glass. Peggy, anticipating the coming toast, raised her glass to gently meet his. Spence looked at Peggy and said, "May our meeting today lead to a wonderful friendship both professional and personal."

Peggy responded. "Yes, I think I would like that."

A relatively short time later, the waiter returned with a large round tray containing plates with silver domes that glistened as the highly polished covers caught the rays of the sun through the nearby tree branches. With a skill from clearly many years of experience, the waiter deftly removed the covers and quietly placed the bowls of mussels and plates of asparagus in front of Peggy and Spence.

As the aromas quickly spread, Spence smiled and commented to Peggy, "Life in Provence is good."

She smiled and with a twinkle in her eye nodded toward their meals as she said, "It will seem even better as you begin to enjoy these wonderful tastes. *Bon appetite*!"

As Spence relaxed with a glass of wine on this beautiful early afternoon in southern France, and, as he thoroughly enjoyed the simple but fine meal, he thought of the lazy summer days growing up in Indiana and the many adventures he had encountered that had brought him to this place and point in time. As he had done so many times before, in his mind he said a quiet prayer of thanks for the many blessings he had been given.

Spence looked up at Peggy. "The food is outstanding."

Peggy smiled and said, "I am pleased that you like the meal." She then continued.

"As you must have already realized, at least hopefully so, in reaching the decision to purchase Villa Rose, the southern part of France will tempt and please all of your senses. The freshness of the food and the range of selections from the local markets coupled with the love of cooking by the French can lead to some memorable meals—sometimes simple in nature but wonderful in creativity and in the complexity of the tastes."

As she spoke, Spence was reminded of Peggy's excellent grasp and use of the English language.

"Peggy, your English is excellent. Where did you learn English so well?" Spence laughed as he continued, "I can only dream of the day when my French might even be reasonably acceptable."

Peggy took another sip of wine.

"I am not perhaps as I appear," she said with what appeared to be a twinkle in her eyes.

She went on.

"I have a law degree from Indiana University and a law degree from the University of Paris. I was born in the United States, but my great-grandparents on my father's side were born and spent their early lives in Provence. They immigrated to the United States when they were both in their late teens. I graduated from high school in three years and spent what would have been my senior year as an exchange student in Liege, Belgium, which is in the predominately French-speaking region of Belgium. I very much enjoyed my experiences in Europe."

Peggy stopped and leisurely enjoyed another sip of wine as Spence refilled both of their glasses.

She continued.

"After graduating from Indiana, I had the opportunity to travel to Europe and made a point of visiting the areas here in southern France with the history of my roots. As so many do, I fell in love with Provence and southern France."

"Should I go on?" she queried.

"Absolutely," Spence responded without hesitation. He was more and more intrigued for a number of reasons and for one reason in particular.

"My French at the time was relatively good—not great—but reasonably functional. My goal became one of finding a way to become self-sufficient and to be able to live in Provence—especially in Aix En Provence."

"I moved to Paris and began business and law classes at the University of Paris, which led to a French law degree. Ultimately I passed the equivalent in France of the bar examination and became licensed to practice law in France. During the process, I applied for and have dual citizenship status."

She smiled. "So, life story!" as she enjoyed another sip of wine.

After a slight pause, she said, "And just who are you, Mr. Spencer Harrington? Tell me who I am sharing this wonderful early afternoon with today."

Spence was prepared for the inquiry knowing that at some point, if for no other reason than polite social courtesy or general curiosity, it was likely she would ask.

He responded to the question. "But, Madame, I am, as you said earlier today, a French land baron!"

They shared laughter together.

Knowing the flip response would not be sufficient, especially to an attorney trained on two continents who might easily suspect that he was more than he appeared, Spence continued.

"I have an accounting and finance background and through some very fortunate investment opportunities now have the ability to travel and to manage a few businesses that I have been able to accumulate around the world."

Moving quickly on so as not to dwell on his background, Spence continued.

"I have a friend who had a wonderful time on a visit to Provence and suggested I visit. Like you, from my first trip to Provence, I fell in love with the area. I began looking for a place in the Provence region that I could call home when I was in Europe, and that place is now Villa Rose."

Spence made a point of looking at his watch and then caught the eye of the waiter and motioned for the check. The waiter promptly delivered the check, and Spence counted out the appropriate number of euros including a nice gratuity.

Spence finished his coffee and said to Peggy, "I do not want to keep you any longer. I have really enjoyed our lunch and the opportunity to get to know you."

He paused and then said, "I look forward to opportunities to meet again—perhaps over lunch or dinner or perhaps to show you Villa Rose after I make some changes."

Peggy smiled. "Yes, I would like that."

Spence noticed that there was no "I think" in her response this time.

As they were walking out of the courtyard of the restaurant and about to head in different directions, Spence said, "Hey, great to meet a Hoosier."

Peggy quickly turned her head toward Spence with a somewhat puzzled but pleasant look.

"I have not heard that term since I have been in France. Brings back good memories."

Spence held her hand and gave her a passing kiss on both cheeks—partly professional and partly personal (who could really tell the difference)—as they wished each other well and then headed in different directions.

As Spence walked lazily up the tree-lined boulevard toward the old section and toward the street where he had parked, he ran through his time with Peggy Mounier. With each step, he became more and more convinced that if she was the person she said she was, then she might be the person he had been looking for to head his organization in Europe.

Four months or so had passed, and Spence, or more accurately the craftsmen that Spence had employed, had completed the remodeling and construction work on the Provence property. Villa Rose was even more appealing and functional than Spence had initially imagined possible. Villa Rose very much captured the essence of Provence.

During the past four months, Spence had visited Aix En Provence on a monthly basis to monitor the construction. On each occasion, he had made a point of telephoning Peggy Mounier and arranging either lunch or dinner. It was clear they enjoyed spending time together. He continued to be impressed with Peggy. She was bright, very personable, had excellent common sense, and seemed to be yearning for a level of adventure beyond the stimulation of just practicing law in France. Beyond all else, she seemed like she could be trusted.

CHAPTER 10

Spence sat reading various confidential reports on the patio at Villa Rose, a nice glass of wine at his beckoning as the shadows from the late afternoon sun began to lengthen. This was his second day at Villa Rose on this trip and the first visit since the work had been completed at Villa Rose. He had been looking forward to this trip and to the week or so that he had allocated from his schedule for France.

The secure telephone rang. From the number that appeared, he knew it was Ginger calling with the morning update from the United States.

Ginger first got in her daily gig on how challenging the relaxing day must have been to this point for Spence. He quickly attempted to convince her that he was really getting some work accomplished. But they both knew that this was a period of quiet time that he needed and clearly time that he enjoyed.

She then briefed Spence on the various matters she deemed of importance or that she knew he would find of interest. He trusted her judgment.

As she was finishing the briefing, she commented. "Oh, and I have the information you requested on Peggy Mounier."

Spence somewhat perked up.

"What did you find?"

"She checks out on all counts. Everything she told you is true." Ginger continued.

"In addition, she is highly respected within the law firm. She is single and has had no serious relationships, but she is not gay. She is frequently called upon by the Paris office of her firm to provide assistance on various matters for clients throughout Europe, and, as a result, she knows how to get around. She has no vices that our people have discovered, and they are, as you know, usually very comprehensive when they do these in-depth reviews. Financially, she lives comfortably within her salary."

Ginger paused and then with light laughter said, "I can give you her bank balances—as well as her measurements, if you would like."

Spence laughed. "No, thanks, but I see our people are complete as usual."

Spence thought for a moment and then said. "I think she could be our person."

"Could well be," Ginger responded.

Based on the conversation, Spence already knew what he would do next. If successful, he had found the person to manage his organization in Europe.

CHAPTER 11

Many, in fact most, times in life the real thing turns out to be far less appealing, interesting, and alluring than the picture it has held in our dreams and expectations. For Spence and Australia, this was not the case. From the moment Spence first visited Sydney several years earlier, he had fallen in love with the beauty of Australia and with the warmth, humor, spirit, and the keen appreciation for adventure of the Australian people.

Spence was a romantic and probably so from birth, he suspected.

He could remember as a young boy in grade school dreaming of what the experience might be like to visit the distant exotic locations he had read about in his geography class. He dreamed of adventure. He dreamed of traveling to some of those far-away places and experiencing the wonders and differences of those places.

For some reason, and he was not sure why, he was especially intrigued by Switzerland and Australia. Perhaps it was the pictures of the snow-covered Alps or the small, quaint villages of Switzerland or the vast open areas of Australia and beautiful quiet beaches that seem to run forever. He also wondered if he would ever see these places or ever have the opportunity to see and visit London or perhaps Gander or Goose Bay or any of the other many places throughout the world that he had read about or been told about.

His father, who had not traveled outside of the United States until the war, had been stationed in London during World War II. He had often spoken of the many areas of interest in London and had told of the airplane flights to England and how the planes would stop for refueling in places like Gander, Newfoundland; and Goose Bay, Labrador. As a young boy, listening to his father and reading the geography books provided a passage to adventure and a passage to other, unlikely to ever reach, parts of the world.

For a young boy growing up in the mid-1960s in the rural Indiana countryside, faraway places could be nothing more than a dream. In addition to his dream of someday being a major league baseball player or, depending on the day, being Davy Crockett or perhaps a swashbuckling pirate, he often wondered what it would be like to be able to step into the pages of his geography book and set foot in the places pictured—especially Switzerland, Australia, and England.

Although he had not fully understood just why he had been drawn to Australia and Switzerland, he seemed to think in later years that perhaps it was because the independent spirit of both the Swiss and the Australians appealed to his own strong independent spirit.

For whatever reasons, those daydreams of his youth had brought him back countless times to these wonderful locations. He had thought then that the extent of his travels would be confined to the limits of the descriptions and pictures of the geography books.

However, here he was—returning again to Australia and the pleasurable satisfaction of anticipating the enjoyable experiences and surprises that lay ahead during the next several days.

His first visit to Australia had been a relatively last-minute thing. He had been on a business trip to Singapore and had successfully concluded his business a few days early. It had been early evening, and he was alone in the famous Long Bar in the Raffles Hotel nursing his second gin and tonic (he had long ago decided that the Singapore sling was really more for the tourists, and he had quickly returned to his favorite drink, which was a gin and tonic). As he relaxed, he pondered whether to spend the next two days in Singapore or whether to perhaps move up his return flight home. He thought of how best to utilize the time that had been freed-up on his schedule.

There was this wonderful seaside restaurant that he often frequented when he was in Singapore, and he had been looking forward to its specialty, which was chili crab. But he had decided that the dinner would have to wait for the next trip to Singapore.

As he sat at the bar, his thoughts took him back to those Indiana days and his boyhood dreams of Australia. He immediately knew how he would spend the next three days as he reached for his telephone to call Carolyn at Primrose Travel in the Chicago area.

At one time, he had known Carolyn's last name, but he was so used to her first name that he had long ago forgotten her last name. Tucker Wolcott had introduced Spence to Carolyn a few years ago, and Spence had found that Carolyn seemed to have a knack of recommending outstanding and unique travel experiences. She had never let him down and was always on the same page of the geography book in his mind.

"Hello, Primrose Travel. This is Carolyn. How may I help you?"

"Carolyn, this is Spence Harrington."

"Spence, it has been awhile. Where are you, and what travel tales do you have to tell?"

Spence was reminded by Carolyn's cheerful voice why he liked working with her so much and why he personally arranged his special travel with Carolyn rather than having one of his assistants make the arrangements. Carolyn was not only very good, she was also always eager to learn if he had enjoyed the experiences she had recommended as much as she thought he would.

"Carolyn, I am sitting here at the Long Bar in Singapore and need your advice."

Spence could picture Carolyn smiling and knew what was coming next.

"Spence, my advice is, as you have come to appreciate, rare and very valuable. This time, you rascal, I want a promise that you will meet me in Singapore for dinner at Raffles—say chili crab and a nice glass of wine!"

Spence laughed as he teased, "You got it young lady!"

Spence knew Carolyn was married to a wonderful guy with some sort of very successful financial career who took very good care of her. But it was still fun to tease. Carolyn reminded him in some ways of Ginger—a highly dedicated and skilled professional full of spirit and fun with a caring personality who took very good care of her clients.

Spence had at one point considered whether to bring Carolyn into his organization, but he already had Tucker Wolcott in Chicago.

"Okay, you met my price. How can I help you?" Carolyn responded.

"Carolyn, I've finished my business in Singapore a few days early and want to go to Australia on my way back to the States. I can spend three days or so in Australia."

Spence paused for a moment and then continued.

"Visiting Australia has been one of the dreams that I never thought as a kid that I would realize."

Carolyn said in a spirited fashion, "Spence, I have come to realize you are one of the world's great romantics!"

Spence quickly replied, "Could be."

"Carolyn, as always, I am in your hands. How can I best spend the next three days finding Australia?"

Carolyn was picturing Spence in Australia and knew just where he needed to spend those three treasured days.

"Spence, give me just a few minutes to check on a couple of things. I have an idea."

This was always the fun part, as anticipation built. Carolyn's recommendations were always so unique, interesting, and so suited to his personality.

A very short time later, Carolyn returned to the phone.

"Spence, can you get to the airport for a flight in about two hours?"

This was more of a statement than a question since Carolyn knew that Spence could easily get from the Raffles hotel, at this time of the evening, to the airport to make a flight within the next two hours. More importantly, she knew that Spence would go to great lengths not to miss a potential adventure even though he did not know what she had in store for him.

Spence was still flying commercial and had not yet purchased his own aircraft, so he was dependent on the commercial airline schedules. On the other hand, he was a premium-class frequent flyer and could move through the check-in lines and the limited security fairly quickly.

"Sure thing," Spence quickly answered not knowing if he could make it to the airport in time.

"I have you booked on Qantas flight 152 at 9:30 p.m. into Cairns in northern Australia. Give me a call when you arrive in Cairns. By then I will have everything else in place."

Spence thanked Carolyn, paid for his drinks, and quickly returned to his room. It did not take long for him to pack since he normally traveled light. He called to the front desk, notified the clerk that he would be checking out within the next fifteen minutes and requested that his bill be updated and that a taxi be reserved for his trip to the airport.

The trip to the airport was uneventful. Spence arrived with more than adequate time to check in at the Qantas counter and then stop for a few minutes at the Qantas lounge for a quick sandwich. He then went to the gate and boarded the flight to Cairns.

The flight from Singapore to Cairns took just over six hours and allowed Spence to get some much-needed sleep.

Upon arrival at the airport in the tropical city of Cairns, Spence cleared Australian immigration and customs and walked out of the terminal into the bright warm sunshine. Something was different but the same, it seemed. Then it dawned on him. Here he was some nine thousand miles from Vermont, but unlike Singapore, here, as he looked about at the people, he could not tell that he was not in America—that is, until he heard the sounds around him and the wonderful, playful Australian voices.

Spence stretched, took in the clean air, and allowed a few minutes to absorb the pleasant breezes and warm air. Although it was still early in the morning in the States, he knew Carolyn would be waiting for his telephone call. He reached for his telephone and dialed the special number she left with him.

"Hello," a somewhat groggy woman's voice answered.

"Carolyn, this is Spence. I am in Cairns enjoying the beautiful morning sunshine."

"Spence, even though it's some strange time in the morning here, you know I thrive on customer service!" she joked as she quickly attempted to clear her head and focus her thinking.

"Okay, here's the plan," she continued.

"Go to the Hertz counter. I have arranged a car for you—a BMW convertible—for the next three days and then a return flight to San Francisco Monday afternoon on Singapore Airlines flight number 84."

With a slight pause, she then quickly continued.

"Oh, and before I forget. If you have not noticed, they drive on the left in Australia. I know you are a quick learner and will pick up the driving quickly, but be careful of the roundabouts. I don't want to be responsible for any damage to your great-looking body on my watch!"

Spence smiled. Even at this early hour, Carolyn was full of spirit.

"Now, three days is not a lot of time, so I want you to make the most of what I think will be an exposure to a wonderfully diverse part of Australia."

Spence jumped back into the conversation.

"Carolyn, have you left time for me to get lost a few times both with respect to directions and also to pursue whatever strikes my fancy?"

After a number of years of assisting Spence with travel services and hearing of many of his travel exploits, she was keenly aware that what he enjoyed most was to just absorb the culture and the scenic beauty of new unexplored worlds—at least worlds that were new to him and that he had not yet explored.

"As always, Spence," she said.

"Tonight I have you booked at the Silky Oakes Lodge at the edge of the Baintree National Park in the rainforest. As you the leave the airport, turn north on Captain Cook Highway toward the town of Port Douglas. You will find the coastal highway to be an absolutely stunningly beautiful drive."

"Saturday and Sunday evenings I have you booked at the Sebel Reef House Resort in Palm Cove on the coast. From the hotel, it is a short drive, assuming you can pull yourself away from the beach, into Cairns. In Cairns, you can take a catamaran to the Great Barrier Reef, take a quaint train ride through the mountains to the town of Kuranda with wonderful overlooks along the way of the ocean and sugar cane fields below, or explore the many other wonderful activities that the area presents."

Spence was eager to head out to experience the adventures that lay ahead. "Sounds great, Carolyn. Any further instructions or advice?"

"No," she said. Spence could not see that she was smiling.

"Well, there is one other thing," Carolyn said.

Carolyn paused for emphasis and then continued.

"It would be a shame for you to be alone for dinner tomorrow evening at the Sebel Reef House—a place that you will find to be a wonderful tropical setting."

Spence thought at first that Carolyn was teasing but sensed there was a somewhat different tone in her voice. His thoughts were interrupted as she continued.

"But first tonight. I have made a dinner reservation for you tonight in the open-air restaurant high in the trees of the rainforest but still beneath the forest canopy overlooking the river at Silky Oakes. The experience will be so relaxing and peaceful with the sounds of the birds and wildlife so nearby that you may never want to leave the restaurant."

"Saturday evening, I have dinner reservations for you and Piper Morgan at the Sebel House for eight o'clock. I have worked with Piper from time to time in Australia, and I think you and Piper will enjoy spending time visiting over dinner."

"Uh-hu," Spence mused.

"Spence, as much as I know you welcome and appreciate your privacy, I just could not think of you being alone in such a wonderful setting. Also, Piper can provide you with additional insights into Australia."

Spence was becoming anxious to begin what sounded like a very exciting experience thanks to the framework for adventure provided by Carolyn, but he had one last question.

Somewhat suspecting and certainly hoping that Piper was female, Spence cautiously posed the question.

"Say, is this Piper a guy or a gal?"

Carolyn laughed as she said, "And the right answer is?"

She paused briefly for added suspense and then removed Spence's fears.

"Piper is a very pleasant lady who enjoys adventures about as much as you. She will meet you at the restaurant. Just in case …," and Carolyn went on to provide Piper's telephone number to Spence.

"Now on your way, you rascal. Enjoy Australia! Call me if you need anything."

Spence thanked Carolyn and wished her well. He then headed back into the terminal to find the Hertz counter and begin to achieve his objective of cramming as many Australian experiences as possible into the next three days.

CHAPTER 12

Cairns is located on the northern coast of the Australian state of Queensland.

Known as the "sunshine state," Queensland offers unparalleled tropical beauty including vast rainforests, some of the world's most beautiful and peaceful beaches, wonderful weather, and one of the natural wonders of the world, the Great Barrier Reef. Cairns truly is a prelude to paradise.

Cairns, a city with a population somewhere in the range of seventy-five thousand, is the northern gateway to the Great Barrier Reef. Cairns is an area where the weather is always warm and temperate, the water is crystal clear, and the opportunities to experience secluded fog-shrouded rainforest mountains, white sandy beaches, the multicolor beauty of coral reefs, and unique wildlife is seemingly limitless. Cairns and northern Queensland are truly located in a tropical paradise.

It was now midafternoon on Friday, and Spence was thinking how quickly the past day and a half had passed. Always a great indicator of how much fun Spence was having was how quickly the time seemed to vanish. He had made a mental note to find something nice to send to Carolyn as thanks for the wonderful travel advice.

The drive north on Captain Cook Highway from the Cairns airport is renowned as one of the best in Australia and one of the most scenic drives in the world. The road winds along the cliffs of the Coral Sea coastline—the turquoise waters of the ocean on one side and the world heritage Daintree Rainforest on the other.

Spence had been given a midnight blue BMW convertible at the airport. *Not bad*, he thought as he got into the car. He registered another note in his mind to thank Carolyn. He had driven north on Captain Cook Highway until he reached the town of Port Douglas. It was not quite lunchtime but close enough. Although he was looking for something Australian, his hunger caused him to stop short in his search as he noticed a small pizza shop. He also wanted to make the stop for lunch relatively quick so he could get to Silky Oaks. He pulled into the lot and parked. The weather was too nice to even think about putting the top up on the convertible.

The shop had somewhat of a weather-worn, wooden planked porch with a window where orders were placed and another window a few feet away where the food was delivered. The outside of the place did not look all that great, but Spence thought, *What the heck*. The place was getting busy although it was still before lunchtime, and it looked clean.

Spence approached the window and read the menu that was hanging on the outside wall just to the right of the window. Spence read through the menu offerings—mostly pizzas with various toppings. He selected the small seafood pizza with scallops, lobster, shrimp, and crab, and thought *Is this heaven or what*? He then quickly thought that he had better wait to make that call until after he tasted the pizza!

He was next in line to order. He had not even thought about what to expect, and had he thought about it, he would never have guessed. Behind the window counter was a very cheerful-appearing man, plump and somewhat balding with graying hair and a white handlebar mustache. He looked like he might have had some Italian heritage in his background, but Spence could not be sure. In any event, he was a neat-looking fellow. He certainly appeared to be fun-loving with an outgoing personality and even more so when he smiled to welcome Spence.

"G'day. What would you like, mate?"

Spence ordered the seafood pizza and a Fosters on draft. Seemed to Spence that it would not be right to be in Australia having a seafood pizza outside in such beautiful weather and not have an Australian beer.

As Spence was enjoying the thin, crisp, crusted pizza with the wonderful seafood, the individual who had taken his order came outside to where Spence was sitting at a table in the shade under one of the nearby trees. He inquired how Spence liked the pizza and if there was anything else he would like.

They struck up a conversation. First about the weather, which led to discussions about the area and then to each of their backgrounds. Spence had found the fellow to have the typical great sense of relaxed humor and sharp wit that he would have expected of Australia. This was his first real encounter with an Australian, and it had been a real pleasure.

After finishing lunch and saying goodbye to his new friend, Spence returned to the convertible and headed north again. He drove through Port Douglas and then another approximately thirty kilometers until he reached the turnoff toward the lodge. The remaining ten minutes or so took him on a single-lane road that wound through a sugar cane plantation. Just as the road entered the rainforest, he saw the sign for Silky Oaks.

Silky Oaks Lodge & Spa is Daintree's ultimate resort and is considered by many to be one of the top ten spa treatment resorts in the world. Nestled on the edge of the Mossman Gorge where the rare wilderness can be enjoyed in elegance and ease, the lodge gives the feeling of having been built in an existing rainforest, with every chalet under delicious assault from the freshly scrubbed aromas of the rainforest and the gentle cacophony of bird, frog, and animal calls.

From the minute Spence pulled up in front of the lodge, he could feel the aura of the rainforest—vast and pristine.

Set on a prime riverfront location, the lodge provides spectacular rainforest views accompanied by the soothing sounds of the Mossman River. This stretch of the Mossman River is too cold for crocodiles, but there are platypuses that live in the lagoon below the veranda restaurant of the lodge.

Spence checked in and was escorted to his room. To his great and pleasant surprise, his accommodation was a beautiful timber tree house. However, this was far from the treehouse that he remembered from his childhood. Set into the rainforest and surrounded by lush gardens, the tree house had been carefully designed to offer privacy and maximum comfort. His tree house bungalow had an understated tropical style with natural tones and timbers that had been used to create a relaxed, comfortable living space. Floor-to-ceiling glass doors opened onto a wide verandah where a hammock was perfectly positioned to make the most of the picturesque views.

It was early afternoon, and Spence wanted to make the most of the remaining time before dinner. He telephoned the concierge to check on the available activities and found that there was still time to take a horseback ride into the rainforest. He quickly changed clothes and headed to the lobby of the lodge where some fifteen minutes or so later he was picked up by a van from "Australian Out-Back Tours" and driven a short distance to a horse ranch.

Spence was assigned a spirited but friendly appearing horse. He was glad that the horse was not the slow, moping type. The group consisted of some fifteen or so folks that Spence suspected were mostly, if not all, tourists like him. The guide was a cute young lady with freckles. Spence guessed she was probably in her midtwenties. An outdoor type.

For the next two hours, they were led through portions of the rainforest, up and over hills and across numerous small streams. A few times, they were allowed to gallop at a quick pace when they reached meadows. It seemed the horses looked forward to both the meadows and to the streams. The guide did an excellent job of pointing out areas of interest, and for the entire two hours the group did not see another human—a few animals and very interesting birds but no humans. With the fog-shrouded rainforest, the cool gurgling streams, the sunlit meadows, and the quiet peacefulness interrupted only by the sounds of the horses and the chirps and sounds of the nearby unseen birds, it seemed they truly were in another world.

The ride had been tiring but very exhilarating. When Spence was dropped off at the lodge, he immediately went to the spa for a massage and relaxing sauna followed by a cool swim.

It was nearing 7:30 p.m. and becoming dark as Spence walked up the sidewalk through the gardens from the spa toward his room. He thought he spotted something move just a few feet from the walk but due to the growing darkness, he was unsure. He was only a short distance from his bungalow, so he quietly and carefully but quickly walked to his room. He remembered that among the items in his luxury suite were a flashlight, pair of binoculars, and a disposable camera.

Grabbing the flashlight and camera, he quickly and quietly retraced his steps and returned along the sidewalk to where he thought he had seen the movement.

He stood and listened. Nothing. He waited. Still nothing. After a few minutes, he was about to leave thinking that he had been mistaken when he heard a slight noise from the ruffling of leaves. He turned in the general direction of the noise and directed the flashlight beam in the same direction.

To his great and pleasant surprise, perhaps no more than eight feet or so away, was a mother wallaby with a junior in her pouch. The little one with its cheerful, inquisitive, mischievous eyes peering out of his mother's pouch and the mother with her more questioning and protective eyes were looking directly at him as if to say, *What sort of strange fellow is this*? Spence remained rigid fearing that any sudden movement would alarm the mother. After several minutes, the mother moved away into the darkness. Spence was so intrigued that he had forgotten to take any pictures.

Spence continued to stand in place for a few moments longer, partly in hopes the wallaby would return, realizing she probably would not, but more to just appreciate the wonderful experience.

Remembering that his dinner reservation was within the hour, he returned to his room and changed into typical tropical dinner attire, which consisted of slacks, white sports shirt, and sports jacket. He then slowly walked down the sidewalk from his bungalow to the main lodge, all the time carefully listening and watching to see if he could spot any wildlife that might be about. No such luck on this walk.

He entered the main lodge and continued through the lobby and on to the Treehouse Restaurant. The Treehouse was an open-air restaurant on three sides with glistening mahogany hardwood floors that reflected the soft golden glow of the candles from the tables. Looking out beyond the polished wooden railings that ran along the perimeter of the restaurant were the upper portions of the large leafy trees of the rainforest and the river below. As Spence was seated, he began to notice the sounds of various nocturnal birds and animals—some monkeys were probably also at play, he suspected. Pleasant light breezes moved the freshness of the rainforest air through the restaurant. The Treehouse was almost as much of a nature viewing and listening post as it was a restaurant. The reputation of the Treehouse, as Spence was about to learn, was that it had one of Northern Queensland's most innovative menus, featuring the freshest local produce and unusual selections.

The waiter arrived with the evening's menu and asked Spence if he would care for a drink.

Spence thought for a moment. "Thank you. I think I would like a nice Australian white wine. I will rely on your judgment."

"Yes, sir," the waiter said as he smiled and walked away.

Spence began to peruse the menu and knew the decision would be difficult from the unusual and interesting items on the menu. Just about the time Spence had made his decisions and laid the menu to the side, the waiter returned with his drink.

"Sir, this is a Chardonnay from the Barabasa Valley north of Melbourne, one of the best wine regions within Australia." The waiter paused for a moment and then continued. "I think you will find this wine very light and pleasing. If not, please let me know."

Spence tempted his senses with the aroma and a slight taste and nodded his approval.

"Have you decided on your dinner choices, or would you like some additional time?"

Spence was ready.

"I will start with the cauliflower and mussel chowder with lobster and paprika oil followed with an appetizer of the smoked crocodile tail with the wilted greens and spinach wafer with the orange sauce." Spence realized that the soup and appetizer together were more than he normally would order, but how could he not try the crocodile tail and the mussel chowder? Both sounded so interesting.

"For the main course, I will have the red curry tiger prawns with pickled ginger and coconut rice."

"Yes, sir; wonderful selections."

Just as Spence was thinking that the meal had been a truly outstanding and unique experience, the waiter returned to inquire if he would care for coffee or perhaps dessert.

Spence knew dessert would mean an early-morning extended workout at the spa but given the menu, the temptation and curiosity were too strong.

"Yes, thank you. I will have a cup of coffee and the caramelized banana and coconut tart with mango ice cream and passion fruit sauce."

Without a comment, the waiter smiled and nodded. A few minutes later the waiter returned with the coffee and the multicolored tropical desert.

Spence returned to his room knowing he would sleep well, and he did. The next morning, he arose relatively early and worked out at the spa. He then walked to the restaurant for a leisurely tropical buffet breakfast, but he was careful to just try small portions, as his trim waistline continued to recover from the wonderful dinner of the prior evening.

After relaxing on the deck of his bungalow for an hour of so peacefully listening to the sounds of the nearby river and absorbing the beauty of Silky Oaks, he packed and walked to the lobby where he checked out.

It was difficult for Spence to leave the peaceful beauty of the rainforest, but then he was curious to see what Carolyn had planned for him next.

CHAPTER 13

The sparkling clean BMW convertible with its top down was waiting for Spence in the drive just outside the lobby. The valet handed Spence the keys and asked if he needed any driving instructions. Spence thought for a moment, not completely sure of the return route south toward Cairns, but then politely declined assistance thinking he could find the way on his own, and if he got lost, well, that was just part of the adventure.

He left Silky Oaks behind and without difficulty ultimately found his way to the main highway and then drove south on Captain Cook Highway back through Port Douglas. He passed the pizza shop. It was now just past lunchtime, but he was far from hungry. He was basking in the sunny pleasant weather as he motored on wondering if the weather was always this nice—almost perfect.

The drive south provided a much better opportunity to look off to his left and take in the beauty of the deep blue ocean and the whitewater surf crashing along the base of the cliffs far below.

Clearly, this was one of the more relaxing automobile drives that Spence could recall. He held his speed within the allowable limit and, in fact, when there was no traffic approaching from behind slowed somewhat so he could catch as many glances as possible of the passing scenery. With the convertible top down, the gentle warmth of the sun, the freshness of the ocean breezes, and the background music from the late '50s and early '60s on the radio, this was indeed an enjoyable drive and one that Spence was hoping would not end soon.

He continued on driving south on Capitan Cook Highway and after another half an hour or so, he reached the Veivers Road turnoff and turned toward the ocean. After a short distance of perhaps two miles or so, he reached the beach community of Palm Cove (some fifteen miles or so north of Cairns) and came to the intersection with Williams Esplanade, an avenue that separates the beach from the palm-tree enshrouded houses and resorts of Palm Cove.

He turned left and drove leisurely south, all the time glancing at the beautiful white sandy beach and the inviting blue waters of the Coral Sea.

Within a few more minutes, Spence reached the Sebel Reef House & Spa and turned into the drive that led to the open-air lobby. He handed the car keys to the valet and headed into the lobby. He was warmly greeted by a cute young lady who he guessed was in her midtwenties and who had a deep but very pleasing Australian accent. She very efficiently took him through the check-in process and provided an overview of the amenities of the Sebel Reef facilities. She explained the location of his room and offered to have the porter show him the way, but Spence declined the offer.

After finding his room and getting settled in, he was off to explore the surroundings. Spence found the Sebel Reef House to be even beyond the expectations Carolyn had briefly described. The Sebel was a luxurious boutique resort with a sophisticated yet relaxed atmosphere situated in the heart of Palm Cove directly opposite the beach. In the distance off the coast, Spence could see the adventuresome-looking and appropriately named "Double Island."

The resort was ideally positioned for exploring this special part of the world. A truly stylish sanctuary nestled among lush private gardens with a waterfall and several pools, the resort and the grounds provided a unique hideaway and an opportunity to lose yourself in the romance of a bygone era.

Before leaving his room to explore, Spence put on a swimsuit and one of his treasured T-shirts. The particular T-shirt he chose was a colorful shirt from the Cheese Days Festival that Spence had attended in Monroe, Wisconsin, (located in the rolling hills of Green County, Wisconsin, the swiss cheese capital of the world) a year or so earlier.

It was a clear, bright, sunny afternoon with relatively low humidity and temperatures in the low to mideighties. In other words, near-perfect weather. The young lady at the reception desk had provided some weather statistics, which had strongly indicated that the beautiful weather he was enjoying was to be almost always expected.

Spence was intent on making the most of the several hours available before his arranged dinner engagement with … he was thinking hard, but could not recall the name and then it came to him: Piper Morgan.

He found a hammock under a palm tree on a secluded part of the beach (not that there were many people on the beach to begin with, which was another reason that this area was so alluring) not far from the resort.

After a short ocean swim, he returned to the hammock, where he relaxed and watched the brilliant small white puffy clouds framed against the deep blue sky lazily float past the bright sunlit green mountain peaks of Double Island in the distance. He could never have imagined how strikingly beautiful this setting would be.

Spence wished he could remain here in this unbelievably comfortable soft hammock gently and slowly rocking with the breeze listening to the waves breaking on the shore, in this perfect weather, with the sounds of some exotic birds in the nearby trees, with this unbelievable view forever. But, he knew that soon, perhaps very soon, for he never knew when, the terrible realities of the real world, which now seemed so foreign and distant, would require his services.

As the afternoon shadows from the nearby palm trees and from the pink and yellow flowering bushes began to lengthen, Spence remembered that he had made an appointment for late afternoon at the spa. Because of his small town background and probably, more importantly, the inherent recollection of how hard his parents had worked to provide for him and his younger brother as they were growing up, he for many years had a feeling that spending money at a spa for something that was so intangible was hard to justify.

Even now, with his enormous wealth, he often felt a pang of guilt after spending money at a spa, but these feelings seemed to be lingering less and passing more quickly as the years passed. Spence was not sure whether this was good and felt in some way the lessened feeling of guilt was a further loss of innocence. He treasured the values of his youth that had been instilled from his parents. The ethics and values of his parents and hard work during the earlier years of his life had ingrained in him the value of a dollar. Although Spence had became the beneficiary of great wealth through his own expertise and skills, he would readily admit that his wealth and good fortune had been the result of more than a sprinkling of good luck.

Even with his wealth, he was always somewhat uncomfortable when he saw the prices he was about to incur when making (although somewhat infrequently) a spa appointment. Spence was a very generous individual, although because of his desire and need not to attract attention most of the beneficiaries never knew the source of the kindness.

Maybe because of the wonderful time he was having, the tropical surroundings, or perhaps the subtle but lingering and now somewhat growing curiosity, as the time for dinner grew closer, about Piper Morgan, Spence had arranged for not only a massage but had also selected what appeared to be a very intriguing and relaxing bath.

Spence knew Carolyn well enough to know that Piper would have to be at least on par with the excellent Australian experiences that Carolyn had already provided. He knew he would not be disappointed. He did not want to be disappointed.

Oh, how much more relaxation can I endure, he thought to himself as the pleasure and pain from the firm hands of the experienced blonde masseuse worked his body. The Sebel House Reef Spa was recognized, as Spence had read on one of the brochures as he was undressing in the men's dressing lounge, as having been voted the number one spa in Australia and all of the South Pacific and one of the top ten spas in the world. The masseuse, with her beauty and skills, did nothing at all to detract from the well-deserved ratings and recognition of the spa.

Spence had selected sixty minutes of "Kodo Body Massage"—described in the brochure as "a wonderful rhythmic full body massage, using ancient aboriginal techniques to tone, realign energy flow, totally reharmonize the mind, body, and spirit, relieve stress and impart greater feelings of well-being.' He thought this better be worth the price of admission and was now admitting that the massage was truly a pleasant and unique experience well worth the time and price.

On top of everything else, the peaceful music in the background, without really registering with Spence, had been a mix of soft jazz and Sinatra selections. Now, softly in the background, Spence could hear "In My Wildest Dreams," by the Doobie Brothers. Could there be any more appropriate music at this moment—certainly nothing that he could think of, and he did not want to spoil the moment by thinking anyway. He became somewhat melancholy realizing that even with all of his wealth and access, moments like this were rare, to be treasured and appreciated. These moments of peaceful pleasure seldom occurred to this degree in a lifetime.

He got up somewhat wobbly from the massage table wrapped in a luxurious soft bathrobe. After regaining his "sea legs," he was led by the masseuse a short distance down the hallway to a pleasant but dimly candle-lit room with windows that looked out into an enclosed private flowering garden. The walls and floor of the room were of smooth stone with a sunken bath with jets of soothing warm water.

To top off the massage, Spence, always being curious about new things, had selected thirty minutes of a lemon myrtle and bush lime bath—described in the literature as "river salts sourced from ancient desert riverbeds blended with ground lemon myrtle leaf and bush lime creating an amazing, uplifting, stress-relieving soak while at the same time acting as an active detoxifying, cleansing, exfoliation treatment." As Spence lay soaking he thought, *If only I were to now be served a cheeseburger and a cold drink, now that would be the final evidence to convince me that I am in paradise.*

After the massage, the sinuous soak, and a crisp cool shower, he was about as rejuvenated, reharmonized and reenergized as one afternoon could provide, he suspected. Other than, he thought, perhaps the glowing feeling from a successful business transaction, or an afternoon of lovemaking with a beautiful woman you loved, or successfully completing a project in his other line of work!

Spence left the spa and quietly and leisurely walked along the stone walkway through the palm-lined gardens, with the sound of waterfalls in the background, to his room. He knew he had only an hour or so before dinner and his encounter with Piper Morgan.

CHAPTER 14

Although Spence only had an hour or so before he was to meet Piper Morgan for dinner, he knew he would only need a few minutes to dress. During his massage and soak, he had considered, dismissed, and ultimately decided on his clothes for the evening.

He stood for a few moments appreciating the fragrant cool air in the stylish elegance of his room looking out beyond the private verandah through the palms to the sea beyond. The sea was quiet and peaceful this late afternoon. He thought for a moment reflecting that times like these can be only truly appreciated when they are shared with a soul mate or a lover, but he knew he could not dwell on this thought.

Spence selected a pair of dark navy slacks pleated at the waist, which would bring attention to his firm waistline and athletic build, a pair of burgundy tasseled loafers without socks (it was the tropics, after all), an elegant light blue shirt that accentuated the dark sculptured features of his face, and a muted yellow tie that projected a warm, inviting, and engaging presence. He then selected a light gray sports jacket that provided a neutral balance and framework for the other colors and brought further attention to his firm trim body and to his cheerful eyes and dark hair.

The models from the pages of *GQ* magazine would have been envious. Spence was, perhaps because of his trim athletic build and features, one of those individuals whose clothes always seemed to fit so well and so naturally and who always seemed so confident and comfortable in his clothes. Unintentionally, he seemed to project a confidence and quiet understated elegance no matter what the setting. It just came naturally to him, and he did not flaunt it. But, to those who knew him, there was no question that he had the "right stuff."

Spence arrived at the Reef House Restaurant about fifteen minutes before 7:00 p.m., and after obtaining assurances from the wait staff that they would direct Ms. Morgan to his table upon her arrival, he allowed the wait staff to lead him to their table for the evening.

The Reef House Restaurant has three major assets: a spectacular setting overlooking the magnificent Coral Sea; a tropical, romantic South Pacific intimate dining room (a room open at one end leading to a large partially covered teak wooden deck beneath towering paperbark trees); and one of the most creative menus in the South Pacific. The restaurant enjoys unsurpassed ocean views, and its tasteful understated décor reflects the colonial charm of the resort—a sophisticated but unpretentious mood of casual elegance. Further, the restaurant has an extraordinary executive chef, admired and respected throughout Australia, who had developed an innovative and eclectic menu with a feeling of Mediterranean, Asian, and traditional South Pacific influences blended to create a truly unique modern Australian cuisine.

As Spence looked about and took in the beauty of the surroundings, he thought the challenge of finding an appropriate thank-you gift for Carolyn at Primrose Travel had just become much greater.

Spence was nursing a wonderful Australian pinot grigio glass of wine as he glanced at his watch and noticed the time was nearing seven in the evening. Across the room, he noticed the waiter subtly motion toward his table as he began to escort a young lady in Spence's direction.

The waiter and young woman were moving toward him but were in an area of the restaurant that was somewhat dimly lit (the sun was still in the sky to the west but portions of the interior of the restaurant were no longer receiving the benefit of sunlight and yet it was too early in the evening for the candles to be lit). Midway through the restaurant, the waiter and Piper Morgan emerged into a stream of remaining sunshine that had continued to find its way through the palm and paperbark trees.

As if a digital picture had been taken and frozen in time, the immediate image of Piper in Spence's eyes was of an Aussie wind-swept surfer beauty. She moved with confidence. Her narrow hips swayed, as she walked across the room. Her alluringly tanned yet nicely endowed athletic body, blonde sandy hair, which fell to the tops of her shoulders, and firm but feminine well-defined pleasant face with a sweet but sensual smile was turning heads and drawing attention as she gracefully moved in Spence's direction. She was wearing a pleated light green and yellow dress, which fell just below her knees, and a designer white blouse that was somewhat seductively cut to provide a tantalizing peek, but only a peek, of her cleavage.

Spence guessed Piper to be in her early thirties. But because of her firm and very attractive tanned body and sparkling eyes she might be, he thought, somewhat older with her age disguised by her youthful, spirited appearance.

As she neared his table and as Spence began to stand to greet her, a momentary fear engulfed him. A fear that did not show and a feeling that was foreign to him since few things caused him fear. He quickly thought, *What if I am mistaken*? *What if this beautiful creature is not Piper Morgan*? He was far less concerned about the possibility of perhaps being embarrassed by a mistaken identify than the possibility of experiencing the great disappointment if this sunlit vision was not Piper Morgan.

His fears were quickly replaced with reassured confidence and gratitude. Just as he stood, but before he had begun to introduce himself, Piper stopped in front of him and extended her hand (a petite, cool, firm, but gentle hand) toward him and initiated the introduction.

"Spence?"

Spence enthusiastically responded, "Piper, so nice to meet you."

He was almost afraid to query if she was Piper Morgan for fear again that just by the act of asking, luck would turn, and she might answer no and turn into someone else.

A warm smile quickly spread across Piper's beautiful face. Spence suspected, at that moment, that he would now have to get a truly wonderful gift for Carolyn at Primrose Travel.

As Spence placed the chair and assisted Piper as she was seated, he was afforded the additional opportunity for his senses to further absorb the beauty and sweet fragrance that surrounded her.

He seated himself across from Piper at what was fortunately an intimate table that kept them close. The table was situated so that they both could have a view of the sun as it was beginning to set. The sunset marked the beginning of the end of another day in what Spence was now convinced must be paradise—cheeseburger or no cheeseburger.

"Piper, what would you like to drink?"

"What are you having, Mr. Bond?" she said and laughed.

Spence was a uniquely handsome man with dark hair, a well-defined jawline with a dimpled chin, and a slight dimple on his right cheek. His eyes suggested mischief but also suggested he was someone of strength and confidence.

Spence wondered if her comment was a subliminal message that she was also immediately attracted to him.

He returned her laughter. "I guess you have quickly sized me up!"

He went on. "I usually have a martini stirred not shaken, but the waiter highly recommended this outstanding Australian pinot grigio."

His eyes twinkled as he said, "I am now quickly falling in love with all things Australian." He seemed to draw out the word *all*, hoping she would notice.

Piper smiled again, "Sounds great to me. I will have the same."

The service, as it would be throughout the evening, was excellent, and within moments the waiter delivered the glass of wine to Piper. Spence raised his glass to Piper's.

"Piper, again, wonderful meeting you. We owe gratitude and thanks to Carolyn for arranging this dinner."

"*Merci beaucoup*!" Piper cheerfully countered.

"You speak French?" Spence asked.

Laughing, Piper replied. "Unfortunately, no."

She went on to explain. "Carolyn and I met during a trip to France. Her French is far better than mine. I know just enough to be dangerous!"

Spence thought to himself, as he absorbed her beauty, *It is not your limited knowledge of French that presents the greatest danger!*

They spent the next fifteen minutes or so providing their respective general backgrounds. Their conversation seemed spontaneous, but unbeknownst to each other, the outline for each of their backgrounds had been carefully scripted. Piper told Spence that she managed investment properties in the Cairns area. Spence told Piper that he provided financial consulting services.

As the sun began setting and with dusk approaching, the candles were lit throughout the restaurant, bringing a warm glow and further enhancing the intimacy of the surroundings.

The waiter refreshed the wine glasses and handed Spence the dinner menus. The waiter, very professionally and efficiently, described the specials for the evening and then quietly left Spence and Piper to their conversations. Spence was in the process of telling Piper of his adventures at Silky Oaks and about the many things he had already experienced during his short time in Australia. She was a good listener.

Occasionally, the warm gentle breezes from the sea would cause the candle flame to flicker, adding to the pleasant setting.

As Spence handed a menu to Piper and began to open his menu, he inquired, "Have you been here often?"

"Not often but when I have been here, I have never been disappointed."

She peeked over the top of her menu with her engaging smile as she continued speaking. "I suspect I will not be disappointed tonight either." Her eyes sparkled.

Spence smiled. "Any recommendations?"

"If you like seafood, you can't go wrong here," she responded.

Just as the exchange ended, the waiter approached. Spence looked at her. "Piper, would you like a few more minutes, or have you decided?"

She turned to the waiter and said, "I'm ready." After a brief pause, she continued. "I will have the blue swimmer crab with avocado salad and chili toast for an appetizer and the tuna steak, medium rare, with the Nicola potato and grilled asparagus."

The waiter smiled as if to say "fine choice," accepted the menu and turned to Spence.

Spence thought for another moment and then gave the waiter his selection. "I will have the crispy fried oysters with the wasabi mayonnaise." Spence turned to Piper smiling. "I could not resist the adventure of something so interesting!" Spence turned back to the waiter. "And the ocean prawns with saffron risotto."

The waiter quietly turned and left Piper and Spence to return to their conversations.

Their dinner arrived, and they continued to find unlimited areas for interesting and mutually enjoyable conversation.

Shortly after they had finished a truly excellent dinner, the waiter returned to inquire about coffee or dessert or perhaps an after-dinner drink. Spence smiled at Piper and took the initiative as he turned to the waiter.

"We can't promise about dessert, but let's at least be tempted by looking at the menu!"

Piper said nothing but returned Spence's smile with a twinkle in her eye, much like the look that might be expected to be found in a young girl who was anticipating a nice surprise.

A few moments later, the waiter returned with the dessert menu. Spence was glad they were not being tempted by a dessert cart. Spence gave Piper the menu and then looked at her smiling.

"What do you think?" he said.

"I don't think so," she replied.

"Me either," he said as he placed the desert menu to the side.

"But," as Piper spontaneously turned to ensure the waiter's continued attention, "I don't see it on the menu, but what I really would like if it is possible and does not cause inconvenience, is a small amount of fruit and berries and a glass of a nice pleasantly sweet wine."

She turned to Spence with a look that was part, "Will you join me?" "Wouldn't this be fun?" and, "Let's not let the evening end just yet."

Spence was further impressed with her spirit and confident nature. Without hesitating for even a moment, he turned to the waiter and said, "I'll have exactly the same, but let's follow it up later with two cups of espresso."

Now he turned to Piper with the same search for approval. Without pausing, she laughed. "Hey, mister, that's a deal!"

When they had finished the espresso, and it appeared they were ready to leave, the waiter quietly arrived and inquired if they would like anything else. Spence responded. "No, thank you very much. The dinner and service has been wonderful." Piper nodded in agreement. "Just the check when you have a chance."

Again, typical of the fine service throughout the evening, the waiter returned within just a few minutes and quietly left the check. Looking quickly at both Piper and Spence, the waiter turned to Spence, "I have enjoyed serving you both this evening. I will return for the check when you are ready. Take your time."

"Thank you," Spence responded.

As the waiter left, Spence reached to pick up the check.

"Here, let me get part of that," Piper challenged as she reached for the check.

"Thanks, but not a chance!" Spence quickly responded with a broad smile as he deftly snatched the check.

"I want you to owe me!" he said as he securely held the check.

"I suspected as much, but how do you know I am credit worthy?" She giggled.

As Spence stood up and began to help move her chair, he gave her a quick look and chuckled. "Hey, maybe I was hoping you can't pay your debt so we would have to work out some other arrangement."

She just chuckled nervously realizing she had been trumped—at least for the moment.

When they were outside the restaurant, Piper turned to Spence with a hopeful but inquiring look. "Would you like to experience a moonlight barefoot walk on a tropical Australian beach?"

Spence laughed. "Only if you accompany me!"

She grabbed his hand and excitedly yelled, "Let's go!" as she led him toward the beach and toward the sound of the incoming waves breaking against the shore in the distance.

Just before reaching the beach, Piper stopped and turned to Spence. "Let's leave our shoes near this palm tree."

As they reached the beach and the shoreline and began to walk along the moonlit water's edge, Piper began to tease as she said, "Watch those big white toes of yours. The sand crabs will think they are a delicacy and go for a bite." She failed to tell Spence that the sand crabs are harmless and frighten easily and scamper away very quickly when they sense people are in the vicinity.

After a lengthy and very enjoyable period of time of slowly walking hand in hand in the moonlight along the water's edge, Spence built up his courage.

"Piper, I think I know of a way for you to repay the dinner debt."

Piper was not sure what to expect, and her hand involuntarily ever so slightly tightened, her pulse quickened, and her bra seemed to begin to have difficulty restraining her breasts as her breathing quickened. She was hoping, praying, that Spence would not notice.

She turned to Spence with a gentle smile and nervously giggled.

"And what might that be?"

She would have been disappointed if he was using such a well-worn and juvenile line to suggest a night of sexual pleasure. But he was so lean and handsome, and with the soft rays of moonlight dancing off the gentle ocean waves, she knew she very likely would have said yes, if asked.

She thought, *It has been a long time.* She had received many offers for romance and had politely rejected such offers, at least for quite some time, but this was different. Spence was different. This had been a wonderful evening, and, quite frankly, she wondered just where it might be leading. She thought she knew where she would like for the evening to lead.

She was becoming attracted to this out of the blue wonderful guy.

Before she could think of a response, Spence continued.

"My flight to Singapore and then on to San Francisco is not until midmorning Monday."

While Spence paused slightly, Piper thought, *Well, nothing wrong with spending the night and the next day and a half in bed*!

Spence grinned.

"I was thinking," he said.

"We had such a great evening together, and you know the area so well. It would be terrific if you could be my guide tomorrow, if you are free and have the time, and show me around this tropical paradise."

She was relieved and disappointed at the same time. Her mind raced as she thought, *Is this guy wonderful or what*?

"Spence, I would love to give you the guided tour. Just promise you won't call and complain to the Australian tourist bureau if you become disappointed with the tour!"

"Great. What do you say we meet at seven for breakfast and then head out? Is that too early?" Spence asked.

Piper thought for a moment. "No. Seven will be perfect. We will need to start early to cover everything I have in mind."

They shared a moonlight smile and turned back toward the lights of the resort. As they walked hand in hand, alone with their thoughts, nothing more was said. The romantic music of the gentle waves began to dissipate in the background as they moved farther away from the beach.

After reaching the resort and stopping briefly near the pool area to wash their feet and put on their shoes, they walked into the open lobby. Spence noticed the sweet fragrant smell of the beautiful and colorful blooming flowers situated throughout the lobby. It was now almost midnight, and the lobby was not totally deserted but was certainly very quiet. Spence could hear the Sinatra song "Strangers in the Night" playing softly in the background and thought, *Appropriate.*

They stood together, silent, both looking at each other and then toward the palm trees and the dimly lit outside gardens just beyond the lobby. There was a tension building from a growing excitement of anticipation. They both sensed it. They gently smiled at each other.

Spence spoke first. "Well, it's getting late, and it sounds like we may have a busy day tomorrow."

He paused. "Piper, thanks again for a wonderful evening."

She smiled. "Spence, I had a great time."

They hugged.

Spence held her hand and led her toward the valet desk near the lobby entrance. She pulled her parking receipt from her purse. Spence graciously reached for the receipt saying, "Let me get this."

In a very short time, the valet pulled up with a dark blue Audi S80 convertible. Spence thought, *Nice car. The business of managing investment properties must be doing well.* As the valet was getting out of the car, Spence and Piper were reaching the driver's side. Spence quietly thanked the valet and slipped him ten dollars Australian. The valet disappeared into the lobby.

Piper reached for Spence's hand. As she did, Spence leaned forward, hugged Piper gently, and gave her a light kiss on the cheek. There was a twinkle in her eye as she looked at him for a moment and smiled. She somewhat reluctantly got in the car hoping he would pull her back.

She turned to Spence, who was standing by the car. "See you in the morning. I will meet you at the poolside restaurant at seven."

With that, Piper began to drive away, turning back for a moment to catch another glimpse of Spence and wave good night. Spence waved as he began walking back toward the lobby and on toward his room. As he walked, he thought, *If tomorrow is anything like this evening, I will owe a very special thanks to Primrose Travel.*

CHAPTER 15

Spence and Piper both slept well that night, but both awoke early the next morning in anticipation of a potentially fun-filled and exciting day.

Spence took an early-morning swim, showered, and was now relaxing with a cup of caramel flavored coffee, one of his few weaknesses, in the tropical garden restaurant near the pool. It was just a few minutes before 6:45 a.m. Piper was not due to arrive for another fifteen minutes or so. He gazed out toward the ocean. It was going to be another beautiful day with bright blue skies. There was music in the background. But this music was being provided by the local kookaburras, cockatoos, sunbirds, and finches.

Spence could see Double Island in the distance. He had read some literature in the lobby describing the history of Double Island and had been intrigued by the beauty and privacy provided by this small island with the double mountain peaks a relatively short distance offshore from Palm Cove. Spence marveled at the peacefulness of this setting and the breathtaking views of the dark green mountains of Double Island with its white sandy beaches lapped by the white surf and blue waters.

Some fifteen minutes or so later, his thoughts were pleasantly interrupted.

"Hope you slept well."

Spence turned toward Piper's voice. "Hey, good morning. I sure did. How about you?"

"Great. Absolutely great! But some coffee sure sounds good," Piper said as she joined Spence at the table.

Spence had guessed correctly in what to wear for the day. He was wearing beige shorts, a colorful green and light yellow tastefully done tropical shirt, and sandals. Piper was wearing much the same with nice shorts, a light summer blouse, which unfortunately did not provide much of a glimpse of what appeared to be reasonably ample but proportionate cleavage, and sandals.

Spence smiled as he looked at Piper "You look terrific." He thought she looked even more beautiful in the morning sunlight than she had in the glow of the candlelight and moonlight of the prior evening—if that was possible.

"Thanks. You don't look bad yourself. Comfortable and ready for adventure, I hope!" She giggled.

Piper looked at her watch and saw it was a little past 7:00 a.m. "We don't have a lot of time for breakfast, so I recommend we have the tropical buffet. I will surprise you with the plan for the day as we enjoy breakfast. The tropical buffet here is really quite nice."

Spence was both hungry and interested and curious about what Piper had planned for the day as he responded, "Okay, then, let's attack the buffet,"

They headed toward the breakfast buffet. Spence found the waiter and ordered coffee for himself and Piper. When they reached the buffet, Spence found that Piper had done a disservice to the Reef House tropical buffet. The buffet was not just quite nice; it was outstanding.

Even with the wide array of selections from the buffet, it seemed they both had somewhat similar tastes since they both selected eggs Benedict, bacon, fruit, and yogurt. Spence could not identify most of the exotic fruit, but Piper had furnished ongoing recommendations as they traversed the buffet lines that ran along the waterfalls near the pool. They returned to their table and to the steaming coffee, which had also just arrived.

Spence looked at Piper. Piper looked at Spence, both with slight grins. Spence finally broke the silence.

"Okay, I give. Don't keep a stranger to your land in suspense any longer. What are we doing today?"

Piper savored the coffee and then put her cup down.

"Well," she responded.

"First, we need to be in the car and on our way no later than seven forty-five or so. On the way to the car, you will need to run to your room and get your swimsuit."

Spence was about to ask how she knew he had a swimsuit but thought that such a question would have been foolish since about anyone coming to the beaches of Australia would have a swimsuit and probably more than one. His immediate next thought, which was involuntary, was a question of what Piper might look like in a swimsuit. He would soon find out, or at least the prospects were sounding promising.

Piper quickly continued. "We need to be at the pier in Cairns no later than eight fifteen. I will drive since I know the way, and we may be a little pressed for time."

Spence looked quizzically at Piper and smiled. "Sounds good to me, but what is at the pier?"

Piper said in a very pleasant but slightly now more serious voice, "Well, since you have agreed to be in my hands today, I thought we could do a couple of neat fun things and experience a couple of truly unique Australian adventures."

Piper then handed Spence a neatly handwritten schedule for the day, which reflected the following:

8:30 a.m. Depart from Cairns by high-speed catamaran to Green Island

9:15 a.m. Arrive Green Island

9:30 a.m. Adventure and explore

11:00 a.m. Lunch and relax at the pool—Green Island Resort

Noon. Depart Green Island by catamaran to Cairns

12:45 p.m. Arrive Cairns
1:30 p.m. Scenic railroad trip to mountain village of Kuranda
3:30 p.m. Tour Kuranda
5:00 p.m. Skyrail to Cairns
7:00 p.m. Dinner—surprise

As Spence began to look at the schedule, he quickly said, "Hey, this looks like fun—I think!?"

Piper jumped back into the conversation. "It will be. The outline is just to keep us on schedule so we can get to Green Island and also to Kuranda. The time will be tight, but we can pull it off. It will be a great day!"

They had finished breakfast and were now walking through the gardens toward the lobby. As they walked, Piper provided Spence with some of the highlights of what their adventures during the balance of the day were likely to bring. As they reached the lobby Piper said, "I will get the car while you get your swimsuit. You need to hurry."

"Okay, I won't be long," Spence responded as he headed through the lobby to his room.

Spence returned to the lobby within a few minutes and found Piper waiting with the convertible. He quickly opened the passenger door and got in as Piper started the engine. They arrived at the dockside parking lot in Cairns some thirty minutes or so later. After having parked the car, they walked to the ticket office and picked up their tickets for the catamaran to Green Island. Piper had reserved their passage earlier in the morning. They boarded the Great Adventures catamaran for the trip to Green Island. The catamaran was actually an ultramodern midsized air-conditioned ship, and due to its high-speed capability, was able to cross the twenty-seven kilometers to Green Island in less than fifty minutes.

CHAPTER 16

Green Island is a true coral cay island sitting like a speck in the Coral Sea. The island is perhaps a mile or so long and approximately a half mile wide at its widest point and is surrounded by a coral reef. Green Island is situated like a sparkling jewel on the Great Barrier Reef. The island offers a rare opportunity to experience both rainforest and pristine reef waters and opportunities to wander paths through the magical lush rainforest, laze on the white coral sands with the blue ocean waters uninterrupted to the horizon, or dive or snorkel among an amazing display of beautiful tropical fish and coral.

The catamaran reached the pier at Green Island, and as the passengers were leaving the ship, Spence stood looking from the railing of the upper level of the ship toward the island and then to Piper, "This place is absolutely beautiful!"

Piper smiled, as the tropical sunlight reflected off her face. "Green Island is one of those rare beautiful places that you cannot imagine but can only experience."

They left the ship and walked down the pier to the beach. They walked down the beach for some distance, and Piper turned to Spence. "Are you ready to get wet? You cannot come to this wonderful place without spending some time in the water!"

Without any hesitation in his voice, Spence responded, "You really didn't have to ask!"

Prior to getting off the catamaran, they had found the respective washrooms on the ship and had put their swimsuits on under their clothes. Piper had a small beach blanket in her bag and spread the blanket out on the beach and then began to take her clothes off.

As Piper began to remove her blouse, Spence thought there could be few things more sensual than being with a beautiful woman on a faraway island beach with the crystal blue Coral Sea waters in the background with anticipation building as she disrobed for the first time. It was like opening presents at Christmas wondering what might be hidden inside and hoping you would be pleased and delighted. Spence, again like so many of his experiences during the past several days in Australia, was not disappointed. Far from disappointed.

Piper quickly finished removing her blouse followed by her shorts and sandals. She neatly folded her clothes on the blanket. Spence had removed his shirt and shorts and placed his clothes next to Piper's on the blanket. She was stunningly beautiful but in a care-free innocent way as if she was not aware of her form and beauty and of the effect it might have on Spence. Piper was wearing a one-piece ocean blue swimsuit that accentuated her lightly tanned firm body. The suit tightly fit her nicely sculptured curves.

"Hey, nice suit," Piper somewhat shouted as an unusually large wave broke onto the beach some twenty feet away. Spence was glad that he had selected the dark, navy, expensive-appearing midlength suit. The swimsuit added focus to his trim body. For the first time in a long time, Spence was at a loss for words or rather he was at a loss for the right words as he continued to absorb her beauty attempting not to appear obvious.

Piper grabbed his hand as she giggled and said, "Let's go!" and began to pull him forward as they raced toward the water.

The sea breeze whipped their hair as they ran, and Piper's breasts gently but noticeably bounced with each footstep into the sand. They spent the next hour or so swimming and playing in the warm crystal clear waters surrounding this exotic paradise far off the Australian shore. Spence was ready to spend all of the available time in the water and had to be reminded of their agreement to stick to the schedule. As they stood neck high in the offshore waters looking toward the white sandy beach and the green forest of the island waiting for a wave to float them toward the shore, Piper yelled out, "One more wave, and then we have to head back to stay on schedule. Race you to the blanket!"

Piper won the race, which was no surprise to her or to Spence. No surprise to Piper because she knew she was a very good swimmer, and no surprise to Spence since he let her win. Letting her see how adept he was at swimming would only lead to unnecessary questions.

As they stood on the beach a few feet away from the blanket, Piper handed Spence a towel.

"I won! What is my prize?" she shouted excitedly.

Before Spence could respond, Piper joked.

"I know! A walk along the beach and then lunch!"

Spence smiled. "It's a deal. You won fair and square, but sometime I want a rematch!"

As Piper bent down to pick up a towel, Spence could not help but see down the front of her swimsuit and marvel at her nicely rounded breasts as he noticed the remaining glistening droplets of water trickle down her cleavage from the smooth, tanned, exposed upper portion of her breasts. He felt somewhat guilty for taking advantage of the momentary opportunity to glance at her enticingly beautiful breasts, but it was only natural curiosity, and he found her very appealing.

They grabbed their clothes and headed up the beach and ultimately onto the path that lead into the forest. After a short distance, they reached the Canopy Grill (casual outdoor dining underneath the canopy of the rainforest and a place with a great selection of the freshest seafood).

"This is the place for lunch!" Piper said as she nodded in the direction of the tables.

They quickly were seated and ordered. As they were eating, Spence thought that this was one of the nicest lunches he could recall. *A glass of wine, prawn salad, picture perfect weather, and a beautiful woman on a Coral Sea island. What could be better—thank you, Carolyn!*

As he was finishing the very relaxing lunch, which had been interrupted from time to time by the sight of various colorful birdlife, Spence turned to Piper. "I was getting hungry. Great lunch and great company!"

"Thanks. Me too, on both counts!"

She pointed toward one of the paths. "We have just enough time to get out of our swimsuits and take a quick shower and then catch the boat back to Cairns. I know the managing director of the Green Island Resort, which is just a short walk from here. We can use the spa facilities to quickly shower."

She laughed, "Just a shower, and that's it. No time for a massage or any other of the great spa treatments that will tempt us!"

Spence had showered and changed and was sitting on a rock ledge along the walkway outside the entrance to the spa. The ledge was lined by large pink and white flowering shrubs. He was enjoying the sweet tropical scents of the flowers when Piper emerged through the entrance to the spa.

As she quickly approached, she said, "Well, that was refreshing. Ready to go?"

Spence contemplated for a moment. "I guess, but I could spend forever here."

Piper smiled. "I know. Me too."

She paused ever so slightly and then continued, "But we have so little time, and today is just a sampler. There are a couple of other special things for you to experience yet today," as she giggled and nudged him off the ledge and down the path.

Spence knew what one was. He was hopeful about the second!

CHAPTER 17

They arrived at the pier with fifteen minutes or so to spare and found nice window seats on the upper level of the catamaran for the forty-five minute trip back to Cairns. Upon the catamaran's arrival at the dock in Cairns, Spence and Piper quickly departed and made their way to the rail station to take the train to Kuranda. The Kuranda scenic railway is a spectacular journey consisting of unsurpassed views of dense rainforest, steep mountains, picturesque waterfalls, and distant views from the mountains of deep green sugar cane fields and of the white beaches and turquoise waters of the Coral Sea far below. The famous railway winds its way on a journey of approximately an hour and forty-five minutes from Cairns to Kuranda, a village in the rainforest.

The Cairns-Kuranda scenic rail line, with its fifteen handmade tunnels and almost forty bridges, was constructed in the 1880s and even now is still considered an engineering feat of tremendous magnitude. The railcars of the Kuranda scenic railway provide a reminder of the age when life was less hectic and passage by rail was intended to be a time of relaxation and perhaps reflection and an opportunity to better appreciate the wonders and beauty of nature. The windows of the coach cars can be opened. The views together with the scents and sounds and the breezes from the cooler mountain air passing through the coaches, as the elevation increases, can prove to be intoxicating.

Near the end of the train ride and after having somewhat excitedly pointed out countless postcard views to Spence, the repetitive rhythm of the tracks coupled with the earlier warm sun and the water activities, lunch, and now the slight mountain breezes floating through the train caused Piper to begin to fight doziness. She finally lost the fight and gently laid her head on Spence's shoulder. She woke as the train came into the Kuranda station. As Piper opened her eyes and got her bearings, she smiled at Spence but did not speak. The smile conveyed a message that Spence understood. *Thank you for watching over me.*

They spent the next couple of hours doing the typical tourist stuff by exploring the rich assortment of first-class and interesting nature-based attractions and unique shopping experiences provided by Kuranda. They then rushed to the Kuranda terminal to the skyrail and the return trip to Cairns. Spanning approximately five miles, the skyrail rainforest cableway glides just above the rainforest canopy in comfortable gondola cabins. The leisurely ride down the mountains in the gondola cars provides a unique vantage point for spectacular and uninterrupted views of the rainforest, tropical Cairns, the Coral Sea, and the lush Cairns highlands. They ultimately arrived back at the parking lot near the dock in Cairns and got into Piper's convertible. It was now close to six in the evening.

Spence looked at Piper and grinned. "What a day. Promise me this is not the end!"

"Well, that's about it for the day," Piper replied as she waited to measure and assess Spence's response.

Spence did his best to not let his disappointment show. He was very skilled at concealing his thoughts and emotions. In his line of work, he had to be since the consequences of not doing so could be devastating. He quickly thought, *Have I misread this? I thought we were having a great time, but it sounds like she is ready to call it a day and send me on my way.*

Piper could not read his look and reaction since there was no noticeable reaction. But, in fear of the remote possibility that he might say something like, "Well, it's been nice to meet you" in response to her attempt to tease, she said, just as he was finishing his thought about maybe misreading her, "But, we have another surprise in store for tonight!"

Spence was relieved—more than relieved! Even though he had encountered more intriguing and dangerous experiences than most men could even dream of encountering during a lifetime, he was now experiencing rare, but very pleasant, feelings of excitement and unfilled anticipation.

Piper continued to speak as she pulled into traffic for the drive back to Palm Cove. "I have some clothes in the trunk, and, if you don't mind, I thought we could go to your room and change and then have dinner."

As soon as Spence heard "to your room," anything after that would have been agreeable.

"Sounds great, but what is the other surprise you mentioned at the pier?"

"You'll see!" she responded with a grin as she played with him.

Spence thought she was not a tease but rather someone who had lots of spirit and enjoyed life and someone who was bright, thoughtful, and compassionate. In other words, he was becoming strongly attracted to Piper, and he felt, or rather he very much hoped, that the attraction and the degree of attraction were mutual.

When they reached his room and closed the door, Piper turned to Spence and gave him a tight hug. He could feel the firmness of her breasts pressing against his chest through his shirt and the firmness of her leg against his as she kissed him on the cheek.

She looked at him and whispered, "It was a wonderful day. Thanks for being such a great sport."

She then stepped back as she said, "Can I use your bathroom to change?"

"Sure. Take your time" Spence said as he pointed in the direction of the bathroom. Piper headed toward the bathroom with her clothes for the evening as she said, looking back with a wink at Spence, "I will be quick."

She laughed. "You probably won't be surprised, but we don't have a lot of time."

Piper was about to close the door to the bathroom when she turned again. "It's a very casual place for dinner, so find something comfortable to wear. See you in a few minutes."

She came out of the bathroom looking freshly scrubbed and sparkling clean. She was wearing a light, airy blouse and a pleated knee-length summer skirt. Spence whistled when he saw her. Piper stuck the tip of her tongue out at him lightheartedly but somewhat seductively.

"Don't run away, you gorgeous Australian!" Spence laughed as he headed for the bathroom. "I won't be long." he promised.

Spence reappeared from the bathroom looking even more tanned and trim wearing dark slacks and a cream-colored sports shirt. This time Piper let out a whistle of her own as they both laughed.

"Now the place for dinner is something special. Nothing fancy but just special—at least for me. Now that I know you, I cannot think of a better place for the evening, especially after the fun we had together today," Piper said as she prompted Spence toward the door.

"Lead the way," Spence said as he anxiously awaited the evening and whatever surprise was in store.

They walked from his room and then along the sidewalk through the gardens to the beach. After walking up the beach for ten minutes or so, they reached Becky's Beach Grill. Piper squeezed Spence's hand and with her free hand she pointed. "We're here!" she announced.

Becky's Beach Grill was a weathered but attractive and well-maintained colorful wooden frame building set back from the beach. The building was surrounded by palm trees with a deck looking out toward the sea. Soft Australian music was playing in the background.

They walked up the wood plank steps onto the deck, where a waiter led them to a table along the railing of the deck with a view of the sea. The sun was in the early stages of setting, and light from the table candles was just beginning to gain prominence.

As Spence looked about, he turned and spoke quietly to Piper. "I can see why this place is so special. It just seems to characterize what the spirit of Australia is all about. Fun-loving, informal, and peaceful yet colorful with a laid back potential for excitement."

"Exactly," Piper quickly replied.

They looked at the menu and reached a consensus to share an order of mudbugs, which are large crayfish from the waters of Queensland, and an order of oysters and turnover-shaped meat pies. The food was outstanding, and the beer they had decided on was ice cold. The evening breezes were pleasantly warm, and they both were enjoying an evening filled with the pleasure of simple conversation.

Dinner was finished, and they were enjoying some sweet-tasting tropical afterdinner drink when Spence looked at Piper and said, "I would like to see a lot more of—" as his eyes gazed at her.

Before he could finish the sentence, Piper quickly interjected, "Hey, sailor!" as she nervously joked not quite knowing where he was leading.

He laughed and nodded to the waiter. "Check, please."

Spence then continued what he had been about to say, "I really want to come back to Australia soon. I can't tell you how wonderful this day has been—thanks to you."

They left the restaurant and walked hand in hand until reaching the point along the lamp-lit garden sidewalk where one direction led to the lobby and then on to the parking lot and Piper's car and the other direction led to Spence's room. Piper turned to Spence. Nothing was said, but nothing needed to be said or remained to be said. The silence was interrupted only by the soft sound of waterfalls in the distance. Their bodies came together as they embraced, followed moments later by passionate kisses as the moonlight filtered through the palm trees.

After several minutes, while still in Spence's arms, Piper softly whispered in Spence's ear as her head was on his shoulder, "I know you have an early-morning flight to the States but ..." as she paused to let her courage build, "would you like for me to spend the night?" It was not really a question being posed as much as an invitation.

Without hesitation, Spence looked into her eyes as he answered with a simple yes, and they kissed passionately again.

He was about to break one of his basic rules, which was to never become intimately involved with a member of the organization or with a potential member of the organization. They took the sidewalk in the direction of Spence's room.

As soon as they reached Spence's room and were inside, they fell into each other's arms. A short time later they were in bed exploring each other's bodies and making passionate love. They fell asleep with Piper's head on Spence's chest, both exhausted from a day of fun-filled exciting adventure and a night of passionate lovemaking.

CHAPTER 18

The early-morning sunlight filtered through the room, and the birds began to make their wake-up calls. Spence was awakened as he felt the fullness of Piper's breasts. She had snuggled along his side with her head on his shoulders and her arm was dangling across his stomach. He lay quietly thinking of the pleasure of the evening and the wonders he had experienced in Australia during the past several days—realizing he must leave for the airport soon and knowing that the business he must attend to could not wait.

Spence was usually an early riser and very much enjoyed the quiet time of early mornings. Early mornings were a time when he could contemplate more complex issues, perhaps attempt to get caught up on reading, and organize his thoughts and priorities for the coming day. It was also a time for peaceful reflection, and this was what he probably enjoyed and appreciated most about the early mornings. He knew he could not linger long this particular morning. He quietly got out of bed, all the time being seriously tempted to return to bed as his eyes traced the outline of curves under the sheet formed by Piper's firm but soft body.

He showered, dressed, and then telephoned room service and arranged for delivery from the in-room menu. He ordered the "Australian breakfast" for two to be delivered forty-five minutes later. He then left a note for Piper on the bed telling her that he would be back in a few minutes.

Spence walked briskly to the lobby and found a telephone. He needed to speak privately.

"Hello. Bluewater Associates." The telephone was answered by a familiar voice.

"Ginger," Spence responded.

"Spence. How is Australia?" Ginger queried.

Spence thought, *What to say*? He paused before answering. "Wonderful," he then replied. "More than I could ever have expected. Having a great time."

He quickly continued. He thought about providing more details, but the details could wait—he needed to get to the purpose of the call and then quickly get back to his room. "I will fill you in when I get back. Anything new?" he asked.

Ginger responded, "Nothing that can't wait."

Spence paused for a moment as he subtly looked about the lobby, "Ginger, I need a deep background check on a Piper Morgan. She is, I believe, a resident of Cairns, Australia, and an Australian citizen."

"Anything I should know, Spence?" she inquired.

"No. Just want to verify my instincts. I will be leaving for the airport and a flight to the United States within the next couple of hours. Just hold the information, and I will look at the report when I get back," Spence advised Ginger.

"Okay, see you soon. Take care," Ginger replied.

"You too!" Spence responded sincerely.

Spence knew that upon his return he would know more about Piper Morgan than Piper could ever imagine possible.

The walk to the lobby and the telephone call had taken some fifteen minutes, and Spence was now almost back to his room. He quietly opened the door and found Piper still asleep. He removed the note from the bed and placed the unopened note in his trouser pocket—no need now to have to explain his brief absence.

Spence quietly began the process of packing. Some thirty minutes or so later, there was a soft knock on the door by the room service attendant as breakfast was delivered. Even though he had experienced what some of the world's best hotels had to offer, and it was truly amazing what some had to offer in terms of service and amenities, he was always reminded of the first time at a hotel in Chicago when room service had arrived. Just like out of the movies. The waiter had been dressed in a black tux and had rolled a silver serving cart into the room, and the plates had been covered with silver dome covers. The room service attendant and the serving cart this morning was similar to that morning in Chicago and reminded him of that first time many years ago when he was just beginning to be exposed to the wonders and experiences that were beyond the horizon of the rural Indiana countryside.

Piper was awakened by the sound of the door closing as the room service attendant left. She rolled over on her back and sat up instinctively pulling the sheet up slightly to cover the lower portion of her breasts. With one hand, she pushed strands of golden hair away from her face. She looked at Spence with a contented peaceful smile.

"Hey, sailor!" announcing she was now awake.

"Thought you were going to sleep all morning!" Spence laughed.

"I am usually an early riser," Piper replied, "but something kept me up late last night," as she winked at Spence.

Before Spence could find a funny line to refocus the conversation, Piper pointed to the room service cart and said, "Is that breakfast I see?" looking at the silver-domed tops covering the plates.

With a devilish smile she said, "What could I possibly have done to deserve such nice treatment—breakfast in bed, no less!"

Spence just smiled.

Not to let such a fine opportunity pass, Piper feigned shyness and pulled the sheet closer to her chin as she said, "Or do you treat all your ladies this nicely? Tell me, sir, is this your standard operating procedure?"

Spence laughed again. "Any more humorous diversions, and we can just forget breakfast and … oh, I don't know, maybe try to improve on last night, if that is even possible!"

"Okay, okay. No more teasing. I am famished, and the smells of breakfast are calling, but your offer is tempting and just so you know, last night was wonderful!" Piper said as snuggled the sheet closer to her chin.

"Give me just a few minutes to take a quick shower and get some clothes," she said as she put her feet on the floor and began getting out of bed. As she headed toward the bathroom with some clothes, she looked back with a grin and said, "Otherwise, we may never finish breakfast, and you may miss your flight."

Spence watched her beautiful tanned and naked body as she left the room. He thought, *Maybe breakfast was not been such a good idea after all!*

He turned on the in-room radio and found a light jazz station and poured a cup of coffee. He then made his way to one of the comfortable padded lounge chairs on the patio. The morning air was still cool, and he was able to leave the patio door open. He could hear the soft music drifting onto the patio from his room. A light breeze danced through the nearby flowering bushes. He could tell that it was going to be another wonderful day in paradise. Unfortunately, his stay in paradise was coming to an end, and the real world would soon call for his return.

Ten minutes or so later, Piper appeared in the doorway to the patio.

"That was quick," as Spence complimented Piper for her quick return.

She smiled. "You look like the type that might wolf down a lady's breakfast if left alone for too long!"

She walked the short distance to where he was stranding and gave him a quick but passionate kiss as they embraced.

"Breakfast!?" Piper announced as she stepped back ever so slightly, hungry but somewhat hoping that he would say, "Forget breakfast." From the feel of his body during their embrace, she would not have been surprised if he had suggested that they forget breakfast.

Not saying a word but with a strength of character and control sensed by Piper, Spence pulled Piper toward him as his arms engulfed her in a warm embrace. He returned the passionate kiss she had given him.

He quietly embraced her as he motioned toward the open door. "Breakfast it is! Let's eat outside on the patio."

"Works for me," Piper replied.

The Australian breakfast with eggs Benedict and outback sausages coupled with tropical fruit and a few traditional Japanese breakfast items including spicy seaweed was outstanding and seemed to more than satisfy their needs. As they were finishing off the last portions of the breakfast and savoring a second cup of coffee, Spence looked at Piper and said, "Piper, the last two days have been wonderful."

She smiled and said, "For me, too."

"I can't tell you how much I want to stay, stay here with you, but I have to get back to the States." The sadness was clear in Spence's voice.

A slight smile spread slowly across her lips. "I know."

She recovered. With her eyes sparkling and her spunky spirit projecting a lightheartedness, she sensed that neither of them wanted to dwell on moments of melancholy.

"Hey, as soon as you are ready, let's get out of here and get you to the airport. Your time in paradise is limited." Piper was doing her best to lift their spirits.

"Don't I know," Spence said smiling.

Piper drove Spence to the Cairns International Airport in her convertible. Spence enjoyed the warmth of the sun's rays and the breezes against his face as they motored toward the airport.

He looked, when he thought she was not looking, at the glow of Piper's face from the reflection of the sun. This was someone he was going to miss.

As they reached the roadway leading to the entrance to the airport, Spence turned again toward Piper. "Are you dropping me at the outside departure entrance?"

For the first time, she struggled with keeping back the tears as she smiled and said, "I would love to walk with you to the departure gate, but it is probably best if we say goodbye at the departure entrance."

She continued driving. Neither said anything further. They were both deep in their own thoughts and exploring and trying to come to grips with their feelings. Piper pulled the Audi into a parking space designated for departure drop-offs outside the entrance to the airport. The space was not all that far from where Spence had walked out of the airport only four days earlier. He thought for a moment, *What surprises life can unfold in such a short time!*

Spence gathered his luggage from the car. They stood on the sidewalk next to the car momentarily waiting for each other to speak first and fearing what they might hear.

Piper broke the silence and spoke first. "Spencer Harrington, will I ever see you again!?"

Spence engulfed her in his arms and pulled her close, as he had on the patio earlier in the morning. They exchanged a warm, long kiss as she ran her fingers through his windblown hair. As they reluctantly released each other from the embrace, Spence smiled as he said, "I will see you again sometime soon. I will call you when I get to the States."

"Take care," she responded in a whisper. She knew then that she would see him again.

He picked up his luggage and walked toward the terminal, stopping a few feet from the entrance to turn and wave to Piper, who was still standing by the side of the car. She returned his wave.

He could not see, in her other hand, the cell phone which had begun to ring and which, she hoped, would provide her with the information she had requested. She turned to glance at the incoming number, and when she looked up, Spence had disappeared into the terminal.

CHAPTER 19

The flights from Cairns to Singapore and on to Montreal from San Francisco had been time-consuming but had provided significant time for Spence to reflect on the evolving structure of the organization. The time also allowed Spence to further develop his thinking with respect to the growth strategies for the future as well as to consider additional actions to enhance security safeguards.

Spence flew business class. In his nicely pressed jeans and sports shirt, he melted in with the many other business travelers in their relaxed attire. Spence could well have afforded first class but he had difficulty accepting the huge price differential for first class when the enhanced service was not worth the price difference, and, more importantly, he did not want to draw attention. He had been very successful—indeed one of the best in the world—and had survived and prospered by avoiding attention. **Some knew of him but not who he was—a very important distinction.**

Although the international business class flights had been very comfortable, and the service had been outstanding (especially on the Singapore Air flight from Singapore to San Francisco), the lengthy time between flights in Singapore and San Francisco and the time involved in clearing immigration in San Francisco and in Montreal reminded Spence that he wanted to seriously look into purchasing his own plane. He made a note to discuss the purchase of a plane with Ginger.

The flights had been uneventful and relatively on schedule. Upon arrival in Montreal, Spence cleared immigration and then gathered his luggage and cleared Canadian customs. He then took the airport shuttle to long-term parking and found his car. For the drive to the airport, Spence had driven his nondescript black Toyota Camry. He paid the parking fee, pulled out of the parking lot, and began the two-hour or so drive to Burlington. After forty-five minutes or so, he reached the border crossing at the small Canadian town of Philipsburg and the northern end of Interstate 89. Without having to get out of the car, he was briefly questioned by the US border patrol agent, his passport was stamped with the date and time of entry, and he was welcomed home by the friendly but no-nonsense agent.

After passing through the border checkpoint, Spence began the drive south on Interstate 89 toward Burlington. He was always intrigued by the fact that a single-lane highway led south through Canada from Montreal to the border and then immediately upon crossing the border the highway became a four-lane superhighway—however, a highway that seldom had much traffic in either direction. He was pleased to know that his tax dollars had been put to good use—a *refreshing thought* as he chuckled to himself. He relished the relaxing scenic drive through the rolling green hills and mountains of northern Vermont to Burlington.

After just short of two hours of driving, he reached the Interstate 89 exit for Route I-89, which led to Burlington. He drove a short distance on I-89 to Shelburne Road and turned south on Shelburne Road and away from Burlington. He continued south on Shelburne Road until he reached Harbor Road. He turned onto Harbor Road, which led to Shelburne Point and home.

He was looking forward to seeing Ginger and McGinnis.

It was now midafternoon—a beautiful, sunny but pleasantly crisp early fall afternoon with deep blue skies. The leaves were in the early stages of turning to their annual multicolors of orange and gold. Spence absorbed the warm rays of sun filtering through the trees as he drove. He took in the various shades of green of the trees and the blue waters of Lake Champlain, through the woods, and as he enjoyed the invigorating scents of the freshness of the pine trees, he was reminded of the vast beauty of the world. Yesterday, or was it the day before, he was in Australia, and now he was in Vermont.

He followed Harbor Road until he reached the secluded lane that led to his estate on Shelburne Point. He followed the winding lane through the woods to his Vermont hideaway.

The lane, as well as the entire property, was guarded with highly sophisticated monitoring equipment. He knew that Ginger had been alerted to his arrival and that she was most likely now watching as he made his way down the lane. As he made the final turn through the woods, he could see the house. Ginger and McGinnis were in the drive waiting to greet him.

As he pulled the car to a stop on the brick circular drive in front of the parking garage, McGinnis ran to welcome him. With one final bound, he was at Spence's feet at the moment Spence got out of the car. A few feet behind was Ginger. Spence knew it was great to be home and to be among trusted friends.

Ginger gave Spence a warm hug. "Welcome back!"

"Thanks," Spence responded.

He smiled at Ginger. "I have some tales to tell, but it's good to be back. How have you been?"

"Things are good," Ginger replied as she helped him with some of his bags.

As they headed up the walk toward the house, Ginger said, "How are you feeling?"

"Actually, great. I was able to get some sleep on the flights. But I think I will just have something light and then get to bed early."

Spence looked at Ginger as he said, "Is there anything that can't wait until tomorrow morning?"

They had reached the house as Ginger replied, "No, some interesting stuff but nothing critical. Everything can wait."

Spence smiled. "Great. Want to join me for dinner?"

"Love to," Ginger responded.

"Give me an hour or so to unpack and take a shower. Sure you have the time?" Spence asked.

"I'm fine. I intentionally kept the evening open not knowing if your flight would be on time. I look forward to hearing about your Australian adventures," Ginger said.

Spence had few secrets from Ginger, but as he walked up the stairs to his bedroom to shower and change, he thought that there was no need to share all of the details about Piper with Ginger. Although he knew he would not be judged by Ginger, there was still a feeling that discretion might be best, and for reasons that were not really clear to him.

CHAPTER 20

The next morning, Spence was up just before dawn and took an early-morning run along the jogging path around a part of the property. He then showered and had a light breakfast before heading to the office wing of the house. After being away for the length of time he had been gone, it was more efficient to work at the house than to go to his downtown Burlington office. Especially since the downtown office was really just to keep up the front and appearances for him—although the handful of employees at the office had enough business activity to convince anyone who might be interested that the business was totally dedicated to investment activities. He wanted to get to his home office, really more of a large comfortable den than an office, to begin getting through some of the correspondence and reports that had accumulated during his absence. When he arrived at the office, he found several neat stacks of papers, documents, reports, and messages that had been arranged by priority for his review by Ginger.

Spence had been in the office for a couple of hours by the time Ginger arrived shortly before 8:00 a.m. He had made a nice dent in the piles of papers and reports. He had also perused the messages and the remaining accumulated papers so at least he had a pretty good idea of what might be lurking within the stacks that remained.

He looked up as he acknowledged Ginger's presence.

"Good morning!" he said as he reached for his coffee cup.

Ginger smiled. "You're amazing!"

With a somewhat puzzled look on his face and yet with a little devilish grin, Spence responded, "Oh, yeah, in what way?"

"Your work ethic for one thing," Ginger quickly replied and then continued as she explained.

"After your long flight yesterday and then the relaxing dinner with the wine last night that kept you up much later than you probably had planned, you had good reason and every opportunity to sleep in this morning. But I can only guess from the apparent decrease in the volume of the various stacks of papers on your desk that I left for you, what time you came in this morning."

Knowing full well how dedicated Ginger was to him and to her work, Spence laughed as he said, "Well someone has to get the work done around here."

He paused and then decided to get additional credit.

"And, you forgot to mention my forty-five-minute run earlier this morning."

Ginger smiled as she ignored his comment about the early-morning run.

"By the way, thanks for last night. Dinner was very enjoyable, and it was great to hear about the adventures in Australia. Also, sure beat the peanut butter and jelly sandwiches I feasted on while you were out and about visiting all sorts of exotic places!"

Both knew that nothing more needed to be said, but it was important to Spence as he continued.

"Ginger, it was great just to be back and to spend relaxed time together away from our projects. Sorry to keep you out so late."

She nodded agreement as she said, "It was fun. Now, let's get you through the stuff that has accumulated."

He knew she meant the items that required his personal attention. Ginger had his confidence and authority to deal with most matters. The items on his desk were for (1) his information, (2) those matters that she wanted to discuss with him and/or to confirm her judgment, and (3) matters that she felt required his direction or decision.

Over the balance of the morning, with Ginger's guidance and assistance, Spence was able to dispose of the balance of the materials. He elected to defer some of the reports for a time of peaceful reading on the deck in the afternoon.

As they were about to finish off the last of the accumulated materials and messages, Ginger, almost as an afterthought, said, "Oh, we just received yesterday afternoon the dossier on Piper Morgan."

Spence thought for a moment.

"Anything worthwhile?"

Ginger handed the half-inch-thick or so bound report, which was stamped on the outside cover "Confidential—Contains Highly Sensitive Information," to Spence.

"Very interesting reading!" she said with an emphasis to catch Spence's attention.

She paused for a moment and then continued.

"She is quite some lady. What's the story?"

Spence's mind was racing as he calculated the pluses and minuses of just how much to share with Ginger at this point. He was not used to making this type of decision when it came to sharing information with Ginger, but this information—this very personal information—was different. He knew he must tell her at some point and soon, but how could he tell Ginger he had slept with Piper? The security of the organization was paramount and was something that both Spence and Ginger knew should not and could not be compromised. He was not ashamed of having made love to Piper. No, it was not that.

The question in his own mind was whether he might have compromised, in some way, the security and confidential knowledge of the existence of the organization by becoming so intimate with someone who he knew so little about. The other question, the real question, was would Ginger feel the same?

He was confident that he had been careful and that he had not disclosed even the smallest shred of information that would have allowed Piper, if she was so inclined, to discern his true identity. But would Ginger agree? He knew that what troubled him most was how she might react to this possible breach of security. They were both highly skilled professionals that trusted and depended on each other. Neither could violate this trust; their lives depended on it.

He had decided to provide all of the details about his affair with Piper only if it appeared that Piper might be a viable candidate to head the Pacific Rim region. He would only have to come clean with Ginger and *pay the piper,* so to speak, if full disclosure was necessary.

After quickly processing his thoughts, he responded to her question.

"I was put in touch with her by Carolyn at Primrose, and she showed me around the Palm Cove area. A very interesting individual. There is something about her that intrigued me."

"Spence, do you think she might be the person to head up the Pacific Rim for the organization?"

"She certainly is bright and has the personal traits—at least from the time I spent with her. But far too early to tell. At least, she is worth a little due diligence."

Spence thought to himself, *For business and personal reasons, the due diligence would be both beneficial and interesting.* He also thought, *Nice to have the resources to be able to learn just about everything possible about an individual without the person ever having a clue or ever knowing.*

Spence was eager to delve into Piper's dossier, but it was almost lunchtime, and, more importantly, he wanted to be able to carefully read through the materials in the dossier at his leisure. Perhaps curled up on the easy chair on the deck after lunch would be a great time, he thought.

Spence placed the dossier on the desk and turned to Ginger.

"This can wait for a while. Let's grab a sandwich or whatever we can find in the kitchen and have lunch outside."

"I like a guy with a plan! I'm ready for lunch."

"After we finish lunch, I need to run into town and visit the office. It might be a nice quiet time for you, if you want, to read through some of the remaining reports and to look at the Morgan dossier," Ginger commented, sensing that Spence wanted to be alone when he reviewed the dossier.

Spence winked. "Good idea."

CHAPTER 21

After they had finished lunch on the deck, Ginger left to drive into Burlington to the office. Spence picked up a stack of reports including the dossier on Piper and went back out to the deck. He found his favorite lounge chair and positioned the chair so that he was shaded from the early fall afternoon sun by one of the nearby trees.

He put all of the reports to the side except for the dossier that he began to read. There was no identification of the author or references for the sources of the information contained within the dossier other than a code number on the bottom of the first page. Spence knew from the code number and from the alpha numeric sequences that followed on the page that the dossier had been prepared in Singapore and that the report included information also from sources in London, Zurich, Hong Kong, and Sydney. He thought, *She must get around,* as he held the report in anticipation of what he was about to learn about one Piper Morgan.

He turned to the second page of the dossier and found the following summary information:

Place of birth: Hong Kong
Date of birth: June 12, 1973
Current age: Thirty-four
Country of residence: Australia (moved to Australia with parents in 1990)

Citizenship: Australian, British, and Hong Kong (carries multiple valid passports)

Parents: English

Siblings: One older sister (married with two children living in Lyme Regis, England)

Married: Never married

Children: No children

Status of parents: Both deceased (Automobile accident in 1995 in Australia)

Residence: Multiple: 1161 Ocean Drive

Palm Cove, Australia

34 Harbor View

Hong Kong

Suite 106

The White Swan Hotel

Guangzhou, China

152 Prince Road

London, England

Education: Elementary school: Sussex, England (Edwards Grammar)

High school: Wellington (Sydney, Australia)

University: London School of Business—graduated with honors

Occupation: Chairman and president—Southern Pacific Trading Company

Ownership of Southern Pacific Trading Company: 100% of the issued and outstanding shares owned by Piper Morgan. **Caution**: Convertible bonds outstanding—refer to page 6.

Net worth: $45 million (US dollars). **Caution:** Refer to page 8.

Close associates: No close business or other associates. **Caution:** refer to page 12.

Relationships: None other than close (but very confidentially maintained) relationship with her sister. No known serious relationships during the last three years. Enjoys sex—not gay.

Personal financial data: Refer to page 15 for detailed credit card history and bank account information.

Cell phone number: Australia (61) 412-555-1214
China (86) 20-5500-6555

Passport numbers: Refer to page 24

After reading the summary, Spence leaned back on the lounge chair as he looked out toward Lake Champlain and thought *Wow, this is one interesting lady.* He immediately turned to the next page of the dossier.

For the next hour or so, Spence reviewed the information and the detailed write-ups in the dossier.

He was pleased and continually impressed with the degree and depth of the confidential and sensitive information that his organization was able to develop and provide on a target. The quality of the information was expected. His resources were highly rewarded and were expected to deliver world-class results. Nothing less was acceptable. Talk about a competitive advantage.

He read the dossier front to back twice and had taken notes of the information of particular interest. He placed the dossier to the side and began to review the notes he had made. He then summarized the more significant observations and opportunities, as follows:

1. Piper had started Southern Pacific Trading Company in Australia at the age of twenty-three shortly after graduation from the London School of Business. She had started the company to import a limited range of items almost as a lark in hopes of providing enough money to enable her to spend most of her time surfing and enjoying outdoor adventures of Australia.
2. To her great surprise, she found that her personality, education, and initiative served her well, and her foreign

trading business began to flourish. She also found that she greatly enjoyed the business.

3. The business had experienced rapid growth and had expanded to include a presence not only in Australia but also offices in Hong Kong, Singapore, China, London, and Ireland. The company's markets included most of the Far East as well as Europe.
4. With the highly profitable growth of the business, Piper had developed and nurtured relationships and had private access to the highest levels within government, financial, and business circles throughout the South Pacific, Far East, and British Isles.
5. From the detailed travel information included in the report, it was evident that she spent a significant portion of her time in Australia and relied upon her carefully created team of managers (the report had detailed resumes of each manager) placed strategically in key markets (Sidney, Singapore, Hong Kong, London, Dublin, and Guangzhou, China).
6. She maintained homes and/or permanent hotel suites in Australia, Hong Kong, London, and Guangzhou.
7. The business had become very profitable. On paper, she was a quite wealthy individual. In financing the growth of the business, the company had issued a significant amount of debt in the form of secured promissory notes. In order to achieve a lower interest rate, the notes contained a provision that, under certain circumstances, allowed the note holder to convert the notes into the company's common stock. Also, the notes were transferable. Spence had underscored the following comment from the report: "the conversion feature of the notes carries a risk that in the event of conversion, Ms. Morgan could lose controlling ownership interest in the company."

8. When Southern Pacific Trading Company had issued the secured promissory notes, the notes had been placed with the Cheshire Oriental Bank of Hong Kong. The notes had been sold to the Cheshire Bank because Piper Morgan had a very strong relationship with the chairman of the Cheshire Bank. Underlying the arrangement was an informal understanding between Piper and the chairman that if the bank should at any time want to dispose of the notes, then she and Southern Pacific would be given the first right to repurchase the notes. In this way, she could protect against some third party acquiring the notes, exercising the conversion rights, and taking control of Southern Pacific. Issuing the notes with conversion rights and with the transferability features contained significant risk, but Southern Pacific was a young company with rapid growth and needed the cash from the lower interest rate notes to continue to grow.
9. The report included a comment in red that there were highly confidential discussions under way that could very likely result in the Cheshire Oriental Bank of Hong Kong being sold to the Royal Bank of Zurich. The report also noted that the Royal Bank of Zurich planned to liquidate some of the Hong Kong bank's investments in order to quickly generate cash to pay down a portion of the debt to be incurred to finance the purchase of the Cheshire Bank. The report indicated that one of the investments on the confidential list of investments to be sold was the Southern Pacific Trading Company secured promissory notes. Spence underscored this information in bold on his notepad.
10. The next section of the report (submitted from sources in Hong Kong) included a copy of a highly confidential Cheshire Bank internal memorandum. In reading the memorandum, Spence found that Liang Guo, chairman

of the Cheshire Oriental Bank of Hong Kong, had met privately on two recent occasions with Piper to inform her that it was likely that Cheshire Bank would be sold and that he would be retiring from the bank. The memorandum had stated that Mr. Guo had offered to arrange to have Cheshire Bank sell the promissory notes back to Southern Pacific at a "fair price."

According to the memorandum, Piper had expressed sincere appreciation and gratitude for the highly confidential information regarding the future of the Cheshire Bank. The memorandum also indicated that Piper had explained to Mr. Guo that even with the rising profitability of Southern Pacific Trading, the company did not have sufficient cash to redeem or to refinance the notes. In three to five years perhaps, but not at this time.

The memorandum further outlined that she had expressed great concern and had reminded Mr. Guo that if the notes were sold and fell into unfriendly hands (for instance one of her competitors) and were to be converted into Southern Pacific Trading common stock, she could lose control of her company.

The memorandum indicated that Mr. Guo had assured her that as long as he controlled Cheshire Bank, she had nothing to worry about. However, he made it clear that the purpose of his visit was to alert her to the fact that it was very likely that the Cheshire Bank would be sold and that he would not be in a position, after the sale of the bank, to guarantee who might control the Southern Pacific notes.

Mr. Guo added another reason for serious concern. He had advised Piper that the Cheshire Bank had been contacted by a broker representing an unidentified party very interested in purchasing the Southern Pacific notes. The broker had informed Cheshire Bank that their client would be willing to pay a significant premium, if necessary, to acquire the notes. Mr. Guo indicated to Piper that due to the willingness of the party to pay a premium, he had suspected the party might be one of Piper's competitors who had somehow found out about the notes and was hoping to take advantage of the conversion feature of the notes and take control of Southern Pacific. He told Piper, according to the memorandum, that the Cheshire Bank had flatly refused to enter into any discussions regarding the notes or to even acknowledge the existence of the notes.

The memorandum went on to state that Mr. Guo had advised Piper that due to the below market interest rates on the notes, it would be very difficult to find any partners, even friendly parties, who would be willing to step in and purchase the notes. Anyone who would want the notes would have one objective, and that would be to exercise the notes and take control of the company.

Spence underscored the next and last point on his notepad. He had quickly recognized the opportunity to convince Piper to join the organization.

11. The answer! If it were to be possible to arrange in advance with the Royal Bank of Zurich to purchase the Southern Pacific notes as soon as Royal Bank acquired Cheshire Bank, then he would be able to ensure that Piper could continue to control her business—subject to his on-going concurrence. If he could purchase the notes, he would have something she dearly wanted. In return, she might be willing to accept his proposal for her to head the Pacific Rim for the organization. A quid pro quo, if you will. Piper had all of the skills and abilities he needed, and Southern Pacific Trading and Piper would be a wonderful cover for the real activities of the organization!

Spence thought for a moment, *This just might work*. He laid the notepad to the side and began to doze in the gentle warmth of the afternoon sun, listening to the birds in the nearby trees as they celebrated the remaining fall days before the onset of winter.

Chapter 22

Ginger returned to check on Spence before heading home for the evening. Spence was still on the deck and was reading the last of the remaining reports.

McGinnis, who had been sleeping near Spence's chair throughout the afternoon awoke and bounded toward his friend Ginger with a great hello as she approached. After giving McGinnis a hug, Ginger turned to Spence, "How was your afternoon?"

Spence was pleased she was back. "Oh, the afternoon was great. Got a lot done including even a brief nap."

"Anything you need before I head for home?" Ginger asked.

Spence looked at his watch. It was only a little after six in the evening in Chicago.

"Yes, there are a couple of things," he said.

"Can you get Tucker Wolcott on the telephone and then reach our folks in Hong Kong and see if we can find out very quickly where Piper Morgan will be during the latter part of next week."

Ginger turned and headed into the house to the office wing.

Within a few minutes, Ginger returned and handed a wireless telephone to Spence.

"Tucker Wolcott is on line one," she said.

"Great. Thanks," Spence replied as he punched in line one.

"Tucker, how are you. I hope I am not interrupting anything important."

After Tucker assured Spence that the call was not an interruption and after Tucker conveyed how pleased he was to hear from Spence, Spence found a break in the conversation to get to the point of his call.

"Tucker, I have a project if you are interested." Spence knew that all he needed to say was, "if you are interested" to get Tucker's attention.

Spence continued. "Cheshire Oriental Bank of Hong Kong holds secured promissory notes of Southern Pacific Trading Company. Cheshire Bank is in the process of being acquired by Royal Bank of Zurich. Cheshire will not sell the Southern Pacific notes because of a strong relationship that the bank's chairman has with the owner of Southern Pacific. However, I have reason to believe that the Royal Bank of Zurich has no interest in holding the notes and, in fact, will sell the notes once they finalize the acquisition of Cheshire Bank."

Tucker quickly commented. "How can I be of help?"

Spence knew this was something right in Tucker's sweet spot given his extensive contacts within the international banking and financial circles. He also knew this was an assignment that would pique Tucker's interest and that Tucker would view as an interesting challenge to be met.

"Tucker, any chance you would be able to meet with the chairman of the Royal Bank of Zurich and arrange for one of my holding companies to have an option to purchase the Southern Pacific notes as soon as Royal Bank acquires Cheshire Bank? I will be willing to pay a premium for the notes so Royal Bank will look good by selling. I believe selling the notes is consistent with their postacquisition plans anyway. I trust your judgment. Do whatever is necessary to get the notes."

Tucker immediately responded. "Spence, I will make some confidential well-placed telephone calls first thing in the morning. I will move quickly, but this may take a few days."

"Understand, and thanks. All the best," Spence said as he wrapped up the conversation.

Just as Spence finished the telephone call with Tucker Wolcott, Ginger returned and advised Spence about the status of the inquiry to Hong Kong.

"Our people in Hong Kong say they will have Piper Morgan's schedule for the next few weeks first thing in the morning."

Spence smiled but raised his eyebrows in a questioning manner.

Ginger shrugged her shoulders and said, "We don't want to know!' referring to how their organization was planning to gain access to Piper's personal and business schedule so quickly, or at all.

Spence had been busy on various matters throughout the following few days and had not given any thought to the Southern Pacific opportunity. He expected that Tucker Wolcott, as good as he was, would still need several days if he was to even be successful in his task. However, midmorning three days later (midafternoon in Europe), while Ginger and Spence were working across from each other at Spence's desk planning upcoming projects, a telephone call came in on the secure line.

Ginger picked up the telephone, listened, and then turned to Spence. "It's Tucker Wolcott," she said as she handed the telephone to Spence.

"Tucker, what's the news?" Spence said with eagerness.

"It's a deal! Tucker said and then went on to explain. "The Royal Bank has agreed to sell the Southern Pacific notes to you as soon as they close on their purchase of the Cheshire Bank. Of course, they do not know it is you, only that the sale will be for cash at a nice premium for the bank to a yet to be named holding company."

"Terrific. Thanks," Spence said with sincerity.

Spence thought for a moment. *Almost anything can be accomplished with money and friends with skills and contacts.*

"Tucker, I would like for you to coordinate and handle the purchase of the notes—standard fee arrangement. Is that okay with you? If not, just let me know."

Without hesitation, Tucker replied, "My pleasure. The fee arrangement is fine."

In closing, Spence said, "Thanks again, Tucker. Just let Ginger know when the deal is ready, and she will work with you on the wire routing instructions and the holding company arrangements for the notes."

As soon as Spence finished the telephone call, he turned to Ginger and smiled, saying "Now, let's see that schedule for Piper Morgan!"

Ginger handed the schedule from Hong Kong with Piper Morgan's schedule for the next two weeks to Spence. After reviewing the schedule, Spence smiled.

"Ginger, book both of us on a flight tomorrow to Guangzhou, China."

CHAPTER 23

Guangzhou, with a population in excess of twelve million people, is the third-largest city in China behind Beijing and Shanghai. Located on the Pearl River in the southern part of the country, Guangzhou lies close to the South China Sea and is approximately 180 kilometers, about 120 miles, from Hong Kong. Guangzhou is in the center of one of the country's most rapidly expanding industrial and commercial areas. The city is an excellent location to have an office for foreign trading activities and, most likely, the reason that Piper had established the China office of Southern Pacific Company in Guangzhou.

The relatively new Guangzhou international airport provides direct air service to many of the major cities in the world including Bangkok, Manila, Singapore, Sidney, and the West Coast of the United States. Guangzhou, known as "the city of flowers," has no real winter, and flowers are in blossom year-round. The city has retained its ancient customs but, at the same time, has emerged as a city full of vigor with great business opportunities and exciting adventure.

The White Swan hotel is located near downtown Guangzhou on historic Shamian Island with the famous and storied expanse of the Pearl River on one side and the magnificent Banyan Gardens on the other. A vibrant yet peaceful setting, the White Swan represents the centerpiece of Guangzhou's luxury hotels. The White Swan, which has both an Asian as well as a Western focus, is an ideal destination for not only leisure but also for international business travelers. With the rapid business expansion in China during the past several years and the vast number of companies from the industrial countries of the world moving manufacturing to China and especially to southern China, the White Swan hotel has been a magnet for international business executives.

The hotel's proximity to the US consulate results in many families in the process of adopting Chinese children staying at the hotel. Other than the dual languages (Chinese and English), it might be difficult to discern at first glance that this beautiful hotel, with its huge waterfall in the lobby, overlooking the vibrant Pearl River, with all sorts of boats and water taxis bustling with activity, is in China. Although, the colorful, brightly lit neon lights of the boats on the river would be a strong clue that something is different, a foreign traveler can easily meld into the background and go unnoticed.

Spence and Ginger arrived at the White Swan late in the afternoon of the following day. They knew from the intelligence reports that Piper would be arriving from Hong Kong and going to her permanent suite at the hotel between seven and nine that evening. Spence also knew that Piper was scheduled to attend various meetings at her Guangzhou office the following day but that she had no dinner plans, at the moment, for the following evening.

After checking into the hotel, Spence and Ginger were taken to their respective rooms. To be safe, they planned to have room service dinner in Spence's room to avoid the possibility, although unlikely, of Spence and Piper accidentally running into each other.

Around 8:30 p.m., as Spence and Ginger were finishing dinner, the telephone rang in Spence's room. Spence answered by saying hello but not giving his name. The individual, a hotel informant, said only that the party had just arrived and was now in her room.

Spence waited an hour or so and then with Ginger still with him, placed a telephone call to Piper's room.

"Hello," Piper answered as the telephone rang.

"Piper, this is Spence Harrington."

There was a pause as Piper gathered her surprised and somewhat alarmed thoughts.

"Spence, how did you know I was here?!"

Spence laughed with the objective of lessening the shock that Piper must be experiencing and hopefully to somewhat disarm Piper's guarded reaction to the surprise and the perhaps perceived intrusion into her privacy.

"I am here in Guangzhou and actually staying at the White Swan for a couple days on business," he said avoiding her question.

"But how did you know how to find me? How did you know that I would be here?" Piper queried again, but this time with more tension and challenge in her voice.

Spence replied, "It's a long story, and I will tell you when we get together. I will be busy most of tomorrow but was hoping we could have dinner tomorrow evening."

The last report provided to Spence was that Piper had not yet scheduled any dinner plans for the next evening. Her next response would be critical. Spence was intent on listening to the tone of her voice almost as importantly as her answer.

He was instantly relieved by her response.

"I am surprised, maybe shocked to receive your call at the hotel, but yes, I want to see you," Piper said in a quiet soft voice.

Spence did not want to risk any change of mind on her part, so he quickly interjected, "Great, wonderful. How does 7:00 p.m. at the Riverside Restaurant here in the hotel sound?"

"Okay, great. I will meet you there. I very much look forward to seeing you," she said.

Spence and Ginger spent the next day sightseeing and taking a boat excursion on the Pearl River. For lunch they had found a nice garden restaurant. As they enjoyed the local cuisine, Spence knew he must tell Ginger everything about Piper, and now would be the time—the discussion could not wait any longer.

"Ginger, before you meet Piper, there's another piece of information you need to know about her."

She looked up from the chili crab she was enjoying for lunch and said, "And what's that?"

Without flinching, Spence said, "Piper Morgan and I spent a night together while I was in Australia."

Her eyes were clear. She hid disappointment well. She accepted reality. She grasped his hand with hers, and he immediately felt the gentle warmth of her hand. She simply said, "How could she resist such a handsome rascal."

She winked slightly and continued, "Who would not want to spend the night with James Bond—even if she did not know it."

Spence started to speak, but Ginger held up her hand to stop him as she said, "I know you do not sleep around, and I trust you. I know you would never disclose any information that would put me or you or the organization at risk."

She thought to herself several times as they finished lunch, *Piper Morgan is one lucky lady.*

Chapter 24

Somewhat before 7:00 p.m., Spence arrived at the Riverside Restaurant, which was two levels below the lobby level but still overlooking the river. He had arranged for a secluded table along one of the windows with a panoramic view of the river. A few minutes before seven, Piper arrived at the restaurant. Spence had been watching for her, and he immediately was up and walking toward her as soon as he saw her arrive. She was wearing black slacks and a blue blouse with narrow white stripes. She had a more professional appearance than he recalled from Australia.

They warmly embraced, and Spence led her to the table. Neither said a word.

As soon as they were seated, Spence smiled and said "I have a lot to tell you."

"Well, I hope so," Piper responded pleasantly but with a distinct seriousness in her voice.

"Piper, first, it is great to see you," Spence said as his eyes darted between her sandy hair, her beautiful eyes and face, and eventually to her blouse, which concealed what he knew to be great breasts.

She smiled. "It's great to see you too—I think."

They ordered a glass of wine each, and then Spence began to explain. No sense for small talk.

"Don't ask me yet to explain why or how, but I know a lot about you. I know that you are at great risk of losing control of your company. I know about the secured promissory notes that were issued by your company, and I know that if the notes fall into your competitors' or other unfriendly, hands, you are at serious risk. I also know a lot about Southern Pacific Trading Company."

Piper looked stunned. She began to ask, "How did you find out so much about—"

Spence quickly interrupted. "I will explain, but what I have to tell you first is good news as well as an opportunity for both of us."

She seemed somewhat less apprehensive by the gentle tone of Spence's voice and his assurances.

Spence then spent the next fifteen minutes or so explaining how he now had a commitment from the Royal Bank of Zurich to allow him to purchase and take control of all of the outstanding Southern Pacific Trading Company secured promissory notes. He assured Piper his planned purchase was entirely benevolent and that his actions were intended to protect Piper and to allow her to continue to maintain control of Southern Pacific.

Piper looked firmly at Spence, her eyes steely and penetrating behind the almost imperceptible tears, which she was doing a great job of attempting to control, for a few moments, and then said, "I have three thoughts.

"First, thanks. I mean, really thanks!

"Second, what's in this for you, and what do you want?

"And, third, who the hell are you?"

Spence knew she was great in bed but now could see that she was probably even better in business. When the chips were down, she was focused and determined. He thought, *No question, she can be tough if necessary, but will she be fair?*

Spence laughed as he said, "Well, as they say, here is the rest of the story."

He trusted Piper based on the time he had spent with her in Australia and based on the extensive background review. But before he went any further and before he shared any information on the organization, he wanted Ginger's concurrence. He trusted

Ginger's judgment—even more so now that she knew he had slept with Piper.

"Piper, I have one of my associates with me on this trip. To give you the full story, I would like for her to join us for dinner. Would you mind?"

Piper's face for the first time betrayed her and allowed her feelings of disappointment to slightly show, but she grinned at Spence as she said, "Well, I was hoping to have you to myself. But, if she will help to explain the mystery of who you are and what this evening is about, then fine with me."

Spence reached across the table and held her hand briefly as he said, "Thanks." He then pulled his cell phone from his jacket and telephoned Ginger's room.

Ten minutes or so later, Spence saw Ginger approaching the table. She seemed even more attractive tonight. Spence quickly rose and introduced Ginger and Piper. Ginger was the first to speak.

"Piper, nice to meet you. Spence has told me a lot about you. I have been looking forward to meeting you."

Piper was very pleasant and gracious with her response. "Ginger, nice to meet you also. Yes, Spence seems to know more about me than I might have thought possible."

They both laughed, and Spence just smiled, his eyes watching Piper closely.

Spence spoke next as he gestured for the waiter. He ordered drinks and then suggested that they look at the menu.

Ginger made her selection quickly, and as she placed the menu to the side commented to Piper, "I bet you have a lot of questions."

Piper replied "Well, yes, I do. For one, who is this seemingly extremely well- informed mystery man?"

"For the moment, let's just say he is one of the good guys," Ginger said as they both then smiled. Piper began to sense that she could like and perhaps trust Ginger.

Ginger continued. “Piper, Spence told me everything about his time with you in Australia. Sounds like you both had a great time. It is not easy to impress Spence!”

Piper looked at Ginger and then at Spence with a somewhat puzzled, worried, and questioning look on her face. She then said to Ginger, “Everything?”

Ginger slightly nodded her head as she quietly and respectfully responded, “Yes.”

Piper was evaluating her emotions and her options as she began to move her chair away from the table as if to leave the table when Ginger quickly continued.

“Piper, you will soon understand why Spence told me. Please trust Spence.”

“Well, this has been one of the strangest evenings so far of my life,” Piper replied somewhat in a state of disbelief.

“I can only guess what is to come, and the evening is still early. My curiosity is winning out, so I will listen,” Piper said in a somewhat unconvinced voice as she sat down in her chair.

Piper did not say anything further, but it went without saying that what she was thinking was, *This had better be good*! as she looked at Spence and then at Ginger.

The waiter returned to the table with their drinks and to take their selections for dinner and in so doing provided a welcome break.

Spence had been very observant but silent but used the break to engage Piper in conversation.

“Piper, Ginger is my most trusted partner. Whatever anyone can tell me, they can tell Ginger. She is privy to everything that occurs within my businesses.”

He could have anticipated, and he certainly could sense the question in Piper’s mind as her eyes measured Ginger. He knew it was not a business question on Piper’s mind. He needed to prompt her further thoughts and quickly said, “Piper, the relationship Ginger and I enjoy and the bond we share is professional. We have shared many interesting adventures and have had a lot of unique experiences, but what Ginger and I have built, we cannot put at risk by letting our feelings go beyond the professional level."

Piper glanced toward Ginger and saw Ginger nod her agreement with Spence's words.

Ginger used this opportunity to deflect the conversation back to Piper as she said, "Piper, Spence has told me somewhat about Southern Pacific Trading Company. Where would you like to take the company, and what do you want to do in the future?"

Piper smiled and said, "Well, the future of Southern Pacific and my control of the company seems, as of earlier this evening, much more secure than I would have thought possible at anytime over the past several months. I really thought I might lose control of my company, but thanks to what Spence told me this evening—"

Ginger interrupted, "What would you like to do in the future?"

Piper thought for a moment as she paused and then said, "The company is doing fine, experiencing rapid profitable growth and is in good hands. I have some great managers who are very capable and who I trust." She paused again and then continued. "The company provides a great foundation with access to opportunities and people that I would never have guessed possible a few years ago."

Just then the waiter delivered the main course. As they began to eat, Piper finished her comment. "I have this yearning to find something new that will be interesting, challenging, and full of adventure, and where my efforts will have an impact."

Piper looked at Spence with an expression that caused Spence to wonder, *Has Piper somehow obtained information on my background*? Well, it soon would not matter.

During dinner, Piper explained in detail the workings of Southern Pacific Trading Company and filled Spence and Ginger in on the holes in her background that had not been covered in the dossier commissioned by Spence. Her story jived with the report that Spence had received.

Spence turned to Ginger. Ginger knew the question. She knew that Spence was asking whether to expose the existence and information about the organization to Piper and whether Ginger thought Piper had the "right stuff" to head the Pacific Rim for the organization.

Ginger smiled and winked and very subtly nodded her concurrence. Spence also nodded.

With Ginger's blessing and after the waiter poured coffee and was out of hearing range, Spence turned to Piper.

"Piper, we are now ready to tell you what you want to know. What we have to say is highly confidential, but we trust you, or we would not be having this conversation."

Piper's interest had reached a new peak as Spence continued. He and Ginger then explained the organization and answered each of her many questions.

When they had finished, Piper leaned back and said, "Wow, who would have thought!"

Piper then continued. "I have one more question."

"Sure," Spence said.

"Why are you telling me all of this?"

Spence looked at Ginger and then at Piper. "Piper, would you be interested in becoming head of the Pacific Rim for the organization?"

Without any hesitation, she answered, "Yes. Yes, I would!"

CHAPTER 25

Spence believed strongly that if you were ethical and worked hard there was a higher probability of experiencing good luck and good fortune. In any event, whether good fortune came his way or not, he was highly ethical and had a strong work ethic. He would let others conjecture on the cause of his good fortune. He only knew that he had been truly blessed.

Spence deeply respected and greatly valued trusted friendships. He was honest and forthright. He was also very intelligent with an uncommon depth of common sense, a high degree of curiosity, and a wonderful sense of humor.

After graduating from Indiana State University with a degree in finance and accounting, Spence had joined the Chicago office of Arthur Andersen & Co. In retrospect, joining Andersen (or the "firm" as it was affectionately referred to) had been one of the many "good luck" events in his life.

Joining Andersen had been happenchance for Spence. He had worked his way through college. In his junior and senior years, he had worked from 10:00 p.m. to 6:00 a.m. in the finance department at the local subsidiary of an international company. He had scheduled only one on-campus interview for postgraduation employment, and that had been with Arthur Andersen. The interview was at ten o'clock one morning in March of his senior year. After leaving work at 6:00 a.m. the morning of the scheduled interview, he thought he would be more refreshed for the interview if he could get a couple of hours of sleep. Unfortunately, he slept through the interview.

When he awoke, he thought, for good reason, that he had probably lost the chance to join one of the Big Eight accounting firms. In the early afternoon, while attending one of his finance classes, the professor asked him to step outside. The professor said he was aware Spence had been a no show for the interview and asked why Spence had not met with the Andersen personnel. Spence explained. The professor told Spence that he was sure the Andersen folks would still like to meet him. Spence looked down at his blue jeans and sweat shirt, at least he thought they were clean, and questioned how he would come across with the partners from such a prestigious and highly respected professional firm when all of the other students who were interviewing were in suits. The professor strongly urged Spence to meet with the Andersen personnel while they were still on campus. Spence went to the interview and explained what had happened.

He left the interview not knowing their reaction, but a few days later he received an outstanding offer to join the firm's Chicago office, and the rest is history.

Much later, Spence would learn that the Andersen partners had been impressed with his honesty and his courage in meeting with them in jeans and a sweatshirt. They had been impressed with his grade level achievements considering that he was working from 10:00 p.m. to 6:00 a.m. five days a week.

For a young man from a small school in southern Indiana to be working in the famous downtown "loop" of Chicago and to be working in the international home office of the largest and most respected accounting firm in the world and one of the great professional firms of the world, it was more than good fortune. It was a whole new world. He was surrounded in this highly ethical environment called Arthur Andersen & Co. by extremely bright, energetic, aggressive, hard-working young individuals. It was also, as is the case with most world class professional firms, a highly competitive environment. He loved it!

Spence also quickly fell in love with Chicago and with the spirit, excitement, vitality, and range of activities of the city. Sitting on the southwestern edge of Lake Michigan, Chicago is the jewel of the Midwest and one of the great cities of the world. Each day brought the possibility for new, exciting, and different experiences for Spence as he walked from the train station along the world-class shopping streets and through the caverns of the skyscrapers of the financial district to the Andersen offices. It was for Spence a love affair truly captured by the Sinatra lyrics "My kind of town, Chicago is, my kind of town, Chicago is ..."

Joining the firm had been one of those good fortune life-changing events.

He had known that the first and foremost "good luck" event in his life had been to have had such wonderful caring parents who had through their honest behavior and caring treatment of others instilled high values in him. His parents had provided a road map of confidence for his life. It was up to him to navigate through the challenges and obstacles of life toward happiness and purpose and to make them proud—proud that no matter the destination or the route traveled, the destination was worthwhile, and that the destination had been achieved without compromising the principles conveyed from his parents and learned in his childhood. And so he had done.

Spence worked his way through college. He had enjoyed the various work experiences and was, he knew, better for the work experiences. Prior to college, he had also worked on Saturdays and during the summers of his high school years at his uncle's grocery store in the small Indiana town. Many times in later years, he would recall how tired he had been working the long hours, but he now longed to be able to return to those times, if only for a few moments. It had been hard work but fun, and he had gained respect for the value of hard work and respect for those who put in an honest day's work. It was a far different time, he thought, than today's world, which seemed to be based on deal-making and the quick buck. Maybe it had always been as it is today, and perhaps he had not seen it. In any event, he had been, in subsequent years, the beneficiary of the deal-making—and in a big way.

He was not political, but he understood the political nature of life. He was trusting but not naïve. He was intensely loyal to his friends, although limited in number, and he expected the same honesty in return. He was compassionate and fair but tough, and he set high standards. He was lean and athletic with dark hair and a quick smile. He had a quick and inquisitive mind.

He was competitive—oh, how he was competitive—but to win through unfair means was unacceptable. Work hard to win and win fairly. Spence viewed life as a game to be played and enjoyed. It was not only acceptable but the right thing to do, to understand the rules of the game better than the next guy but to play by the rules. He was continually reminded of the sayings "it's okay to lose, until you lose"; "never let them see you sweat"; "success demands great execution"; and, most importantly, "what I do today is important because I am paying a day of life for it. What I accomplish must be worthwhile because the price is high."

He appreciated individuals who were sensitive to those less fortunate. He did not tolerate liars and cheats; nor did he tolerate people who attempted to take advantage of those who, through no fault of their own, were on a lower level of life's scale of success. He also did not tolerate those who found or attempted to find success by bypassing the rules of the game. Such success, he knew, was fleeting and short-lived.

He often wondered why we are who we are, and he always felt, upon such reflection, blessed that he was who he was. Life had been good to Spencer Harrington, but he had earned his good fortune.

Work hard and do the right thing. Spence had followed the philosophy and expectation of Arthur Andersen & Co. (an approach driven into each new recruit from the first day with the firm) and a philosophy captured by the firm's anthem of "think straight and talk straight." The firm's philosophy had been consistent with his own beliefs and values. Not only was the right thing to do the best approach, but in doing so, he believed good things would come your way, and at the most unexpected times. He also believed that your honorable actions of today, in even the most seemingly inconsequential ways, and the decisions made, including the hardly recognizable and apparently most insignificant decisions, can result in significant beneficial opportunities in the future. Just another way of saying, "How you live your life today is a reflection of your tomorrow."

Spence had an inner-strength, and it was clear he had the "right stuff." A quite unassuming individual and yet an individual who was very astute and very observant, his adversaries had learned through painful experience that he should not be taken lightly.

Behind the nice exterior was a tough competitor with a high sense of adventure.

Chapter 26

Like most of us, Spence, during times of reflection, often yearned to be able to return, if even for a few precious moments, to his young adult years. He wished he could again sit on the porch swing of his family's hillside home. He longed to be able to again sit with his father and mother. To sit with them on a quiet, peaceful, warm summer's afternoon with the birds singing in the background and the butterflies fluttering in the meadow across the way, as he remembered, or perhaps in the evening near dusk with the sounds of crickets and locusts chirping. Oh, to be able to ask the questions of his parents now that he should have asked when he was younger, when they were still alive, or to have listened more closely to them or to have more clearly retained in his recollections the times spent with them.

He wished he could have better understood their aspirations and how they viewed their life's experiences (the challenges, the disappointments—he hoped there had been few, and the joys—he hoped there had been many). He also wished they could see him now and that, hopefully, they would be proud of him and that they would know his success was because of them. He wanted just to say thanks.

He would often recall those times when his father would talk about the times he spent with the US Army in London during World War II. His father had been a cryptographer during the war. Coupled with Spence's natural curiosity, the retold experiences of his father while in England and his father's classified activities during the war further fostered Spence's desire for adventure and exposure to new and exciting experiences. The city of Chicago and the firm, with its wide range of clients, and the international scope of the firm had provided the opportunity for such experiences.

Spence had excelled within the firm and advanced up the ranks. He became highly skilled in the areas of purchase investigations, creative financial structures, and forensic financial reviews. His client roster consisted of large multinational corporations serving a wide range of industries across several continents. His natural curiosity, highly developed level of expertise and healthy intellectual skepticism coupled with a keen sense of smell through experience for what just did not seem right had served him well. Although he could have stepped out of the pages of *GQ* magazine, he had the skills of a financial detective, if you will, with world-class financial and business experience and expertise. He was sought out for his advice and counsel from the highest levels within corporate boardrooms—usually to deal with potentially embarrassing and highly sensitive matters on a confidential and need-to-know basis.

Because of his expertise and the many opportunities to delve into mischievous financial activities, he had become extremely skilled in assessing people—who could be trusted and who were less trustworthy. He was creative, but he was also pragmatic and believed in the sayings "anything that can go wrong, will go wrong!" attributed to one Mr. Murphy, and the saying that Ronald Reagan made famous: "Trust but verify."

To best summarize Spence Harrington is through comparison. When Her Majesty's Secret Service had a unique challenge, James Bond was called. When the firm had a client with a highly sensitive or delicate risk, a call went out to Spencer Harrington.

Spence was on the upward path but was restless. As much as he loved the firm, he wanted to control his own destiny. As a result, in the early 1990s, when he was approached by an investment bank and offered the opportunity to become the chief executive of a high-tech company, he jumped at the chance.

He had been careful in his due diligence and was convinced that the company's new products, although still in the early development phases, could be breakthrough products with tremendous high-margin sales potential. Although he was not necessarily motivated by money, but rather by the challenge to succeed, the huge number of stock options he had been granted had the potential of making him a wealthy man if the company achieved the level of success he envisioned and thought possible. On the other hand, he recognized that with great opportunity came great risk. He realized he could devote to this fledgling start-up business his talent, time, and energy for the next several years only to experience financial failure. This was not to be the case.

Spence led the company to spectacular profitable growth and great success. Five years after becoming chief executive, the company was taken public and "overnight" Spence was worth in excess of $200 million. As importantly, he was having fun. However, his instincts told him that the high-tech easy money would not, could not, last forever. Trusting his instincts, Spence resigned from the company and cashed in his stock holdings in the company.

With the funds from the sale of his stock, he established a number of interrelated trusts that ultimately led to him as the beneficiary. However, the structures of the trust relationships were such that his identify, as the ultimate beneficial owner, had been carefully concealed and would be extremely difficult for anyone to discern. Acting through the trusts and using the proceeds from the sale of his stock, he purchased a manufacturing company that had businesses in the United States, Canada, and Europe. With the balance of his funds, he aggressively invested in the high-tech market. His objective was to significantly grow the value of his investments and to attempt to exit the market before the bubble burst. He took a huge risk, but he timed the market well and was hugely successful!

Excluding his ownership of the manufacturing company, his stock investments had grown in value on an after-tax basis to well in excess of $500 million. Because the investments were handled through the trusts, no one knew of his financial worth. Six months before the high-tech bubble burst, Spence sold all of his stock market holdings and "retired." He was indeed, at a relatively young age, an immensely wealthy man. Better yet, because the vast majority of his wealth was secreted within the trusts, no one would easily know the degree of his wealth.

Even with the immense wealth, Spence continued to maintain a relatively conservative lifestyle. However, there were now a few exceptions. After selling all of the shareholdings, other than the manufacturing company, Spence took six months to travel, including a Mediterranean cruise, to relax, and to spend time on a hammock, under the pine trees, just swaying peacefully listening to the breaking waves and enjoying the gentle ocean breezes on a beach in Jamaica.

Spence also took some time to indulge and purchase two automobiles. On his travels, two different automobiles had especially caught his eye, and, after several test drives, he had been seduced.

His two toys were a hunter green British Morgan roadster and a deep blue Esparante sports car.

The Morgan roadster convertible was made of the highest-quality materials—leather, aluminum, and seasoned ash. The roadster had been built to his personalized specifications. This British classic paired the hand-assembled craftsmanship of a bygone era with advanced design dynamics making the Morgan marquee legendary. Driving the Morgan on the open road was unequivocally emotionally sensational. With its low center of gravity and near perfect weight distribution, the car had outstanding balance and poise. The Morgan provided an unparalleled driving experience.

Spence developed a special relationship with the car. He loved those times when he was able to peer down the long bonnet, accelerate, enjoy the rush of the passing landscape, and indulge his senses. Driving the Morgan was nothing short of exhilarating.

His Esparante was just as enjoyable. The beautifully styled, limited-edition sports car with the distinctive green clover leaf insignia was just as much of a treat to drive.

In addition to the cars, after recent trips to Australia and the Far East, Spence arranged for one of the trusts to create an aviation company through which he purchased and staffed a Falcon 900 EX jet aircraft. The plane could carry eight passengers and crew very comfortably. The sleek tri-engine plane had a range of forty-five hundred nautical miles, nonstop, and could access virtually any business airport around the world with a minimum number of refueling stops.

For some, the plane might have been considered an indulgence, and there was no question the plane provided luxury. The cabin included a full bathroom as well as a section that converted into a private bedroom area. There was a galley with the capability for the preparation of hot meals as well as holding areas for a wide range of cold drinks and food. The spacious, quiet, and pleasingly proportioned cabin had glistening veneer woods and soft, elegant carpeting throughout. Two dozen windows flooded the cabin with natural light, and the panoramic vistas that flowed across the windows on the world—the lights of Paris by night, the Australian coast, the Grand Canyon, and Mount Hood by day—could be enjoyed in luxurious peaceful silence while dining with excellent wine and a wonderful meal. The cabin included luxury supple leather, swivel reclining chairs with electronic controls for selecting the perfect position for work or relaxation or for a pleasant nap as the crisp bright sunlight filtered through the windows with the deep blue horizon in the background. State of the art climate controls provided an extremely comfortable mix of temperature and humidity. The cabin had video and audio systems capable of securing radio, television, and satellite broadcasts and had an on-screen flight route tracking system with full flight status information similar to the information on international commercial flights.

The plane had leading-edge avionics with advanced technologies and had the capability to fly at speeds of over five hundred miles per hour and at heights well in excess of forty thousand feet. The plane had also been equipped with radar-evading stealth systems.

Perhaps most rewarding of all was the convenience, privacy, and personal space to work, relax, or sleep in luxurious comfort above the clouds on journeys to destinations around the globe. Spence suspected that the plane would be a great asset and would provide him with valuable options in the years ahead. The plane was also equipped with encrypted fax, telephone, and satellite communications.

As he lazily spent the afternoons almost floating in air on the hammock in Jamaica, he contemplated what to do with the rest of his life. He had a strong feeling that money, especially once you had it, was the least important component of wealth and happiness.

How could he keep himself entertained? He knew he must build something that would have worthwhile purpose and that would also provide the opportunity for great adventures. It was during those relaxed sunny days in the shade of the pine trees on the beach with the ocean breezes gently moving through the branches that the objective and the outline of the "organization" began to take shape in his mind. He had been blessed with the financial resources necessary to bring his plans to reality. With his plans firmly in mind, he was convinced the future now held the possibility for great adventure. It was now up to him to make it happen!

Chapter 27

Warren Buffet had given a significant portion of his accumulated wealth to the Bill and Melinda Gates Foundation to further the focus on and to prompt cures for diseases, to reduce global poverty, and to improve American schools. But long before this huge philanthropic contribution, Spence had recognized, as he later suspected that both Buffet and Gates also realized, that while it takes money to make the world a better place, money alone cannot get the job done.

As he relaxed in the hammock during those lazy days in Jamaica, Spence contemplated transferring significant portions of his wealth to charitable organizations, but he realized that he was far too young to give up control of his assets. As importantly, his vision for the organization was taking form, and it held the promise, at least the potential, for justice and good coupled with the prospect for intrigue and adventure.

The premise was simple! The purpose and the objective of the organization would be to identify and solve interesting and baffling crimes throughout the world and to neutralize significant threats from criminal and terrorist groups. The organization would not only thwart sophisticated criminals but "sting" them in such a way that they would be left guessing by whom and how they had been outsmarted. Spence recognized that life was a game—all a game. He smiled as the theme from *The Sting*, the great movie with Paul Newman and Robert Redford, came floating through his mind.

Spence did not, and clearly would never, need the earnings and cash flow from Shamrock Enterprises (the holding company for his worldwide manufacturing and financial services companies). What he did want and need was an ingenious plan, and indeed such a plan was coming together.

The plan encompassed growing Shamrock Enterprises and funneling, through a complicated and complex series of international holding companies, a portion of the free cash flow of the businesses to support a secret organization with worldwide reach. Even more importantly, Shamrock Enterprises, with its strategic international locations, would provide a wonderful cover for the "organization." At one level and at a very visible level, Shamrock would be a thriving group of companies with virtually all of the employees striving to profitably grow the companies unaware of the real and secondary purpose of the umbrella protection and resources afforded to the "organization" by the Shamrock companies.

Spence, through firsthand experience, had the highest respect for the New Scotland Yard, Her Majesty's Secret Service (MI-6 and the various other highly secret branches), and the US Secret Service. But the bad guys continued to seem to win big all too often, and he wanted, in whatever way possible, to more effectively level the playing field. His plan would be to match the talents, resources, and secrecy of the organization against the wit of the world-class criminals.

Spence would combine his forensic, financial, and other highly developed skills with the specialized and unique skills, expertise, and access to confidential and critical information that the other members and resources of the organization would provide.

Over time, he created an organization that now consisted of himself and Ginger Martin together with the following "key assets":

Peggy Mounier—responsibility for the European Continent.

Piper Morgan—responsibility for the Pacific Rim, China, and Asia

Megan O'Malley—responsibility for the British Isles (England, Scotland, and Ireland). Megan was a dual agent. She was on the roster of a top-secret branch of Her Majesty's Secret Service, but she also moonlighted and was deeply loyal to Spence. He had saved her parents from bankruptcy several years earlier. Megan, who was a dark-haired, blue-eyed beauty in her early thirties, maintained residences in both London and Ireland.

Rafael Posada—responsibility for Latin and South America. Rafael, fluent in English, Spanish, and Portuguese, was based in Sao Paulo, Brazil. He had attended college in the United States and had a master's degree in communications technology. He had spent ten years with the US Central Intelligence Agency based in San Francisco and New York before returning to Brazil to become owner and president of a very successful company focused on leading-edge advanced telecommunications technology products. Rafael and Spence had met many years earlier while working on a joint case involving international wire transfer fraud. They had become instant friends. Rafael, who was trim and lean and in his early forties, knew the cities of Latin and South America extremely well. He was someone who you wanted on your side. Handsome, with dark hair and a killer smile, keen intelligence, and savvy as a fox. He was also very experienced with disguises and, when necessary, had accomplished his objectives through a number of means including various forms of deception.

Jack Andrews—responsibility for the Caribbean. Jack had served ten years or so in special operations for the British navy. He was a free spirit, highly ethical, highly skilled, and still a relatively young man in his early forties. Although he had been stationed in the Falkland Islands the last five years before leaving the navy, he had been on classified missions throughout the world with a focus on South America and the Caribbean. He fell in love with the laid-back lifestyle of the Caribbean and with the pirate history and lore of the region. When he left the service, he purchased a charter air service and had grown the business to the point where his air charter service, based in the Cayman Islands, now serviced most of the islands throughout the Caribbean and parts of northern South America. Spence had met Jack several years ago in Aruba on a project, and they had stayed in touch hoping to find an opportunity to work together. The air service business provided an ideal cover for activities in the Caribbean and could conceal trips from island to island.

When Spence began to form the organization, Jack was one of the first individuals he recruited. When Jack was not in the office or flying, he could be found most other times enjoying the camaraderie and "scenery" of the watering holes throughout the islands—places like Senior Frog's, Carlos and Charley's, El Squid, or the Lounge at Greycliff in Nassau, the poolside restaurant and bar on the beach at the Four Seasons in Nevis, or perhaps the Hyatt poolside bar in Aruba. Much like Rafael Posada knew Latin and South America, Jack knew the islands of the Caribbean, and he had a vast network of contacts. Not many things occurred throughout the islands that did not come to Jack's attention.

When Spence began to form the organization, after Ginger, Jack Andrews, Rafael Posada, and Megan O'Malley were the first to join, and each had unquestioned loyalty to Spence and to the organization's purpose—that being to ferret out criminals and to have fun and camaraderie in doing so.

Spence had previously known, and from experience trusted Ginger, Jack, Rafael, and Megan. Finding someone (Peggy Mounier) to head the European Continent and someone (Piper Morgan) to head the Pacific Rim regions had taken much longer than Spence had anticipated and had been much more difficult. But now, with both Peggy and Piper on board, he had the key areas of the world covered—and covered with people that he trusted.

It was a great organization. People! Spence knew that people were always the key to success in any undertaking, and this would be no exception. The individual team members were all unique, but each shared a passion for success and adventure. They were each highly skilled with highly developed curiosity and healthy intellectual skepticism.

Each of the team members brought to the organization a network of contacts and very talented resources such as Tucker Wolcott in Chicago.

In the boardrooms of the world, highly skilled professionals utilized state-of- the-art strategies and methods to develop and achieve their business objectives and plans. Spence would use similar advanced methods and technologies coupled with still-classified operational methods to develop strategies and tactical approaches to outsmart the bad guys.

The equipment utilized within the organization was some of the most advanced within the world and out of reach of all but a few of the world's intelligence agencies. For instance, in the area of communications, all of the organization's key posts throughout the world had been equipped with wireless voice, video, and data transmission capabilities, state of the art voice emulators, and multiband encryption software and communication diversion routers. As a result, it was impossible for anyone to intercept or interrupt communications to or within the organization.

So there you have it! The organization pretty much as Spence had outlined it to Piper Morgan during their meeting in China and the basis on which Piper made her decision to enthusiastically join Spence and the organization.

With the organization now in place, Spence had no idea of when the adventures would arise or where the adventures would lead, but he was certain he had the right team in place, and he was convinced the rest of his life would not lack for adventure!

Spence knew time had long since passed since he had been that young boy growing up in rural Indiana. The once young boy with the dreams of one day visiting exotic places was now bringing to realization the potential for further experiences of unimaginable intrigue and adventure. Little could he have ever guessed then that one day he would travel to and become familiar with many of the exotic locations of the world and that his code name would aptly be "Travelin' Man."

Chapter 28

The red light on Ginger's telephone console began to flash. She could tell from her computer screen that the call had been placed to Evergreen Associates, one of the organization's forwarding companies with an address in Farmington, Connecticut (a community west of Hartford). The communication diversion routers had automatically scrambled the routing and redirected the call on an untraceable basis to Ginger's office.

"Evergreen Associates. How may I help you?" Ginger answered in a very pleasant and professional voice.

"I have been given this number and told to ask for the Travelin' Man," the voice on the telephone responded.

Ginger quickly, as always, politely responded but also in a coded fashion challenged the caller by saying, "I'm sorry. You must have the wrong number. There is no one here that provides travel assistance."

The caller replied with the correct response to the challenge.

"Oh, I was hoping someone could help me change my train reservation to Williams, Arizona."

Ginger knew that Williams was one of the unique locations on the current validation list. She also knew by the location that this caller was, or was representing, a high-ranking or very important party. She knew this because Williams, Arizona, is the gateway to the Grand Canyon, and "grand" was the code word designated for extremely important contacts.

"Just a moment," Ginger said as she immediately pulled up another communication screen on her computer.

The computerized communication system was filtering and analyzing the telephone call for numerous characteristics. She reviewed the diagnostics of the call to ensure there was no evidence of interference or line taping, although with the organization's advanced telecommunication safeguards that were in place, the possibility of interception was virtually impossible. The diagnostics screen showed everything was fine.

Ginger also ran a parallel trace and saw the telephone call was from an "unregistered" personal cell phone, which generally meant one thing—a high-level government intelligence official.

Ginger returned to the caller.

"I'm sorry to keep you waiting. May I ask your name and your train ticket number?"

As an additional safeguard, only those on a need-to-know basis or those individuals who had been given restricted access for a term-specific duration were given access identification numbers.

Even then, the identification number only permitted access to the special Evergreen Associates telephone number. Once given the restricted access number, a caller was prequalified. However, the caller would have been given no further information on who controlled the telephone number he or she was calling other than the caller would have been told that whoever answered the telephone might be capable and willing to be of assistance.

In this case, the ticket number was the disguised identification number.

"My Amtrak ticket number is 595 812 072681," replied the caller.

Ginger validated the identification number as having been assigned to a Jill Winslow at the request of the secretary of the treasury. The secretary of the treasury was a longtime and trusted friend of Spence's.

The caller continued, "And my name is Jill Winslow, deputy director of the Bureau of Special Investigations for the United States Department of Treasury."

As Ms. Winslow was speaking, Ginger was running the voice authentication digital analysis software in the background to match the caller's voice with the voice sample on file. The system showed a 98 percent match, which was well within the range of acceptance.

In order to protect against the possibility of a recorded voice being used or perhaps some other creative method of falsifying the voice, there was one additional safeguard.

Ginger challenged the caller one further time.

"Do you have one of today's newspapers with you?"

Anyone who was given access to the special telephone number was told to have one of the national newspapers (*Wall Street Journal, Financial Times, USA Today* or the *New York Times*) with them when they telephoned.

"Yes, I have the *Wall Street Journal* and the *New York Times*," the caller answered.

Ginger picked up her copy of the *New York Times* and randomly turned to page 6 of section B and then gave the caller the following instruction.

"Please turn to page 6 of Section B of the *New York Times* and read the first and fourth lines of the third paragraph and then give me the current time."

The caller responded.

"Huckleberry cobbler is a wonderful summer treat ... and from line four ... found in the mountains and hillsides of Montana and many of the western parts of the United States. The time is 3:05 p.m."

The words matched exactly with Ginger's copy of the *New York Times*. With the match, Ginger was assured the caller's voice not only matched the authentic voice that the organization had on file but also that the voice had not been prerecorded.

"Yes, Ms. Winslow. Thank you for being so patient with our verification process."

Jill Winslow gratefully thanked Ginger.

"I fully understand and appreciate the very through security safeguards. I know the safeguards are in place for our mutual protection."

"How can we help you, Ms. Winslow?" Ginger asked.

There was concern and a sense of urgency in Jill Winslow's voice as she replied.

"We, the US Treasury Department, believe we have a very serious problem. I would like to discuss this highly sensitive matter with the Travelin' Man and determine if he would be willing to be of assistance."

Jill Winslow had no idea with whom she was speaking or the identification of the Travelin' Man. She only knew that a potential national security level problem had been identified and that, in her judgment, skills and expertise even beyond her elevated grade level were required.

The highly skilled Special Investigations Unit had exhausted its limited leads and had reached an apparent dead end. The secretary of the treasury had given the special telephone number to Jill and requested—no, instructed—her to contact this mystery man. The secretary had also assured Jill that the "Travelin' Man" was discreet and could be trusted, that he had access to an unbelievable array of contacts and resources throughout the world, and, most importantly, that he produced results. Jill had been sworn to secrecy by the secretary.

After speaking with the secretary, her curiosity had piqued as she left the lush deep carpeting and the rich, dark wood paneling of the secretary's office. She walked to her office, which was a short distance away. Not only did she have great curiosity about this secret "off the books" resource held in such high esteem by the secretary, but there was a growing sense of excitement on her part as she had began to dial the special telephone number the secretary had given her.

Jill had heard whispered rumors of some sort of secret resource but had never been able to clarify the nature of the resource or to verify the existence of such shadow resources that had the capabilities to provide the assistance she now required.

"Ms. Winslow, we appreciate your call. I will arrange for the Travelin' Man to contact you soon," Ginger advised.

"What do you mean by *soon*?" Winslow asked in a pleasant but firm voice.

Ginger could tell that Winslow was a professional. She suspected that Winslow could be a feisty rascal. She liked that.

"Soon—very soon. We take your call very seriously. Wait to be contacted. We have your cell phone number," Ginger instructed.

Jill was momentary surprised that they had her confidential cell phone number. She then thought that if they were as good as they needed to be, then she should not be surprised that they had ways to obtain all sorts of information, including what was, she thought to be, a highly confidential cell phone number.

Winslow, realizing the conversation—perhaps a stretch, Winslow thought, to consider the dialogue a conversation—had been concluded, replied, "Thank you. I will wait for the call. Thanks again."

As soon as the call was terminated, Jill Winslow hit the intercom button on her desk and asked her security officer to meet with her immediately. A few moments later, a disguised door in the middle of a custom-built bookcase opened along one wall of her office. The security officer walked into her office as the bookcase door closed behind him.

"Well?" Winslow asked.

"No luck," the security officer answered.

"What do you mean? I kept her on the line long enough for the trace," Winslow said with a look of disbelief on her face.

"Even with the black art top-secret communications stuff we have, we were no match. They are using some sort of diversion routers. They certainly fooled us. Our folks are some of the best in the world, and they are saying they have never seen anything like it," the security officer responded.

"Sounds like we are dealing with some very smart dudes," Winslow said, somewhat as a question but more in admiration.

"I would say so," the security officer said as he turned to leave Winslow's office through the secret passageway.

"Tom, thanks. Let's keep this just between you and me. Okay?" Winslow cautioned.

The security officer turned toward Jill Winslow for a moment and nodded his concurrence as he stepped through the doorway.

Jill Winslow was good at what she did—indeed very good, one of the very best. She knew there were not many better. She had a growing suspicion that she was about to encounter, hopefully encounter, someone far better. But she also thought that she knew all of the major players in the world. It was her job to know. Who was this "Travelin' Man" and why all of the mystery and why did she not know that he existed?

As she turned in the leather chair and pondered, she also knew, given the completely unsuccessful attempt to line track the telephone call, that she could not do anything other than wait at this point—wait for hopefully a return telephone call. She was not accustomed to waiting, but her growing anticipation and curiosity far outweighed her impatience at the moment.

Chapter 29

"What are you doing?" Ginger asked in a spirited fashion as Spence answered his cell phone. Ginger knew that Spence would want to know as soon as possible about the telephone call received from Jill Winslow on behalf of the secretary of the treasury.

There had been a legitimate business need for Spence to be in Portland, Oregon. At the conclusion of his business meetings, he had decided to tack on a couple of days and spend time relaxing at one of the quaint hideaways on the rugged and stunningly beautiful Oregon coast.

The weather was gorgeous. The temperature was in the low seventies with wonderfully blue skies. In the silver Audi convertible rental car, Spence had driven west from downtown Portland (the "Rose City"), until he reached Route 26. He turned onto Route 26 through the tunnel and then up the mountain overlooking the beautiful city of Portland, now behind him to the east. When he reached the plateau, he could see in his rearview mirror Mt. Hood to the southeast.

Green. Everything was so green and lush. He continued west toward the mountain range that separated the wheat fields, orchards, vineyards, and rolling countryside west of Portland from the Pacific Ocean. His visits to Portland more often than not had included rain, but for this trip, the skies were crystal clear with only a very few brilliantly white small puffy clouds. He could only imagine how nice it must be along the coast.

Spence continued west on the four-lane Route 26, the main highway to the west from Portland to the ocean beaches, through Beaverton and Hillsboro, suburbs of Portland but vibrant independent communities of their own, until he reached the exit for Route 6. Spence turned onto Route 6 and continued west through the foothills and through the mountain range passing over and along the Wilson River. He crossed the river several times as the highway wound through the valleys and mountain passes. As he was on the downward leg of the drive through the mountains, Spence noticed, at several points below through breaks in the pine trees, the sun reflecting from the rippling waters of the Wilson River, really a large stream in the summer. Occasionally, he could see sunbathers, rafters, and other water activities in the stream as he drove along. Spence made a mental note to think about stopping for a swim, in what very much appeared to be a cool mountain stream, the next time he had the opportunity to make the drive.

Spence was taking Route 6 to the coast, rather than continuing on Route 26, which was a much quicker route to the coast, for a very specific reason. Still a kid at heart and because of his natural curiosity, he was looking forward to visiting Tillamook—the home of Tillamook Cheese. Best known for its delectable cheddar cheese, the town of Tillamook is also one of the gateways to the northwest Oregon coast.

For nearly one hundred years, award-winning cheeses have been produced by the Tillamook Creamery Association. The Tillamook cheese visitors' center is located on Highway 101 a couple of miles north of downtown Tillamook. As Spence turned into the vast parking lot of Tillamook Cheese, he could quickly see why Tillamook Cheese was one of the top ten Oregon tourist locations. Tillamook is a mecca not only for cheese lovers; Tillamook provides both an educational and a fun time for visitors of all ages. The visitors' center is a showcase for a wide range of Pacific Northwest cheese and other products. The center also provides an education in the creamery's history and the cheese-making process. The upstairs glass-walled observation areas provide viewing into the cheese-making rooms and provide an opportunity for the visitors to watch the numerous ongoing activities as cheese moves quickly down the Tillamook packaging lines.

As Spence watched the rapid progression of the vast quantity of cheese move down the packaging lines, he could not help but wonder, *Where in the world is all this cheese going*?' knowing that long after he left, and continuing seven days a week, the facility would continue to constantly package cheese. The Tillamook Creamery visitors' center was a neat place. Tillamook Cheese even had somewhat of a Disney feel. Spence could tell that Tillamook was a great place for families and certainly a great place for adults who were kids at heart.

Not to be overlooked was the world famous, or at least Oregon famous, Tillamook ice cream. It appeared to Spence that for most of the visitors, Tillamook was more of a religious experience than a cheese visit. There was a large number of visitors, and all seemed to be having a wonderful time. As Spence wandered about, it seemed that almost all were enjoying the ice cream in one form or another. The place was amazing. Spence counted at least ten servers behind the ice cream counters on the main floor and another three or four servers behind the ice cream counter on the second-floor observation level.

Spence's curiosity got the better of him. He could not resist any longer. He got in line for ice cream. The selections, which were listed on a large blue and yellow overhead board, were numerous and included many unusual flavors. When he finally reached the counter, he had his selection well in mind after having considered many combinations. He selected a scoop of Mountain Huckleberry and a scoop of Peach Cream. He was reminded of the cartoon series from his childhood—the great cartoon *Huckleberry Hound*.

He immediately understood why the lines for ice cream were long and why most everyone was eating ice cream at Tillamook.

The ice cream was outstanding—truly outstanding. He finished the ice cream and thought about trying another flavor (who knew if he would ever come this way again), but he looked at the line and then at his still trim but challenging waistline and thought better. He walked out of the visitors' center, refreshed, and into the bright sunshine and cool Tillamook air.

From Tillamook, Spence drove north on Highway 101 approximately forty miles until he reached the beach community of Cannon Beach.

He was looking forward to the next two days of total relaxation with a little exploring along the great Pacific Northwest Oregon coastline.

He turned off Highway 101 onto the coastal road that led through the pine trees into the community of Cannon Beach. The salt-air breeze was refreshing as it pushed through the open-air Audi convertible.

Cannon Beach, nestled between the Pacific Ocean and the coastal mountain range, is famous for its forested headlands, towering monoliths, and vast stretches of pristine, sandy beaches. Located just a few miles south of the junction of Route 26 and Route 101 some eighty miles west of Portland and some twenty-five miles south of Astoria, Cannon Beach is surrounded like no other place by the rugged natural beauty of dense forests, wide ocean beaches, and meandering rivers. The community has become a haven for artists, with numerous galleries and shops. While the community of Seaside, some ten miles to the north, is a boisterous beach community, Cannon Beach provides a peaceful, relaxing environment of serenity.

The streets and yards are lined and replete with all types of colorful and beautiful flowers emitting an inviting cheerfulness as if begging to be captured on canvas. Spence noticed a lady with a camera being dropped off in front of one of the white frame homes for the apparent sole purpose of taking pictures of the flowers. He noticed the car had rental plates and suspected that she was from the Midwest, perhaps from the Chicago area since there was such an emphasis and appreciation in the Chicago and surrounding areas for beautiful flowers. Spence had fallen in love with the uniqueness and beauty of Cannon Beach.

Traveling north, he continued on the beach frontage road until he reached the short street that led to the Stephanie Inn—his home base for the next two days and nights. As he pulled onto the stone drive in front of the inn, he could not help but see the huge pink and deep blue azaleas, some of the largest daisies he could ever recall seeing, and a wide array of stunningly beautiful wildflowers. It seemed that almost any type of flower loved to habitat and thrive in this area.

While driving from Portland, Spence had pulled together a list of five things he wanted to accomplish over the next couple days:

1. Sit on the beach and watch the sunset the next two evenings.
2. Have dinner at Mo's on the beach (informal place famous for chowder).
3. Visit the community of Astoria (where the Columbia River flows into the Pacific Ocean) and visit the Lewis and Clark site at Cape Tribulation (across the bridge from Astoria in Washington where Lewis and Clark reached the Pacific Ocean).
4. Have lunch at the Ship Inn in Astoria.
5. Relax and enjoy the peaceful beauty of Cannon Beach.

He had just mentally completed the final version of his list as he pulled onto the stone drive of the Stephanie Inn.

The Stephanie Inn had become a favorite hideaway for Spence when he was on the West Coast and when time permitted. The Stephanie Inn had a subdued elegance. He recalled with anticipation the description from the inn's brochure. The language in the brochure clearly captured the essence of the beautifully relaxing inn and described well the beauty of its location overlooking the ocean.

> On the Oregon coast, the sea is never the same. The ever-changing seascape may be bright and sparkling, calm and pensive, or gray and tempestuous, but never boring, always evocative.

The brochure went on to describe the inn.

> Situated on its very edge, the Stephanie Inn observes the rhythm of the sea, but remains constant, never changing in the pursuit of excellence. Ours is a place of repose, respite, calm sanctuary from the unnatural rhythms of a hectic world. Here you will find the elegance of the finest hostelries of Europe combined with the charm and seclusion of an enchanting New England inn.
>
> A soothing and romantic atmosphere. Striking architecture, tastefully appointed in the finest tradition and crafted in natural word and stone from the region, creates a warm and serene ambiance. Quiet and cozy. Sink into an overstuffed chair in front of the fireplace; look out the windows and reflect on the spectacular ocean. Whatever the reason, this is the place to be. The view is dramatic and captivating during stormy weather, endlessly blue and seductive during clear days.

Spence entered the lobby and found a very pleasant young lady at the check-in desk just to the left of the fireplace. After exchanging pleasantries, his room reservation was confirmed, and his check-in was quickly and efficiently processed.

It was clear the attractive young lady at the desk was sophisticated, professional, and discreet, but it was also clear, given Spence's trim build and attractive appearance,

> that she was showing great restraint in not inquiring as to whether he would require a second key—perhaps for a Mrs. Harrington.
>
> To add to her day and perhaps to her fantasies, when she handed the room key to Spence, he smiled and ever so slightly but noticeably winked as he thanked her.

He had reserved a room on the first floor with a walk-out patio framed by a short stretch of warm, inviting, dark-green manicured lawn that bordered the edge of the sandy beach. As Spence entered his room, he began to question the list of activities he had planned. Relaxation was quickly moved up the list and given more time and greater priority. His room was spacious, elegantly furnished—a cozy hideaway with a glowing fireplace and a soothing Jacuzzi. The room provided a wonderful view and sounds of the sea; it was truly an inspiring sanctuary for relaxation and enjoyment.

The room was indeed soothing and handsomely furnished. The owners of the inn had spared no detail. He propped his feet up as he enjoyed a glass of fine wine and watched the waves and the surf break onto the beach in the distance with the soft music of Kenny G playing in the background. Now, Spence thought, *This is nice! What could be better*?

Well, certainly the curves and companionship of a spirited woman to share this time and place would be great, he thought, just before waking from the trance of watching the waves. Spence wondered for a passing moment what the young lady at the front desk might have planned for the evening, but he thought better knowing that he did not need or want any type of complication but rather just wanted the freedom to relax and explore alone and on his own.

Spence spent the next two days and nights doing what he had planned—relaxing and exploring. He had dinner each evening at Mo's restaurant on the beach. Each evening he sat at one of the tables on the oceanfront patio and enjoyed the fabulous views of

Haystack Rock, indescribably beautiful sunsets, and the early-evening campfires along the beach below. Although there were many very good restaurants along the coast, as well as in Cannon Beach, Mo's was an extremely popular location (advertised as "world famous" as well!) with a laid-back, informal beach attitude. But, not to be mistaken, Mo's focused on great service and great food. Spence had two favorites on the menu at Mo's, and, therefore, two nights were set aside for dinner at Mo's.

The first night, Spence ordered what Mo's claimed was "world famous" clam chowder together with clam fritters. The clam fritters were really pan-fried clam cakes with a light, crispy outside layer. Both were wonderfully good and fully satisfied Spence's sea breeze enhanced appetite. The second night, Spence ordered Mo's special chopped cabbage salad that included a light ranch dressing garnished with small shrimp. For his main course, he ordered the bouillabaisse consisting of clams, crabs, shrimp, halibut, large oysters, and other Pacific Northwest seafood that had been simmered together in a tomato basil broth. Accompanied, of course, by a cold beer. The meal was outstanding. Mo's was the place to come to enjoy great food in an informal beach atmosphere with the added benefit of great scenery.

The next morning Spence left the Stephanie Inn around eight o'clock and drove the twenty-five miles or so to the Astoria area. He wanted to spend several hours visiting Astoria and Cape Tribulation on the southern coast of Washington State and still get back to Cannon Beach by midafternoon to enjoy some time on the beach.

Astoria, the oldest permanent American settlement west of the Rockies, is a nationally acclaimed historic site at the western end of the world-renowned Lewis and Clark Trail. Just a few miles from the Pacific Ocean, Astoria is a pleasant, quaint town set along the beautiful Columbia River. The huge Astoria Bridge, almost three miles in length, provides access across the wide expanse of the Columbia River to southern Washington.

Spence reached Astoria, crossed over the breathtaking Astoria Bridge into Washington State and drove to the small town of Ilwaco—the gateway to Cape Tribulation Park. He knew that Lewis and Clark's arrival at the Pacific Ocean was one of the most dramatic episodes of their expedition. Perched on a cliff 160 feet above the junction of the Pacific Ocean and the Columbia River, the Lewis and Clark National Historic Center at Cape Tribulation recounts the story of Lewis and Clark's journey from St. Lewis to the Pacific Ocean. As Spence stood on the cliff looking west at the stunning vistas of the Pacific Ocean, he marveled at the beauty of this setting and only wished that he could have been with the Lewis and Clark party when their eyes first set sight on this view as they rejoiced in accomplishing their goal of reaching the end of the trail.

When Spence returned to Astoria, it was just before 1:00 p.m. After crossing the bridge on Highway 101 coming south into Astoria, he turned east on Highway 30 for a few blocks until he reached The Ship Inn restaurant. The Ship Inn was nothing fancy. It was just an informal restaurant on the dock at the water's edge with a fabulous view of the Columbia River and far in the distance to the north the shoreline of Washington State. Almost as important as the views was the fact that the restaurant had wonderful (make that outstanding) clam chowder and great seafood. Almost all of the coastal restaurants advertised their clam chowder to be either "world famous," "the best," "critically acclaimed," or "authentic," but Spence had found that The Ship Inn and Mo's as well as Dodger's Seafood restaurant in Seaside all delivered on their promises as having truly great clam chowder.

Returning to Cannon Beach, Spence arrived back at the Stephanie Inn around 3:00 p.m. He found the big, cushioned lounge chair on the patio calling his name. He curled up and enjoyed the peaceful melody of the ocean breezes. He was intermittingly dozing, which was hard to avoid with the soothing sounds of the breaking ocean waves in the background, when an hour or so later the telephone rang.

CHAPTER 30

"Hello," Spence answered as he stretched in the lounge chair and glanced to see if there was anyone on the grassy knoll adjacent to his patio.

"What are you doing?" Ginger asked.

"Most likely a lot of your work!" Spence jokingly replied.

"Hey, don't forget I am the one person who knows where you are and what you are doing!" she jabbed back.

"Oh, yeah. So what do you think I am doing right at this moment? You little clairvoyant rascal," Spence challenged as he laughed.

Ginger was now in a corner and had to quickly gather her thoughts. She did not want to lose the sparring match—never did—but she also did not want to hear if Spence was engaged in any intimate encounter. She thought this was highly unlikely after Spence's relationship with Piper Morgan, but she could not—could not completely—be sure.

"Nothing!" she said—she hopefully guessed.

"You know me all too well!" he answered.

"I have had a wonderful couple of days. I've seen some beautiful scenery here, as always, and achieved my clam chowder quota!"

"Well, it's back to work for you," Ginger replied in a much more serious voice.

"What's up?" Spence asked.

Ginger outlined to Spence the telephone call she had received from Jill Winslow.

"Assume her credentials and security passwords all check out," Spence asked knowing full well that the nature of Ginger's call would have been far different had Winslow's telephone call not been valid.

"Yes," Ginger replied.

"What do you think?" Spence questioned.

"She sounds like an interesting individual, and if this is something the US Treasury Special Investigations Unit has not been able to solve, well, could be fun!" Ginger responded.

"Looks like Jill Winslow will have the pleasure of at least making our acquaintance and perhaps getting some of our help," Spence said, more as an observation than a statement.

"Let's use the Naperville location for the meet. It's been a couple of years since we have been to Naperville, and it will be nice to return. Also, the locations we can select from provide excellent cover and very good flexibility. What do you think?" Spence asked.

"Great location. Want to use Quigleys for the meet?" Ginger offered.

"Yes."

"When?" Ginger queried.

"See if Winslow can make it tomorrow evening at seven o'clock. Give her the standard drill," Spence said, somewhat thinking out loud.

"Got it," Ginger quickly responded. "I will make all of the necessary arrangements in Naperville."

"I will call you once I get to Chicago. I suspect I will get to Chicago sometime midafternoon. I will alert the pilots to be ready to leave early tomorrow morning from the Portland airport for the flight to Chicago's Midway Airport. I will have the pilots arrange to have a car at Midway for my drive to Naperville," Spence said.

He was about to hang up the telephone and then remembered, "Say, let's rendezvous in Skaneateles on Saturday evening for dinner and debrief. Book me into room 28 at the Sherwood Inn, and make a dinner reservation for us at the inn for say 8:00 p.m."

"Sounds great. I love that place!" Ginger said very pleased.

She continued, "I'll book my room at the Mirbeau."

Spence smiled. "Oh, you mean at the Mirbeau Spa and Resort!"

Ginger laughed. "You know the saying, "All work and no play ... there has to be some perks for all that I endure!"

Spence laughed and then said, "See you in Naperville tomorrow evening" as he wrapped up the conversation.

Chapter 31

"Hello," Jill Winslow said as she answered the telephone.

"Miss Winslow, this is the travel service you requested."

With only a slight pause, Ginger continued as she questioned Winslow. "Are you still in need of our services?"

"Very much so!" Jill Winslow answered.

"Good. We have arranged a meeting for you with the Travelin' Man in the Chicago area tomorrow evening. Can you make it?" Ginger asked.

"Yes. Where and when?"

Ginger then explained.

"You need to be at the Starbucks on Chicago Avenue in downtown Naperville, Illinois, no later than six thirty tomorrow evening. Tell the counter person your name and order a vinte caramel macchiato."

"Anything else?" Jill questioned.

"Yes. Come alone and no shadows. Do not bring your cell phone or any other electronic equipment," Ginger advised and cautioned.

Jill thought for a moment and then asked, "Say, isn't Naperville the community that is consistently rated as one of the best communities in America? I seem to recall the rankings in *USA Today* and *Money Magazine* as well as perhaps some other publications. A far western suburb of Chicago."

"Yes," Ginger answered. "A lovely place."

Ginger continued. "Take a commercial flight to Chicago's O'Hare Airport and rent a car for the forty-five-minute or so drive to Naperville. Take Interstate 294 South to Interstate 88 West and continue west to the Naperville Road exit. Take Naperville Road south until you reach Ogden Avenue. Take Ogden west until you reach Washington Street. Turn left (south) on Washington Street and continue south until you reach Chicago Avenue. Chicago Avenue runs east and west through part of the heart of downtown Naperville. When you reach Chicago Avenue, turn left and then less than a block to the east turn into the shopping area on your right. You will see the Starbucks nestled among various shops and restaurants."

"Got it," Jill replied.

Jill Winslow's flight to Chicago's O'Hare International Airport had been on schedule and uneventful. She had been careful to follow the instructions given to her and knew from the careful design of the security safeguards that these were not people to be taken lightly. She would be in their hands, and, as much as she wanted to have her normal backup, she could not take the risk of jeopardizing the opportunity of obtaining their assistance. She needed them too much to take the risk.

CHAPTER 32

Jill was now in the rental car driving west on Interstate 88 and nearing the exit for Naperville. She had googled "Naperville" on the web as soon as she had received the telephone call with the meeting instructions. She had been extremely impressed with what she had learned about Naperville.

In her research, Winslow had found that Naperville was located in the Illinois Technology and Research Corridor along Interstate 88, approximately thirty miles west of Chicago. She was intrigued with what her research had provided.

Naperville, founded in 1831, is today one of the most affluent and vibrant communities in America. Ranked as one of the best places to live in America, Naperville consistently is considered one of the top communities to raise children. The city boasts nationally acclaimed schools, the best public library system in the country, and an exceptionally low crime rate. The community works hard to maintain and enjoys a world-class parks and trails system (including the treasured tree-lined Riverwalk that runs through downtown Naperville along the DuPage River—a large stream). On a nice day, droves of families and lovers stroll along the picturesque Riverwalk or frolic at Centennial Beach (a one-time quarry that has been converted into a beautiful beach and swimming facility).

Although Winslow found that Naperville, with a population nearing 150,000, had all of the amenities of a modern community, including world-class shopping and dining, she also was delighted to find that Naperville had maintained a great respect for history and that the downtown residential area included several blocks of well-maintained and highly sought-after Victorian and early twentieth century homes.

As she read on further into the research, she became convinced that Naperville was truly an interesting place. She noticed that the community celebrated Saint Patrick's Day with a large parade, celebrated the past with Civil War Days (with reenactments held at Naper Settlement—a beautifully restored settlement in downtown Naperville), celebrated the Fourth of July with a parade and with RibFest (an outdoor food festival, with an emphasis on barbecued ribs and family entertainment), Oktoberfest and Last Fling (held over the Labor Day holiday to celebrate the end of summer—the last fling, if you will).

She was beginning to envision what this beautiful and unique place must be like. She was looking forward to the destination.

Chapter 33

Ten minutes or so after exiting Interstate 88, Jill had found her way onto Washington Street and was now driving through downtown Naperville. She thought out loud to herself, *What a quaint, vibrant, wonderful community*. The sidewalks were filled with strollers and shoppers, and the tree-lined streets seemed to shelter all sorts of restaurants and interesting shops. At any other time, she would have been tempted to stop and explore.

She found Chicago Avenue and turned east, following the instructions. Almost immediately, she came upon the entrance to the shopping area that had been described. She quickly turned to her right and into the parking lot. She found one of the few open parking spaces—one of several designated for fifteen-minute parking. She relaxed for a moment and then got out of the car and walked the short distance across the drive and entered the Starbucks.

This particular Starbucks had a very relaxed feel, perhaps caused by the fireplace, the brick and wood interior, or the subdued lighting. Although it was not the season, and the fireplace was not lit, there was still a very comfortable feel.

In quickly assessing the surroundings, as she had been taught to do, she noticed what appeared to be a couple of businesswomen with computers, an older couple, a mother with two small children, and a number of young people who she guessed were most likely college students. In checking out Naperville using Google, she had also learned that among other distinctions, Naperville was the home of North Central College. She also learned that the college was on the eastern edge of downtown Naperville and, in fact, just a couple of blocks from the Starbucks.

She approached the counter and said hello to the young lady behind the counter. She introduced herself and ordered a vinte caramel macchiato. The young lady nodded and accepted the five-dollar bill from Jill and provided change. The young lady then stepped away for a just a few moments and returned to take the order from the next person in line.

Jill moved to the far end of the counter. In a very short time, the counter person handed her the large container of coffee and also discreetly handed her a small sealed envelope with Jill Winslow's name printed on the outside. She found a somewhat secluded overstuffed chair in the corner near the window and sat down. She opened the envelope and found the following typed message:

> Return to your car with your coffee and then immediately drive to the Edward Hospital Health Club. Take Washington Street south to Martin Avenue. Turn west on Martin Avenue until you reach Brom Drive (approximately three blocks), turn left and go two blocks, and the health club will be on your right. There will be a four-story parking garage on your left. Pull into the parking garage and park on the third floor as close as possible to the elevator. Take the elevator to the ground floor and then walk across the drive and across the health club parking lot to the Edward Health Club. When you enter the club, proceed to the front desk and give your name and inquire if one of the members left an envelope for you.

She left the Starbucks parking area and turned west on Chicago Avenue, then south on Washington Street. She crossed the bridge of the DuPage River (really a large stream) in downtown

Naperville and continued a few more blocks until she reached Martin Avenue. She turned west and followed the instructions until she reached the Edward Hospital north parking garage. She could tell by the nicely landscaped areas and the preponderance of high-priced cars that Naperville was indeed a very affluent area. It was nearing 6:45 p.m. Not knowing what to expect, she quickly checked her hair in the mirror and did the best she could to freshen her appearance.

Winslow took the elevator to the ground floor and then walked the relatively short distance to the club entrance and approached the front desk. Rather than instruct her to park in the Health Club parking lot, she had been instructed to park in the hospital parking garage across the drive from the health club parking lot. As she walked, she knew there was a reason why she was instructed to park in the garage and not in the more convenient parking lot adjacent to the club. She also knew that she did not know the reason.

As instructed, she gave her name to the attendant at the counter when she entered the health club.

"Hi, my name is Jill Winslow. I believe one of the members left an envelope for me to pick up. Can you check for me?"

"Oh, yes," the young man at the counter said as he smiled and quickly handed the envelope to Jill. As she took the envelope, he seemed somewhat disappointed, perhaps at the thought that she would not be changing into some sort of body-hugging workout outfit that would reveal what clearly was a hot body.

"Thanks," Jill said as she returned the smile and sat down in a chair near the door and opened the envelope. The typed instruction read as follows:

> Walk back to your car and drive north on Washington Street to Jefferson Street (which intersects with Washington Street in downtown Naperville one block north of Chicago Avenue). Turn right (east) on Jefferson and drive one block,

> then turn right onto the ramp leading to the open air, top floor of the municipal parking garage. Park your car and then walk back across Jefferson Street to Quigley's Irish Pub. Once inside, go to the second "snug" (enclosed booth) and take a seat (the table will have a "reserved" sign. Disregard the sign and take a seat). You must arrive no later than 7:00 p.m. If you have complied in all respects with the instructions, you will be joined. **If you have not complied, wait fifteen minutes and order dinner, if you wish, or leave if you wish because you will not be joined, and our discussions will be terminated**!

Unbeknownst to Jill, when she gave her name to the counter person at Starbucks and was handed the envelope, the purpose was merely to provide Ginger with the opportunity to observe Jill depart and to identify the car Jill was driving. As soon as Jill pulled away from the Starbucks parking area, Ginger telephoned the communications specialist who was sitting in a van in the same parking lot.

As Jill pulled out of the parking lot for the drive to the Edward Health Club, the van pulled out of the same parking area and followed a couple of cars behind. Inside the van, the communications specialist was running a series of scans to determine if either Jill or the car had any beacon or signal-transmitting devices.. No signals were being transmitted electronically or via infrared from Jill's car.

The north parking garage at Edward Hospital was four stories high and provided an excellent vantage point to observe automobiles entering the hospital complex area and entering the parking lot for the health club across the street. From the top floor, it was very easy to observe whether Jill was being shadowed or had a backup. Since there were only three ways into the hospital complex and into the health club, any backup (without the ability to monitor Winslow's movements electronically) would have had to maintain visual contact with Winslow, and such monitoring could be observed from the parking garage. The fourth-floor level of the parking garage was an excellent surveillance location—well chosen.

As one last safeguard, while Winslow was away from her car and in the health club, a jamming device was quickly installed under the car to ensure she could not signal her position, just in case the van's electronic scanners had missed something.

Following the typed instructions, Winslow left the health club and returned to her car in the parking garage. She followed the new set of instructions and reached Quigley's just before 7:00 p.m. She entered the pub and found the enclosed booth, just as described in the instructions.

Chapter 34

Craic is a Gaelic term that describes the feeling you should get in an Irish Pub—fun, good conversation, good music and food, and great people. Quigley's Irish Pub had great craic!

As Jill Winslow walked from the street and across Quigley's stone patio entryway, she noticed the lovely detail and charm of the place. Situated back from the street, the pub resides in the lower level of the historic Jefferson Hill Building, which was built in 1845, three years before the potato famine in Ireland. The words *Kilkenny, Quigley's* and *Guiness* appear under the attractive windows with etched glass in cabinet maker frames.

Once inside, Jill was vicariously transported to a traditional pub in Ireland, complete with an antique fireplace, hand-etched and colored custom glasswork, original Irish prints, Iroko teak wood, inlaid tiles, dark green and tan ceilings, and a large wooden bar with eight lovely and colorful beer taps.

The pub had been designed, built, and shipped over from Ireland to Naperville. The antiquc fireplace and bookcases had been brought over from Dublin. The entire pub had been intentionally divided into several intimate areas and small rooms to provide couples and groups their own space for private conversations. Throughout the pub, the original hand-hewn beams and foundation from 1845 can be seen. Among all else, laughter and good conversation is the hallmark of Quigley's. *Cozy* is another way of thinking of this place.

The long beautiful wooden bar is located in the Victorian room which is the main room of the pub. Also, located in the Victorian room is a fireplace, several heavy wooden tables, and two enclosed booths called "snugs." In Ireland, "snugs" had doors and were the only areas within pubs where women were allowed to drink. Women are now welcomed in all areas of the pubs in Ireland. However, the snugs gained such popularity that they became highly sought locations to enjoy a refreshment and a great meal and were places for quite secluded conversations.

The snugs also provide an environment where private conversations that need to be confidential are not overheard.

After enjoying the welcoming interior and adjusting her vision to the soft glow of the pub's candle lights, Jill found the snug with the "reserved" place card on the table. As instructed, she stepped inside the snug and sat down on the padded bench seat on one side of the six-foot-long table. She could hear the soft melody of Irish music in the background, coming most likely, she thought, from one of the small rooms within the pub.

Shortly after Jill sat down, a waiter approached the snug and stepped inside and with a strong but pleasant and engaging Irish accent, extended a friendly welcome.

"Hello, are you Miss Winslow?"

"Yes," Jill answered.

"Lovely!" the waiter replied with a smile. "The other party will be joining you shortly. The gentleman has already ordered dinner and has asked that you peruse the menu and make your dinner selection. He is having the pan boxty as an appetizer (grilled patties of mashed potatoes crispy on the outside with parsley sauce) and the Irish lamb stew for the main course and a glass of Blue Moon with a slice of orange."

The waiter handed Jill a menu and a beer list, which included a fine selection of draft beers as well as an extensive selection of unusual imported beers.

"It would be my pleasure to get you something to drink," the waiter said as he pleasantly, by the tone of his voice, encouraged her to place a drink order.

Jill quickly scanned the listing of beers and was about to select by default a glass of Guiness (Guiness she thought, *seems to be the beer to order when in an Irish pub*) when at the last moment she was pleasantly surprised to see that Quigley's served Leinenkugel's—a great beer brewed in Chippewa Falls, Wisconsin.

"I will have a Leinenkugel's!"

The waiter nodded with an approving smile. "I will return in a few moments for your dinner order."

Jill picked up the menu, read the "blarney" about the history of the pub and then moved on to the decision of what to have for dinner. Although she had not eaten much during the day, her appetite had been suppressed by the anxiety of anticipation. *Who,* she thought again, *is the person I am about to meet, and will I receive the help I need?*

However, she was now beginning to take notice of the delicious aromas within the pub, and her appetite began to become aroused as she opened the menu and scanned the listings. The menu seemed to capture the essence of the food within an authentic Irish pub, and she found the menu included the following:

Corned beef and cabbage

Fish and chips

Classic shepherd's pie (described as a timeless classic prepared with ground Angus beef, diced carrots, leeks, and celery, braised in a demi-glace, topped with champ and baked to perfection).

Bangers and mash (described as Irish sausages served over champ with a unique blend of sautéed onions, green and red peppers, topped with a white cream sauce).

Quigley's Guiness beef (described as beef tenderloin braised in our homemade Guiness sauce, served with champ and sautéed vegetables).

Irish lamb stew (described as a hearty mixture of fresh lamb, garlic potatoes, carrots, and herbs served with fried toast points).

Traditional Irish breakfast (described as grilled Irish bacon, black and white pudding, two eggs, two bangers, served with golden fried mushrooms, fresh grilled tomatoes, and English beans. Served with HP sauce and light rye toast).

Corned beef hash (described as corned beef hash, two eggs, served with grilled tomatoes and fried toast).

She immediately selected the traditional Irish breakfast only to be disappointed to discover in small print on the menu that the Irish breakfast and the corned beef hash were available only on Saturdays and Sundays until 5:00 p.m. She looked at the menu again and thought to herself, *The shepherd's pie might be a little too heavy, but the Guiness beef sounds interesting.*

The waiter returned with a tall frosted glass of Leinenkugel's. He placed the glass gently on the table to the side of Jill.

"Do you have any questions on the menu?" the waiter asked.

"I was thinking of trying the Guiness beef. What do you think?" she asked.

"It's excellent, very tender with a smooth yet slightly tangy sauce. I think you would be very pleased."

"Great. I will start with the cucumber sandwiches and then the Guiness beef."

The waiter nodded and then said as he turned to step out of the snug, "Your party will be joining you soon."

CHAPTER 35

Jill Winslow looked at her watch. It was now a little before 7:15 p.m. She reached with great anticipation for the cold, frosted glass of Leinenkugel.

Hello, old friend, she thought with fondness. As she enjoyed the first smooth taste of the beer, her mind was flooded with wonderful memories of her times spent in Wisconsin.

Jill had obtained a master's and doctorate in criminal investigation from the University of Wisconsin in Madison several years earlier. Upon receiving her doctorate, she had been recruited to join the Department of Treasury—Special Investigations Section. She was bright, energetic, and athletic with a firm body, a highly curious mind and a great sense of humor. She was also extremely attractive in an understated fashion. She had become well respected and highly regarded within the Treasury Department and in a short time, she had moved up the ranks with increasingly higher levels of responsibility and authority.

Her internal highly confidential résumé reflected the fact that she was qualified to carry and extremely proficient with a wide range of firearms. Her résumé also outlined the numerous cases she and her team had "broken." Winslow was single and in her late thirties. Her work and the requirements to travel, sometimes for extended periods and on short notice, had precluded the opportunity for any serious relationships. She loved the excitement of her work, but she, at times—more and more often now it seemed—longed for a companion. She longed for love, and she knew she was not, as they say, "getting any younger." She was hoping that in the eyes of any prospective suitors she would, like good wine, improve with age. In the meantime, she would continue to crack the tough cases and broaden her overall domestic and international financial expertise with the possibility of one day, hopefully in the not too distant future, take on an even greater role within the Treasury Department.

She considered, as she sat in the cozy snug conversing with her old friend Leinenkugel, *Will I regret in the years to come the cost to my personal life of my professional commitment?* She always knew the answer.

She was deep in fond recollections of the wonderful times in Madison with the beautiful lakes, the lively spirit of the town, the quaint little cafes, the crisp golden fall days, the Saturday morning markets on the square, and the cold Leinenkugel beer on late summer evenings with close friends. Again, she thought, *Hello, old friend*, as she sat alone and as she took a long, slow drink of the cold, smooth Leinenkugel.

At that moment, when she was in deepest pleasure of remembering the good times, her thoughts were interrupted.

"Miss Winslow. I believe I am the individual you are looking to meet."

Jill Winslow looked up, and her eyes met those of the tall, lean stranger with a devilish smile. Jill Winslow had made her first contact with Spencer Harrington.

Spence stepped into the snug and took a seat on the padded bench across the table from Jill.

Following behind Spence was the waiter. The waiter delivered the Blue Moon for Spence, a fresh Leinenkugel for Jill, and the cucumber sandwiches and pan boxty.

When the waiter had left and was out of hearing distance, which was not far given the growing noise levels within the pub from the increased number of folks gathering throughout the pub either at the tables or at the bar as the evening aged, Spence turned to Jill.

"I hope that all of this cloak and dagger stuff has not been unsettling. We tried to make the instructions as straight-forward as possible and yet at the same time provide the appropriate levels of protection," Spence said knowing better about the instructions and knowing that she knew better.

"Oh, I just thought the reason you brought me all the way to this pub was that maybe you owned the place!" she retorted as she grinned. Her comment brought back to mind Spence's long desire to someday have his own quiet pub where he could hang out in a comfortable private back room with a separate entrance near the kitchen.

"By the way, this is a wonderful place!" she immediately interjected.

"This place serves its purpose well," Spence replied as he tipped his glass to hers.

"I do apologize for the various steps you had to take, but I can assure you, you were never in any danger of getting lost," Spence said.

Jill burst out in laughter as did Spence. She understood the subtle humor among two highly skilled professionals. She clearly knew that Spence was saying that she had been observed and followed throughout the instruction process on her travels through Naperville.

"Well, in any event, thank you for meeting me," Jill said.

"How could I not!" Spence said as he smiled and allowed his eyes to quickly travel from her face down her body to the top of the table where his view then became limited in such a way that she knew he was expressing a well-deserved compliment.

"Please, let's enjoy the cucumbers and boxty and start to get to know each other. Our dinners will be here soon," Spence said as he snatched one of her small cucumber sandwiches and offered her a portion of his pan boxty.

"Nice to meet you, Jill Winslow!" Spence said as he again raised his glass toward her.

Jill touched her glass to his and asked, "And what name do you go by?"

"Oh, I think Travelin' Man will be fine for the time being, if you don't mind," Spence answered with a grin.

Jill smiled knowing that she had little choice and that to pursue her quest for his true identity would be fruitless and nonproductive at this point.

"Okay, Travelin' Man, what would you like to know about me that you do not already know! Want my bra size? I bet you know just about everything else."

It was Spence's turn to laugh as he offered, "Oh, we know that!"

Jill laughed. "But did you know that before you met me earlier tonight!" she challenged.

Jill was passing along a not so subtle acknowledgement to Spence that she knew, that he wanted her to know, that he had made a visual assessment of her a short time earlier.

"Okay, Okay. Enough sparring—at least until dinner arrives!" Spence said as he grinned.

They spent the time, as they enjoyed the appetizers, discussing Jill's background—not the specifics of her background because as Jill suspected, Spence was fully apprised of her background. Rather, they discussed the Madison area and Wisconsin in general. Spence was sincerely interested and, at the same time, drawing the "subject," in this case Jill Winslow, into discussing areas with which the subject had an in-depth knowledge and where the subject was very comfortable. The "conversation" approach was an old trick of putting a subject at ease.

Jill recognized the procedure. She had used the same approach many times herself. She was not offended and was willing to play the game, and, in fact, she enjoyed being an ambassador for the

Madison area and promoting the wonderful laid-back lifestyle of the area.

By the questions about Wisconsin, and Madison in particular, that Spence was asking, Jill could tell that Spence had a very curious mind and enjoyed absorbing and assessing information. She also thought, by the extent of his inquiries, that he had never been to Madison. That was, until near the end of her discussion of her love affair with the years she had spent in Madison, when he asked the question, "And how did you like Pasqual's?"

She froze for a moment. She knew he was testing her reactions to a surprise, and she knew that she must control her reactions. She knew that he was trying to throw her off her game by surprising her with the fact that he, after all, knew the Madison area very well. Anyone who knew of the quaint, Mexican, hippy restaurant of Pasqual's, which was known and frequented primarily by locals, must be very familiar with Madison.

"Oh, have you been to Pasqual's?" she asked turning the question back to him.

"Once upon a time during one of my travels. Neat place with great food," he said without further comment. She gave a knowing smile letting him know that she understood the tactic, that she was not fazed, and that she was still in the game, if there was to be a game. He returned her smile.

Their meals arrived with the wonderful Irish aromas engulfing the snug.

"Care for another Leinenkugel?" Spence asked as he measured her response. Had she accepted his invitation, he most likely would have passed on her offer for assistance. He had learned many years ago never to rely on anyone, no matter how charming or convincing and no matter how much in need, who could not control his or her drinking or who had other serious vices. Given enough time, such individuals would lose control and either disclose critical information or would fall under the grasps of others who often had ulterior motives and, as a result, potentially could jeopardize him and the organization.

"No, thank you. But a cup of coffee would be great," she replied. Spence was pleased and relieved. He thought, *Would have been a shame to have come this distance and to have met what appears to be a very bright and engaging, and certainly attractive, lady, only to have to subtly terminate the project.*

Spence caught the waiter's attention, and as the waiter approached the table, Spence nodded toward Jill and then to the waiter and said, "Two cups of coffee when you have a chance."

"Now," Spence said as he turned back toward Jill.

He looked firmly at Jill. "What is the nature of the assistance you need?" and then he savored a fork full of the Irish beef stew.

"We seem to have misplaced $10 million in cash," Jill said somewhat with a wry sense of humor in the hopes of deflecting any challenges about the Treasury Department's ability to keep control over the banking system.

"Some pretty poor housekeeping, I would say." Spence smiled as he invited her to continue and as he forked another piece of the beef.

"The First Metropolitan Bank of Pittsburgh reported the loss in mid-September, two months ago, and the theft appears to be the 'perfect crime,'" she said now in a much more somber tone.

Spence looked up from the last remnants of the beef stew as he thought, *To the best of my knowledge, there has yet to be the perfect crime—just crimes waiting to be solved, and some are much more challenging than others.*

"Go on," he said with growing curiosity.

"Well, the ten million was stolen over Labor Day weekend. First Metropolitan did not report the loss for ten days to the Feds, to the US Treasury, or to the FBI. At the beginning, First Metropolitan assumed that the discrepancy had to be a clerical or system error in its records and that somewhere the "1" digit had been dropped. They thought that given their security safeguards that surely the difference must be due to some sort of error within the bank's complex computer systems."

She smiled and then went on. "Did I mention that over the Labor Day weekend, First Metropolitan went through a conversion to a new financial enterprise computer system?"

"So how did they become convinced that the ten million was missing?" Spence questioned.

"Well, here's the beauty of it as well as the mystery," Jill said as she drew out her words.

CHAPTER 36

It was now almost eight thirty in the evening. The waiter refreshed their coffees and inquired about dessert. He assumed since they were relatively young and were both very attractive, perhaps lovers or perhaps hoping to explore such a possibility, that dessert might be a good likelihood.

"May I suggest the Irish Crème Bash Pie," the waiter said as he looked for approval first from Jill and then from Spence.

Jill reached for the dessert menu and turned to Spence. "What do you think?" as she began to read from the menu.

"The decadent Irish Crème Bash Pie is a rich mélange of cream cheese, white and dark chocolate, Irish crème liquor, sour cream, and Devonshire extract in a chocolate crumb crust."

Spence turned to the waiter, "Are you really sure that this is an authentic Irish dessert?"

"Yeah, what say you?" Jill giggled good-naturedly as she looked at the waiter.

The waiter just smiled but the message was clear—"probably not."

"Sounds great—really great, but I think I will pass."

"Me too" said Spence.

"Then perhaps warm caramel apple pie?" the waiter asked, stressing and drawing out the question with hopes one or both would be seduced by the dessert temptation.

Spence and Jill looked at each other and both nodded no to each other and then to the waiter.

"Thanks, but not tonight," Spence said in a polite but firm fashion. The waiter could read the message that Spence and Jill wanted privacy.

Ginger had arranged for the snug to be available, if needed, until closing, so Spence knew that he and Jill would not be hurried.

"So how," Spence asked again, "did the bank become convinced the ten million was really missing and was not just an unidentified computer conversion error?"

Jill took another sip of coffee, sat the cup down, settled into a comfortable position, and readied herself to relate to Spence the facts that were known about the missing funds.

"The cash was in the bank's main vault. At the close of business on the Friday before the Labor Day weekend, the vault was closed and under timer lockdown until the opening of business on the following Tuesday morning."

"So! A lot of seemingly impregnable, time-controlled vault locks have been 'cracked' over the years."

"Well, we know the vault was not 'cracked,'" Jill said emphatically.

She went on to explain.

"There are two independent camera monitoring systems within the bank's vault area. One camera is within the vault, and a second camera-based monitoring system is located on the outside of the vault with the camera trained on the huge vault door. The monitoring systems are linked through a dedicated direct line to the bank's security office."

Jill continued as Spence listened intently for flaws in the "perfect crime." He did not anticipate identifying any great insights or any "ah-ha's." He could tell Jill was very good. If she and her team had not broken the case, it just meant that the case would be another worthy challenge for the "organization." He continued to listen.

"Because of the computer system conversion, the camera system within the vault had been turned off for the long Labor Day weekend. Since the vault was in lockdown, and no one would be in the vault over the weekend, the bank's security group approved turning off the camera system within the vault. In fact, this was part of the SOP (standard operating procedures). Nothing unusual at this point."

Jill continued. "However, the more important camera monitoring system—the system focused on the outside vault door—operated all weekend. We know that the camera system worked fine and that the system was not compromised."

"How can you be sure?" Spence asked.

Jill smiled. "Yeah, that was one of my first questions too!"

"The bank security personnel were clever when they installed the camera system. The camera view captures the entire outside of the vault door but also captures the real-time movement of a digital clock attached to the top of the vault."

Jill went on. "It gets even better," she said.

"In addition, there was a television set on a stand to the side of the vault door within view of the camera. The television was set to CNN. We have verified and matched the CNN programming throughout the Labor Day weekend to the digital clock. The digital clock and the television are closed independent systems, and it is clear the systems were not compromised. We know the vault door was not opened between its closing at the close of business on the Friday evening before the Labor Day weekend and when it was opened for business on the following Tuesday morning."

"So maybe the ten million was not there when the vault was closed on Friday," Spence questioned.

"We had the same thought," Jill said as she concurred with his line of thinking.

"But the internal camera system clearly shows a cart (one of over fifty carts within the vault) loaded with currency when the vault was closed on Friday. When the vault was opened Tuesday morning, and the camera began running, the film clearly shows the one cart, in exactly the same location, to be missing the cash!"

"So there lies the mystery—the 'perfect crime'?" Spence questioned and observed.

"Yes, the mystery indeed!" Jill said.

"So other than the unresolved challenge and perhaps the self-imposed embarrassment of not being able to solve the theft, why is this case involving the highest grade levels, at this point, of the US Treasury? Why not let the FBI work the case?" Spence questioned"

"I'm sure at your level, you have far greater things to worry about," Spence observed.

Jill smiled. "Thanks for the compliment, I think!"

"Well, first, $10 million is even still today not an insignificant amount of cash to be missing," she said.

"But more importantly, far more importantly, we clearly do not know how they, whoever they are, pulled it off. And as long as we do not know how they pulled off the theft, then similar thefts could occur, and the banking system could be at risk. Who is to say that next time the theft will not be for even far larger amounts?"

"As I thought," Spence said.

"So can you be of help, and if so, how?" Jill came right to the point and asked the direct question.

"We normally are focused on problems that are more international in scope and that either have or have the potential to have a bearing on the country's national interests. However, since the federal agencies have not been able to determine how this crime was performed, and since the impact could, if not addressed, have the potential to undermine the country's banking system, we will take the case.

"Yes, we will take the case. How could we not!" Spence assured Jill.

"But keep in mind that there are no guarantees regarding the results. There can never be any assurances or guarantees other than we will do our best."

"Understood," Jill said as she accepted the assistance of this man who was still an unknown stranger to her.

She paused and then somewhat challenged Spence, through the inquiry to Spence that followed.

"Our very best people and the very best people in the FBI have worked this case over the last two months without any success—not even the smallest progress. Why would you have any better chance?"

"Don't know," Spence honestly replied.

"But we have some uniquely qualified and experienced folks who have been very successful in the past on matters that at first seemed to provide no clues. We thrive on challenges!"

Jill smiled. "Any thoughts?" she asked.

"None at the moment," Spence said, hoping his lie would not be detected by any body language giveaways.

"How do we proceed?" Jill asked.

"Nothing more to do now. We will get back to you as soon as we have something to report."

Spence turned and caught the waiter's eye and motioned for the check. Jill noticed, but was not surprised, that he paid in cash. No credit card trail for her to follow up on later.

Spence escorted Jill to her car on the top level of the municipal parking garage across the street from Quigley's. They stopped for a few moments to look at the nighttime lights of downtown Naperville.

"We have a paid reservation for a room tonight for you at the Hyatt just off the Interstate. Maybe a fifteen-minute-or-so drive to the hotel at this time of night."

"Paid in cash, I bet!" Jill said and laughed.

"Nice feature about cash is that it limits the opportunities for curiosity," Spence said jokingly.

Part of her wanted to say, "Will you be joining me?" She was really becoming attracted to this man. She wondered, *Is it the fact that he is so attractive, or his confidence, or his keen sense of humor, or is it just the fact that he is such a mysterious individual?*

However, she turned and said, "Wherever this leads, if even anywhere, thanks for a great evening, Travelin' Man. I enjoyed the evening."

Spence nodded in a fashion of one professional to another, but he sensed a real affection for Jill; he liked her spirit.

As she drove down the ramp of the parking garage, she looked back. Spence had already disappeared into the shadows of the night.

CHAPTER 37

Spence arrived at the Sherwood Inn in Skanateles, New York, around three in the afternoon and checked into his favorite room—room 28.

The village of Skanateles with a population of somewhere in the range of three thousand (more in the summer, less in the winter) sets on the shore of a jewel—a clear lake in the Finger Lakes region of central New York State. Skanateles is a village of rare charm with lovely old homes, quaint shops, and interesting galleries. The village has been a vacation spot for one of the former first families of the United States as well as for many other families for generations. The summers on and along Skanateles Lake are like no others, and the winters, especially during November and December with the annual Dickens Christmas celebrations throughout the village, are an enchanting time. In the historic downtown district of the village, the shops and galleries are housed in restored buildings dating back to 1796.

Located in this charming village is the Sherwood Inn. The inn is located in the heart of Skanateles, which is known as the eastern gateway to the Finger Lakes region. The inn is located on the north shore of Skanateles Lake, one of the most beautiful and cleanest bodies of water in the world.

For almost two centuries, travelers have rested and relaxed in the inn's comfortable guest rooms. Each of the inn's rooms has been carefully restored and uniquely decorated to retain the inn's original charm. Many of the rooms overlook beautiful Skanateles Lake.

The inn's lobby is a throwback to those times when life was to be savored in peaceful relaxation. The lobby, with numerous overstuffed chairs, provides the opportunity to just sit and watch the lake, particularly inviting during the winter months with snow on the ground and the fireplace crackling in the background with the Dickens characters singing around the large beautifully decorated Christmas tree.

The wooden stairway, which overlooks the lobby, leads to the rooms on the second floor and then up the remaining flight to the third-floor rooms.

By pure luck, Spence had wandered into Skanateles and into the Sherwood Inn a few years earlier on one of his business trips to the Syracuse area. He had been able to spend only one night at the Sherwood Inn on that first visit to Skanateles, but he had fallen in love with the quaint charm of the inn. He had found room 28, a corner room looking out toward downtown Skanateles from the side windows and with views of the lake from the front windows, to be a beautiful room with a comfortable, relaxing environment. He had always requested room 28 on his subsequent visits. Sometimes he had been successful but most times not, since the inn was a very popular destination for all of the same reasons that caused Spence to enjoy this unique place so much. He was very pleased that Ginger had been able to reserve room 28 for this stay.

After checking in at the front desk, Spence settled into room 28 and sat near the front window, enjoying the warmth of the afternoon sun, marveling, as he always did, at the beauty of the sparkling blue waters of Skanateles Lake. After a few minutes, he telephoned the Mireau Spa and Resort. The resort was a mile or two from the Sherwood Inn. He asked to be connected with Ginger Martin's room. The Mireau is a Bavarian-themed upscale spa and hotel, not something that had in the past appealed to Spence.

Although with his spa experience in Australia, the thought of spending time at a spa was becoming more and more appealing to him. But in his view, nothing could match the Sherwood Inn for peaceful refreshment of body and soul.

"Hello," Ginger answered.

"I know I took a wild chance that maybe you would be in your room and not at one of the spa treatments," Spence joked.

"Assume you made it to Skanateles okay?" he asked.

"Fine. Everything went well."

"Were you able to listen to all of the tapes?" Spence asked. He was referring to the tapes of his dinner conversation with Jill Winslow at Quigley's in Naperville.

"Yes. Very interesting."

"Think you can break away around six for dinner?" Spence asked.

"Kinda, sorta," Ginger replied. *Kinda, sorta* was a phrase that Ginger used occasionally without thinking. Spence thought the term when used by Ginger was somewhat endearing and a reflection of her spirited nature.

He also suspected, no he was really pretty sure, that the use by Ginger of "kinda, sorta" in the context of their conversation meant only one thing—that she had another spa treatment scheduled in the evening.

"Hey, I think we can cover what happened in Naperville over a quick dinner. I have some thoughts on how we might proceed."

"Dinner sounds great," Ginger said with renewed enthusiasm.

Spence could tell his use of the word *quick* had registered with Ginger and had signaled to her that there would be plenty of time after dinner for her return visit to the spa.

"Anyplace you would like to go?" he asked.

"Let's see. Quick and local with great food and a wonderful atmosphere!?" she teased.

She knew that her favorite place was also Spence's favorite place. There were several wonderful restaurants in the Skanateles area including an excellent pub and an excellent restaurant at the Sherwood Inn. In addition, there was an outstanding gourmet restaurant at the Mireau. But nothing captured the quaint charm of Skanateles like Doug's Fish Fry.

"How about Doug's!" Ginger phrased more as a statement than a question.

"Oh, I don't know," Spence teased in response.

"Okay, if I confess about the spa treatment I have scheduled for later this evening, will you agree to Doug's?"

"It's a deal. Let's meet in the Sherwood lobby at five forty-five."

"Works for me," Ginger said. "See you then."

CHAPTER 38

Doug's Fish Fry is just a small place in downtown Skaneateles but a place with a laid-back casual atmosphere that has developed a mystique and an extremely loyal following. Doug's is a short three- or four-block walk from the Sherwood Inn. Although small, people flock to this "hole-in-the-wall" for the great food. There's often a line outside the door and down the sidewalk waiting to get in and to place an order for the fried haddock fish sandwich. The portion of fish is twice the size of the bun, and the bun is large, and the accompanying golden french fries and cole slaw both taste great with a dash of seaman's vinegar and a refreshing drink.

There are no waitresses and no tipping. Pay five cents for a Doug's postcard, and Doug's will mail the postcard anywhere in the world free of charge. The entryway walls are plastered with pictures taken of folks visiting various parts of the world where they are photographed holding up T-shirts with the Doug's logo.

Once inside Doug's, there are two booths that look out onto the street and a small narrow counter facing the wall with stools for seating. However, if you go out the back door and to the left, there is an adjacent two-story building that provides significant additional seating. Doug's popularity is principally the result of 1) the colorful, quaint, casual atmosphere, and 2) the fresh quality and wonderfully prepared seafood. For many years, those who know of the place have had fun and have feasted on live lobsters, steamed clams, creamy chowder, Boston scrod, onion rings, lobster rolls, fried oysters, cold beer, and milk shakes. Doug's milk shakes are made with hard ice cream, fresh whole milk, flavored syrup, and powered malt (no premade mush mix at Doug's). Everything is fresh just seconds before being served.

Spence and Ginger arrived at Doug's a little before six in the evening, and to their surprise, one of the booths was available. The booth had not yet been bussed, but knowing the value of a booth at Doug's, Ginger immediately sat down to lay claim while Spence secured a place in line to order.

A short time later, Spence returned with a bowl of oyster soup, a bowl of clam chowder, a large fish sandwich, a large order of onion rings, a lobster roll, and two steins of beer.

As Ginger eagerly eyed the morsels now on the clean table, she said, "It's all your fault that I have to spend time at the spa!"

"Oh, you thought some of this was for you?!" Spence joked as he feigned pulling the tray with the food toward his side of the table.

"I know we both like all of this stuff, so I thought we could divide everything in half except the soup. Please take whichever soup you want."

"Thanks," Ginger said as she began to cut the lobster roll in half.

"Well, what did you think about Jill Winslow?" Spence asked.

Between bites, Ginger responded thoughtfully and in a very serious tone. It was all business now.

"No question, she's a solid, experienced pro. I liked her. Not the political type."

"I agree." Spence said as he reached for his stein of beer.

"Nice on the eyes too, if, you are into that sort of thing," Ginger said as she effectively shifted out of the all-business mode and prodded Spence.

Spence raised his eyebrows in mock surprise. Ginger, seeing his facial expression, quickly interjected, "Which, I am not!"

Ginger regained her composure and smoothly shifted back to the business subject. "Seems like a fun challenge," she said.

"I would say so."

"Any thoughts on how they pulled it off?" Ginger asked.

"No. But, there is this one theft some thirty or so years ago at one of the banks in Chicago that seems vaguely familiar. I just can't remember the details," Spence said as he continued to attempt to probe his memory.

They continued to enjoy the rest of their dinner talking about the operational tactics used in Naperville and attempting to identify any opportunities for improvement.

As they walked leisurely back toward the Sherwood Inn after finishing dinner, Spence turned to Ginger.

"Ginger, if you have some time before your spa treatment tonight, can you see if you can reach Tucker Wolcott in Chicago? Ask him if he can remember or if he can find out the details about a theft in the midseventies at one of the major downtown banks. I think it might have been First National."

"I'll make sure I have the time," she said.

"Thanks."

"When will you arrive back in Burlington?" Spence asked.

"Midafternoon tomorrow. I have an early-morning flight out of Syracuse and then will drive from Boston. How about you?" Ginger asked. They made a point of never traveling together except on the company plane.

"I get back into Burlington tomorrow night. I will see you early the following morning. Hopefully, Tucker will have something for us by then."

CHAPTER 39

Ginger and Spence were reviewing various correspondences when the telephone rang in the office at Spence's home on the lake in Burlington. Ginger answered the telephone.

"Yes. Oh, hello, Tucker. Nice to hear from you so soon. Yes, he is right here."

Spence nodded and asked Ginger to place the call on the speaker.

"Tucker, great to hear your voice. I have you on the speaker with me and Ginger. Find anything out of interest?"

"Well, your memory is quite good," Tucker Wolcott began by saying.

He continued. "Over Labor Day weekend in 1976, there was a theft of exactly $1 million from the vault at the prestigious First National Bank of Chicago."

Tucker paused for a moment and then said, "It was ingenious!"

Knowing the answer but to generate discussion, Spence asked, "Why was the theft of $1 million so ingenious?"

Tucker laughed. "Because it was exactly one million! The bank took almost a week before they reported the missing funds to the federal authorities,"

"Let me guess," Spence said, "They kept thinking that it must have been a clerical error or some sort of transposition error where the digit "1" was added or subtracted by the accountants in error."

"Exactly!" Tucker said with emphasis.

"The bank has been sold and changed names several times since then, but I would think that to this day many of the old-timers who were around then still adamantly believe that it was nothing more than a clerical error and that no theft ever occurred," Tucker went on to say.

"Well, was there a theft?" Ginger asked.

"Yes. Yes, there was," Tucker answered.

"How do you know for sure?" Ginger queried.

"I am starting to remember more of the case now. But, as I recall, the supposed theft was never solved," Spence said.

"Well, that's what the bank wanted everyone to understand," Tucker added.

"What do you mean?" Ginger asked.

Tucker then explained. "In early 1978, I was providing some specialized services to the Treasury Services group within the bank. I was sitting alone at a table in the bank's executive dining room having lunch. By the way, that executive dining room was a great place. But back to the story. There were very few people in the dining room that early afternoon, but there were two bank executives just finishing lunch at the table next to me, and they were in deep conversation when I sat down. Apparently, they did not notice that I had sat down at the table next to them. I heard the two senior-level executives discussing the theft and the fact that the thief had been identified. Apparently, it had been the bank's good fortune that one small stack of fifty-dollar bills included within the missing million had been marked and the serial numbers registered. Some of the marked fifty-dollar bills began to surface and were ultimately traced back to the thief."

"What happened next?" Ginger asked.

"Nothing. Absolutely nothing!" Tucker said, stressing the word *nothing*.

Tucker continued. "The thief refused to acknowledge he had stolen any money and claimed he had found the stack of fifties on the street. He refused to say how the heist had been pulled off or to even acknowledge he was part of such a theft in any way. However, and it was never disclosed, the FBI had found one set of fingerprints in the vault that they had never been able to match until this guy was arrested and fingerprinted. The prints matched, so they were certain that they had the guy."

Tucker paused for emphasis and then continued. "The limited few top bank officials who knew about the situation were so embarrassed for the bank, and for themselves as top officers of the bank, that they decided to keep the fact that the theft actually occurred a secret, especially since they could never explain how the theft happened!"

"Do you know how they pulled it off?" Spence asked.

"No. But I may know who does," Tucker said.

"Almost as good," Spence said. "Who?" he asked.

"A guy named "FTC." That was the name I overheard at lunch that day back in 1978. But, unfortunately, that's all I know," Tucker explained.

Spence thought for a few moments and then said, "Tucker, it would be very helpful if you could determine the whereabouts of this Mr. FTC. I would like to speak with him."

"I know not to ask," Tucker said, "but is there anything else I should know?"

Spence paused for a moment and then explained. "I would just like to see if we can find out who FTC is, and if, in fact, FTC was involved in the theft and, if so, what was his *modus operandi.*"

"Really a long shot, but I will do the best I can to track him down. Keep in mind that it has been almost thirty years. I will get back to you as soon as I can."

"Great, thanks Tucker," Spence said as he ended the conversation.

"Well, that was interesting. Think there is any connection, after all these years, with the bank theft in Pittsburgh?" Ginger asked.

"Good question," Spence said as he moved on to think about other matters and other information that was continually being surfaced by the organization.

Chapter 40

The next day was the second Wednesday of the month, which meant that Spence and Ginger would be busy most of the day with telephone briefing updates from the heads of each of the organization's regions. It was a time that Spence looked forward to each month because the update briefings provided a scheduled opportunity to speak first with Piper Morgan in Australia (given the time difference, she was always scheduled early in the mornings) followed by Penny Mounier in France and Megan O'Malley in Ireland, followed then by the heads of the South American and Caribbean regions.

During the briefings, Megan O'Malley had mentioned that she was beginning to hear that forged corporate bearer bonds of US corporations were being offered for sale on the black market in Europe. A few weeks earlier, Jack Andrews, during the update briefing from the Caribbean region, had told Spence that he had heard a rumor that some high-quality US corporate bonds were being forged somewhere in the Caribbean and that the forgeries were of such high quality that they were undetectable to all but the most experienced investment managers.

During the update briefings, Spence asked Megan and Jack to discreetly follow up on the rumors. He knew that if the rumors were true, then this was, indeed, the type of criminal activity that was right in line with the type of activities that the organization was committed to solve on behalf of the federal authorities. Spence advised the heads of the other regions to be alert for any forged US financial instruments surfacing in their regions. He went on to ask the regions to squeeze their informants and other sources for "talk on the street" for any information about high-quality financial forgeries.

Chapter 41

"Spence, it's Tucker Wolcott on the phone."

"Thanks." Spence said to Ginger as he quickly picked up the telephone.

"Tucker, how is life in Chicago today?"

"Great, I would guess. I have been too busy on your project the last week or so to know!" he laughed.

Spence immediately knew from the inflection in Wolcott's voice that Wolcott had discovered something of interest.

"I hope all of that work resulted in something worthwhile," Spence said as he gently prodded Wolcott to share the news.

"Spence, the heist was almost thirty years ago. There were no known trails at the time other than the inadvertent conversation that I overheard between the two senior bank officials. Tracking down someone who does not want to be found is not easy, especially so many years later and especially if the individual or individuals were experienced in covering their tracks. Also, memories fade and can become misleading; key links in the trail fall away and can, and more often than not do, result in frustrating dead ends."

"I know, I know!" Spence somewhat impatiently interjected.

This was not like Wolcott. He usually got right to the point. As soon as Spence interrupted, he immediately regretted his comments. He knew that Tucker was one of the best and that there must be a very good reason for the extended dialogue.

"I'm sorry. Please continue. I am just anxious to know if you have good news, bad news, or no news," Spence said.

"Well, none of our extensive matrix searches identified a first, middle, and last name combination with the letters FTC for an individual with a background that would suggest the potential probability of being the mastermind for a high-precision bank heist. Clearly, the individual who pulled off the heist had to have had more than a working knowledge of bank safeguards and operating procedures."

"So I guess it is bad news!" Spence said.

"Well, it would have been, but that's not why you use me," Tucker said and laughed.

Unfazed, Tucker continued. "We were about to give up and then had the idea of running the initials FTC against the old Interpol European alias data base files."

"How—" Ginger began to ask.

"Don't ask," Tucker quickly scolded with a chuckle and then joked. "If I give up the secrets of my trade, you two might go into competition with me!"

Tucker continued. "FTC was not the initials for a proper name but rather the initials for an alias. We are highly confident that FTC stands for "Felix the Cat." When we ran the simultaneous matrix match programs against the Interpol files from the mid- to late 1970s and inserted the search criteria 'FTC, Chicago, financial fraud, and banks,' the following relationship was identified:

"FTC or Felix the Cat or Frank Thorne, born Chicago, Illinois. Experience—bank safeguards consultant.

"Without the enhanced search and comparative capabilities of the much more robust software currently available that did not exist back in the '70s, we could never have made the match."

"Sounds like he could be our guy," Spence offered.

"Yes, we are convinced, based on what we then found once we had identified the starting point."

"And all this leads to Frank Thorne?" Spence questioned hopefully.

"Frank Thorne is dead," Tucker said.

"But he left a trail, we think," Tucker quickly added.

Tucker went on to explain. "In late 1977, Frank Thorne relocated from Chicago to London, where he started a bank fraud consulting business. He also opened investment accounts at three separate banks in central London with aggregate deposits of five hundred thousand pounds sterling. The US dollar/pound sterling exchange rate in early 1978 was approximately 1.95, making the US Dollar equivalent of the deposits approximately $975,000. It's probably more than coincidental that $1 million US dollars less say $25,000 for expenses equals the $975,000 deposited in England within a year or so after the bank theft in Chicago of $1 million.

"After about ten years living in England, Thorne moved to the Bahamas, where he opened a beachside restaurant called the Dirty Turtle featuring seafood, specializing in fresh conch and grouper from the local waters as well as American-style hamburgers and pub food."

Tucker paused for a moment waiting for any questions or observations and then continued. "Thorne died from natural causes about five years ago."

"And I bet he didn't leave any written prose outlining his life's story!" Spence observed.

"Oh, but he may have!"

"How so?" Spence inquired, his hopes for information rising.

"Thorne had a son, now in his forties, who is now living in St. Kitts. His son's name is Tony—Tony Thorne. But that is as far as we have taken the trail. With more time, we can pursue the trail if you wish."

"Tucker, we can take it from here. Great job. Thanks." Spence turned to Ginger with the type of smile that a cat might have after having just devoured a nice canary.

CHAPTER 42

Jack Tracey was just finishing a nice tropical breakfast when the telephone rang. He was sitting on his patio with a cup of coffee looking out toward the Caribbean from his home in the Cayman Islands. The blue waters of the Caribbean were peaceful this morning, and the skies were clear. A good day for flying.

"Hello."

"Jack, it's Spence."

"Hey, I knew my day needed a little spice. What's up?"

"Have you heard of a Frank or Felix Thorne or a Tony Thorne?" Spence asked.

"Oh, yeah. Quite a pair. What do you want to know?" Jack offered.

Not waiting for Spence to respond, Jack quickly continued. "Felix, his real name was Frank, owned a restaurant in Nassau called the Dirty Turtle. Not a bad place. In fact, the food was above average. He catered to the beach crowd. There was always something hazy about his background, but he seemed a decent enough guy. He ran a clean operation and kept out of trouble. He was an American from somewhere in the Midwest, the best I can recall, but he had lived in England for a number of years. Thorne died four or five years ago."

"What about the son?" Spence asked.

"Well, that's another story!" Jack responded with a noticeable sound of disgust in his voice.

"Tony Thorne was a real disappointment to his old man. The kid has drifted around the Caribbean getting into one sort of trouble or another everywhere he has landed. Nothing serious, but he is always looking for the easy money. He's a flashy dresser and always trying to impress those who don't know him that he has some level of influence. Truth is that he is lucky to have more that a buck to his name at any one point in time. He seems to always be on the verge, if you listen to him, of the next get-rich scheme. A minor leaguer who wants badly to be in the big leagues, if you know what I mean. He is not someone you would want to do business with."

Jack paused. "Here's the real problem. The kid loves the casinos, and the casinos love him! He is just a good enough gambler to think he is good but not good enough to know when to cut his losses. He has a few big wins from time to time but invariably hangs around long enough for the casinos to win it all back plus a lot."

"Loses a lot?" Spence asked.

"Big time!"

"It was only Felix and the kid. The old man had nobody else as far as I know. Felix would cover the kid's gambling losses, but the old man made it clear to the casino owners that there must be a limit on the kid's losses. Like I said, Felix was an okay guy, so the owners worked with him and did not let the kid's losses accumulate."

"What happened after the old man left the scene?"

"You can probably guess!" Jack said with a tone of seriousness but with a tinge of laughter.

"Left to his own devices and without his old man around to provide cover, the lure of the casinos beckoned, and the kid became easy prey. As the old saying goes, *'A fool is soon separated from his money,'* or something along those lines. In this case, the fool was soon separated from his father's money. The kid gambled away his inherited ownership of the Dirty Turtle as well as essentially everything else left to him from his father."

"So what is he doing these days?"

"He hangs out in St. Kitts trying to find the next get-rich scheme and trying to keep his head above the waterline with the casino owners throughout the islands."

"Not a bad place to hang out," Spence said as he remembered his days in the hammock under the pine trees on the beach in Jamaica. He quickly thought, *St. Kitts is a far better place to hang out than Jamaica.*

"Oh, and one more thing," Jack said, almost having forgotten. "Word has it that the kid just pulled off some sort of big score and has paid off all of his outstanding debts from his last round of gambling losses. He is clean with the casinos. For the last couple of years, he had been laying low and trying to hide out from the casinos' collections guys. But recently, he has been resurfacing and beginning to show up at his old watering holes."

"Anything else?" Spence inquired.

"Yeah, one last thing. If you get more than a couple of drinks into young Tony Thorne and find a way to put him in a stressful situation, he becomes like a Hewlett-Packard printer—he can't spit out information fast enough."

"Jack, thanks. We need to find out what the kid knows about his old man's background, especially the time period just before they moved to London."

Spence thought out loud for a moment as he said, "We need a plan to work Tony Thorne."

"How about a squeeze play?" Ginger suggested.

"Exactly my thoughts," Jack concurred.

"I agree," Spence said.

CHAPTER 43

The Four Seasons Resort on the island of Nevis is an award-winning, five diamond resort surrounded by coconut palms, quiet beaches, and a full spectrum of facilities in a secluded haven nestled against a wide stretch of sugary white sand. Sunset dining and charming gingerbread guest cottages, in addition to the main resort tower, are a short walk across the beach from the blue waters of the Caribbean. The resort provides the opportunity to see endangered sea turtles, to scout for green vervet monkeys in the nearby rainforest, to stretch out in the garden-wrapped serenity by the infinity-edge pools, to experience the Caribbean's number one spa, or to fall asleep to the tune of tree frogs. The Four Seasons Nevis promotes the message "to stay, play, and relax in luxury" on a small exotic island.

As Spence and Ginger, together with assistance from Jack Tracey, began to develop the plan to put the squeeze on Tony Thorne for information, they decided, for a number of reasons, to stage the "sting" on the island of Nevis. One of the reasons to locate the sting operation in Nevis was that Tony Thorne was reported to be living in St. Kitts, which is a relatively short ocean ferry trip of less than an hour from Nevis. Also, Nevis is a beautiful, somewhat secluded island, and it provided Spence and Ginger a great opportunity to indulge themselves in the warmth of an exotic Caribbean adventure wrapped in the luxury provided by the Four Seasons Resort.

St. Kitts and Nevis are located in the northern part of the Leeward Islands off the coast of South America some twelve hundred miles south of Miami. The island of St. Kitts is twenty-three miles long and five miles across at its widest. Nevis, the smaller island, is approximately seven miles in diameter. The yearly temperature for both islands is slightly less than eighty degrees, humidity is low, and constant northeast trade winds keep the islands cool and very pleasant.

St. Kitts and Nevis, like no other islands in the Caribbean, seem to embody a kind of lush tropical paradise usually associated with the South Pacific. The atmosphere is palpably luxuriant: an intoxicating blend of sunlight, sea air, fantastically abundant vegetation, and brilliant tropical flowers. And yet, nature is only a small part of the wonder of these small, relatively undiscovered destinations.

The peaceful calm of St. Kitts and Nevis—the tranquil atmosphere that is Nevis especially edges toward slumber—suggests nothing of the extraordinary histories of these two islands. For centuries, St. Kitts and Nevis occupied a critical position in the European struggle for the West Indies, combining exceptional wealth as sugar colonies with a vital strategic position as gateways to the Caribbean. It is thought that Christopher Columbus provided both St. Kitts and Nevis with their European names when he first arrived on the islands in 1493. As the story goes, the Great Navigator dubbed the larger of the two islands St. Christopher, in honor of the patron saint of travelers. Although it may not have been Columbus who named the island of St. Kitts, it was almost certainly British sailors who shortened St. Christopher to the familiar St. Kitts. Whatever its origins, the gesture toward St. Christopher makes sense, as the islands' visibility and position—as well as their comforts—made them common first targets for early trans-Atlantic navigators.

Long ago, St. Kitts and Nevis were the pearls of the British Caribbean, rich and enormously important islands that were celebrated throughout Europe. Nevis, the "Queen of the Caribbees," possessed unimaginable wealth from its superproductive sugar industry. Of course, prosperity brought its own problems. The island became a magnet for pirates and privateers, who sought to ambush richly laden merchant ships. In fact, pirates harassed Nevis until the nineteenth century, until they finally disappeared along with the island's great sugar wealth.

Dominating the center of Nevis's thirty-six square miles is Mount Nevis. The summit of Mount Nevis is almost perpetually cloaked in mist, giving it the appearance of being snow-capped. The slopes of Mount Nevis and surrounding foothills are covered with lush vegetation—trees, flowers, and fruits of every description. The island's shores are fringed by miles of quiet, secluded beaches, including Pinney's Beach—where the lush luxurious Four Seasons Resort is located, acknowledged worldwide as one of the Caribbean's best resorts and best beaches.

Still largely undiscovered, despite its extraordinary beauty, remarkable history, and unmatched charm, Nevis offers a rare opportunity to visit the "secret Caribbean." Nevis is special, a place that will seduce you and tug at your heartstrings long after you leave.

Spence and Ginger were looking forward to spending time in Nevis—almost as much as they were looking forward to determining what information could be gleaned from Tony Thorne.

It had taken a couple of weeks for Jack Tracey to circulate the word through his contacts "on the street" in such a way that Tony Thorne became aware that a big poker game was about to occur at the Four Seasons Resort casino in Nevis—in his backyard! Jack made sure that Tony heard that there were to be a number of wealthy dumb fishes at the game and that there was still an open seat or two for the game. It would seem to be easy pickings to be had for a quick-thinking gambler. Even better pickings, it would seem, for a lowlife like Tony Thorne.

As expected, Tony Thorne took the bait and called the telephone number that was circulating on the street.

"Hello," Jack said as he answered the dedicated telephone line knowing, because of the dedicated line, that the call was in response to the "game."

"Are you handling Nevis?" Thorne sheepishly inquired.

"Yeah, who's calling?" Jack challenged.

"Tony Thorne. I get around the islands and heard you are working a big game in Nevis."

"That's right. This Saturday night. You interested?"

"Might be," Thorne answered.

"Five card draw poker," Jack said and then quickly added, "Hundred thousand to get into the game. Some business types from the States on vacation want a game. They probably have been watching too much of the television poker tournaments!" They shared a laugh.

"I'm in!" Thorne said without hearing more.

"Hold on," Jack said. "I like your eagerness, but we need some references. This is a clean game."

"Check with the Sunset Casino in Nassau and the Crystal Casino in Aruba. They will vouch for me."

"Okay. Show up at 8:00 p.m. Saturday at the Four Seasons casino in Nevis with the hundred thousand. The game is in a private room in the casino. Ask for Tom Wilmont. If your references check out, you will be in the game."

"You Wilmont?" Thorne asked.

"No, a friend of his. Just tell the concierge in the lobby of the Four Seasons that you are there to meet Mr. Wilmont. He will see that you and Wilmont find each other. Wilmont will see that you have a seat at the table, assuming your references check out and so long as you have the entry fee with you in cash."

"Thanks," Thorne said.

"Good luck!"

"Thanks," Thorne said as he thought to himself, *Luck will not be necessary.*

CHAPTER 44

As soon as the telephone call with Tony Thorne had concluded, Jack placed a call to Spence.

"Ginger, it's Jack." Ginger heard the familiar voice of Jack Tracey when she answered the telephone.

"Is Spence available?" he asked.

"I will see. Just a moment," she answered, knowing full well that Spence was nearby and was free to take any call if he cared to.

"It's our Caribbean friend Jack Tracey," Ginger said as she turned smiling toward Spence. Spence nodded that he would take the call.

"Jack, any luck?" Spence asked.

"Oh yeah! Thorne is on for this Saturday night in Nevis."

Spence thought for a moment. "Gives us four days. That should be plenty of time to finalize the arrangements. We have the team on standby and prepped. There should not be much we have to do in Nevis other than to run through the layout and the plan a couple of times."

"Thorne said he would take the boat over from St. Kitts late Saturday afternoon," Jack added.

"Great. Let's all plan to get to Nevis no later than tomorrow night. Everyone has been provided with background credentials, and each member of the team knows to take on his or her role upon leaving for Nevis. Should Thorne arrive early, and he sees people who will be in the game before the game, they will appear to be normal tourists, and he should not become suspicious. Ginger has already made reservations for six rooms at the Four Seasons. Can you pick the two of us up at Miami International and fly on direct to Nevis?" Spence asked.

"Sure thing."

"Since some folks know you throughout the islands, you know the rest of your role will need to be limited to just flying us into and out of Nevis," Spence advised and cautioned.

"I understand," Jack said.

"Jack, great job," Spence said in a very grateful voice.

"Looking forward to seeing you in Miami," Jack said.

"Same here," Spence and Ginger both responded.

"Ginger will get our arrival times into Miami to you later today," Spence said as Ginger nodded in agreement.

As Spence put down the telephone, he turned to Ginger and asked, "How's your poker skills?" He knew quite well that she could hold her own in any poker game and could bluff with the best.

"Explain a full house to me again, will you?" she teased with a girlish innocent look on her face.

The plan that Spence and Ginger had developed, again with the overall input from Jack Tracey, included having Spence and Ginger in the poker game together with three individuals from the US branch of the organization. Tony Thorne would be the sixth player at the table. The three individuals from the United States had been given chief executive officer titles and backgrounds and had been fully briefed on the Nevis plan, which had been code named "Grouper."

"Alert the Grouper team to get to Nevis by tomorrow evening," Spence said to Ginger as soon as they had completed the telephone call with Jack Tracey.

"Got it," Ginger said in a reserved but energetic fashion. *The thrill of the hunt*, she thought as she began to experience a growing level of excitement. Of course, she was also being drawn by the thought of spending time in exotic Nevis and catching some time at the spa and on the beach. The overall anticipation of adventure was gaining a growing presence.

CHAPTER 45

Spence and Ginger were sitting at the outdoor Pool Cabana café at the Nevis Four Seasons Resort enjoying a light lunch along the beach, shaded by the nearby palm trees. It was Saturday afternoon and a few hours before the poker game "sting" with Tony Thorne. All of the Grouper team had arrived, were trained, and were in place.

The Four Seasons Resort in Nevis can best be described in a word or two by "relaxed elegance." Spence sat somewhat lounging at the café table near the tree- and flower-surrounded pool at the edge of the beach enjoying Long Island Ice Tea and a wonderful lunch. He looked at the broad beautiful beach, the blue waters of the Caribbean, and the imagined visions of colorful pirates in the distance and Ginger in her bikini. He thought, again, how far away this place was from his days of childhood and dreams of adventure in the small rural area of Indiana that he still so loved.

His next thought was, *As soon as this job is completed, I am off to Australia!* He knew there was someone special waiting for him there.

Ginger looked at Spence and could tell he was deep in thought. "What are you thinking?" she prodded carefully.

"Oh, just hoping that this guy Thorne shows and that he really knows something that will be helpful."

"Even if he is a bust, this is not bad duty!" Ginger laughed looking at the sun, sand, and breaking surf, and at the last of her lunch.

Ginger and Spence had shared an order of Drunken Tiger Shrimp. Ginger had then ordered the jerk-marinated swordfish sandwich and Spence had ordered a grouper sandwich. The food was terrific and certainly was enhanced by the wonderful surroundings and great service.

"Boy, have you got that right!" Spence said and smiled as he finished the last bite of his sandwich. "This is a wonderful place."

"Are we all set?" he questioned again, knowing that if Ginger was in a bikini and enjoying a relaxing lunch that everything was under control.

"Yes, the room is all set, and everyone is ready. Now just waiting for the fun to start," Ginger said.

She thought for a moment and then said half jokingly, "So, it is game on!"

"Yes, game on!" Spence said in a more serious tone and then smiled and winked at Ginger.

Chapter 46

It was almost 7:30 p.m., and the level of activity was growing within the casino. Spence and the three other players from the organization were in one of the private players' rooms off the main floor of the casino.

Ginger was relaxing in one of the overstuffed chairs in the open-air lobby. The luxurious lobby was enclosed but, like most upscale resorts in the Caribbean, the entrance was open as well as the side overlooking the pools and the beach. Ginger found the early-evening Caribbean Sea breezes to be very refreshing, especially after an afternoon in the sun and after a quick late-afternoon jaunt to the spa, as the light breeze mixed with and distributed the fragrances of the many fresh-cut flowers located throughout the lobby.

From her position in the lobby, Ginger had a good view of the concierge's desk. She knew, given the ferry schedule from St. Kitts to Nevis and the ten-minute or so cab ride from the dock, that if Thorne was going to show, he should be arriving soon. About ten minutes later, she noticed a very tanned, lean, well-dressed man in his midforties, she guessed, approach the concierge. A few moments later, she saw the concierge nod in her direction. From the photographs she and Spence and the team had studied, she knew Tony Thorne was heading her way.

"Hi, I'm Tony Thorne. They told me you will take me to Tom Wilmont," Thorne said somewhat with a smirk as he gave her a careful once-over, stopping briefly to dwell on her chest and then her thin, shapely hips.

"Yes, follow me," Ginger said, maintaining control over her initial disgust with the weasel.

"He your boss?" Thorne asked as they began walking with Thorne trailing Ginger toward the casino entrance, which was just off the right of the large lobby area.

"Who?" Ginger asked knowing what he meant.

"Wilmont," Thorne clarified needlessly.

Ginger did not reply but rather keep walking. She led Thorne into the casino, past the rows of noisy slot machines, past the roulette tables, and to the private area of the casino where an attendant was stationed to guard the entrance to one of the private VIP rooms. As Ginger approached the assigned private room, another attendant nodded acknowledgment to Ginger without saying a word and opened the door to the private room for Ginger and Thorne. Thorne quickly, upon entering the room, evaluated the room as if sizing up the fishes and calculating how much of a payday this evening might represent. Within the room was a large green felt table with seven chairs—six for the players and a chair for the dealer—and a large bar serviced by a dedicated bartender that Thorne assumed came with the room. At the far end of the room was a door that Thorne guessed led to a washroom.

Spence walked up to Thorne and extended his hand. "Hello, I'm Tom Wilmont."

"Tony Thorne," Thorne answered as he shook Spence's hand.

One by one the other players introduced themselves to Thorne—all using their fictitious names.

"Everyone ready to get started?" Wilmont (Spence) said more as a strong suggestion than as a question. There were a series of concurring agreements in the form of "all set," "I'm ready," and "good to go."

With the concurrence of all of the players, Spence said to everyone in general and to no one in particular, "Grab a seat at the table. The waiter will refresh your drinks or get a drink for anyone who would like a drink."

Thorne, Spence, and the other three players each took a seat, and then Ginger took the last remaining seat at the table. As Ginger sat down, there was an expression of surprise, perhaps shock, on Thorne's face, and he almost involuntarily blurted out, "Hey, Wilmont, what's your assistant, the chick, doing in the game!"

Spence smiled as he calmly responded, "Oh, I apologize. Forgive me. I guess I did not provide a proper introduction."

Spence paused for emphasis. "Tony, let me introduce you to Susan Thatcher." Spence then whispered. "Susan is not my assistant. I only wish!" He turned his head slightly and shared a private wink and made his best attempt at a lecherous smile toward Tony. Spence knew that this is the type of observation that would be welcomed by Thorne.

In a more normal voice level, Spence then continued. "Susan is a senior executive with a Silicon Valley high-tech company. She is here on vacation, single, and loves to play with the big boys!"

Thorne turned toward Ginger (a.k.a "Susan"). "Sorry," he said.

Ginger smiled as she said to Thorne in a tone to undermine his already falsely based confidence, "I hope for your sake that your poker 'reads' are better than your people judgment and assessments." She smiled as the other players shared a laugh at Thorne's expense.

Skill is important in poker, and surely without question luck plays an important part—perhaps critical at any specific point in the play, but confidence, the ability to "read" opponents, and getting the physiological edge on an opponent are acquired skills—something that Tony Thorne had never mastered. And as a result, Thorne was always at a distinct disadvantage in any poker game that involved more experienced and savvy players. However, in his own mind, Thorne consistently greatly overestimated his own skills and abilities—a very dangerous thing to do in most situations and especially in the game of poker when the lack of understanding, poor common sense, and poor judgment can lead, and usually does as well demonstrated with Thorne's history, to a costly conclusion.

For the first couple of hours, Spence and his crew allowed the game to proceed in a direction that carefully built Thorne's confidence. No big wins for Tony, but clearly he was allowed to have a trend of successes. After four hours or so, near midnight, two of the players had lost most of each of their $100,000 and excused themselves from the game. In other words, they had been cleaned out. Spence (a.ka. Tom Wilmont) and Ginger (a.k.a. Susan Thatcher), Thorne, and one of the other "players" remained in the game. A short time later, Ginger went all in on one hand, lost, and left the game followed, as planned, a half hour or so later by Spence. Two remaining players were left in the game, Tony Thorne and one of the organization's "players." Thorne had, as planned, also begun to lose, and his chips had dwindled. Although he still had more chips than he had started the evening with, the value of his chips had been reduced from almost $500,000 at the high to now $150,000. The other remaining player had chips with a value of $450,000. Although there was now a relatively significant advantage in chips for the "player" in comparison to Thorne's position, Thorne was still, as he had been all evening, very cocky, and he felt the big hand was just waiting for him. He came to win and to win big.

A few hands more were played with no significant change in chips between the two remaining players. Thorne then bluffed a hand and won the next pot, moving $25,000 of the "player's" chips to Thorne's side of the table and bringing the balances to approximately $175,000 for Thorne and $425,000 for the "player."

It was now almost one in the morning. Spence knew that now was the time to move. The entire evening and the sequence of play had been to position the vulnerable Tony Thorne to this point—to a point where his greed and overconfidence could be used against him in a big way.

Each player received two cards. Thorne received a king of hearts and an ace of spades. The "player" received a queen of diamonds and a nine of diamonds. Both players, as usual, guarded their cards carefully. Thorne bet $20,000 and the "player" raised the bet by an additional $30,000. Thorne received another card, a king of hearts, and raised $40,000. The "player" received a card and raised the bet another $25,000. Thorne received his last card, a king of spades, and with three kings, he raised $40,000.

The dealer now began to turn the cards up on the table for the "river." In this type of poker, the "river" is four cards that are available for each of the players to utilize in their hand to combine with and make the best five-card hand. The "river" contained the following cards:

King of clubs
Nine of spades
Four of diamonds
Ace of diamonds

It was taking all the restraint Thorne could muster to not let his excitement show. The odds were overwhelming that he had the winning hand. By winning this hand, he would cripple his opponent and could be well on his way to taking all of the chips within, hopefully, just a couple more hands.

With the last card, a jack of hearts, the "player" raised by pushing his entire pile of remaining chips toward the middle of the table. This was the moment. Thorne had only $10,000 of chips left, but he knew he had the hand of a lifetime—at least, so far in his lifetime. He wanted this win. He just could not fold. How could he fold with such a winning hand? He needed credit to stay in the game, and he needed the credit now. He needed a backer.

Thorne looked at the huge pile of chips near the middle of the table (a pile that already included $165,000 of his chips) and then looked at his puny pile of chips that totaled $10,000. Yes, he needed credit. He could not give up on this great winning hand and just could not say goodbye to so many of his chips. He must play on, but how? He needed time—time to think, time to get help.

Thorne looked at the "player" and then said, "I'm a little short, but I'm good for it. I am not folding!"

"How short?" the "player" responded very cordially knowing they had Thorne, or he would have folded and cut his losses.

"I plan to stay in and win this hand. So, assuming you stay the course, I would need probably $250,000," replied Thorne.

"Sorry, no help here," said the "player." "I have the winning hand, and I don't want to worry about having to chase you around the islands trying to collect when you lose."

Thorne was convinced that the "player" was using this opportunity to bluff Thorne into folding. He thought for a moment and then said, "I need a five-minute break. Okay?"

"Okay, but five minutes and then either fold or call with the additional cash," the player admonished in a pleasant but firm voice.

Thorne got up from the table and walked a few feet away, always keeping a close eye on the table with the cards and the chips. Thorne asked Spence, who with Ginger and the other "players" who had already dropped out of the game and who had been watching what now appeared to perhaps be the final hand, to come to where Thorne was standing.

"Tom," Thorne whispered. "I need the $250,000. I have the winning hand!"

"What makes you so sure?" Spence asked.

"With the king on the table, I have four of a kind. Four kings and an ace high," Thorne excitedly answered.

"What if he has a flush?" Spence challenged.

"Could be, but do you know what the odds are against that—huge!" Thorne said as he tried to build his case for help.

"How do I know you are good for the $250,000?" Spence asked.

"First, float me the loan for two minutes, and I will give you $25,000. Second, I will put up my ownership in the Dirty Turtle restaurant in Nassau as collateral." Thorne showed Spence a stock certificate and other documents in an effort to convince Spence that Thorne was good for the $250,000. Of course, Spence knew that Thorne had a couple of years earlier gambled away his ownership of the Dirty Turtle.

"Okay," Spence said, "but I want $50,000 of the winnings, not $25,000."

"Done," Thorne said with a huge smile as he shook Spence's hand.

"Give me a few minutes to get the casino manager. I will need to get the $250,000 against my open line of credit," Spence said to Thorne.

Thorne immediately stepped back to the table and announced to the other player, "I call but I need an additional five minutes or so to get the cash."

"I can wait five minutes," the "player" said as he nodded agreement.

Spence disappeared and less than ten minutes later returned with a guard and $250,000 of cash. The guard and the cash were both from the organization. There had been no involvement from the casino.

Thorne was convinced he had the winning hand but was too nervous to sit down. He remained standing as he turned his cards over on the table. He was smiling ear to ear and about to pounce on the pile of chips and pull the chips to his side of the table. There was a stern look on the face of the "player," a look that Thorne could not read, but there was a twinkle in the eye of the "player" that Thorne could also not see.

The "player" turned his cards over slowly one by one, and with the last card, Thorne knew his luck had run out. He was beaten by the flush of the "player." Tony Thorne had been beaten by the odds. He was both devastated and terrified. He had bet and lost $250,000 that he did not have. Thorne staggered from the table toward the door without muttering a word. The only sound was the sound from the chips of the "player" gathering in his winnings.

As Tony Thorne entered the hallway and began to walk toward the casino floor, Spence caught up with him. "Hey, what about my $250,000!" Spence shouted.

"I guess you are now the owner of the Dirty Turtle," Thorne responded.

"Well, we have a problem, or, should I say, you have a problem Mr. Thorne. A big problem!" Spence said.

"Listen, Wilmont!" Thorne said, "it was bad luck, and I am sorry I lost the money, but I am a man of honor. The Dirty Turtle is worth well more than the $250,000, and the Dirty Turtle is yours. Run it, sell it, or whatever you want to do with it, but you have your $250,000."

"Could be," Spence replied, "if you were really the owner. I happen to know you lost your ownership a few years ago."

Thorne was now sweating profusely. "Who are you?!" he asked defiantly as he looked at Spence.

"The guy you owe $250,000!" Spence said sternly.

"I don't have $250,000 or anything close. I just need some time," Thorne pleaded.

"Time won't help you," Spence said leaving no room left for negotiation.

"Then you're out of luck," Thorne said trying to muster all of his courage with one last bluff.

"No, sir! You are the one who is out of luck and out of time!"

"You will be fine fish bait!" Spence said as two of the "players" grabbed Thorne by the arms and pinned his arms behind his back.

"Wait, wait!" Thorne begged. "Can't we work something out!" He fell to his knees crying, "Please, please, anything you want."

Thorne was pulled into the now darkened room where he had just lost the $250,000 that he did not have.

"Well, there is one thing," Spence said as the two men applied greater pressure on Thorne's arms signaling they were dead serious and were standing ready to carry out Tom Wilmont's instructions once given.

"Anything, anything," Thorne yelled.

A light—a very bright light—was directed at Thorne's face as Spence directed his next words in a very firm and nonemotional voice to Thorne. "How did your father pull off the First National job?"

Thorne's face literally turned a pale gray with shock as he almost silently muttered, "Oh no, not again."

"What do you mean, 'not again'?" Spence questioned as he turned the light directly into Thorne's eyes and as he motioned for the two men to further tighten their grasp on Thorne's arms. Thorne began to whimper again from the pain in his arms. If it had not been clear before, it was now becoming quite clear to him that these people were serious—dead serious.

Spence asked again, and it was clear in his voice that his patience was nearing an end, "What do you mean, 'not again'!" Again, there was no response from Thorne.

With a further motion from Spence, the two men then applied the Chinese ear squeeze to Thorne's left ear and the french finger hold to the index finger of Thorne's right hand. Thorne yelled out in excruciating pain.

"Please stop, please, please," Throne cried. He had never experienced such pain. The french finger hold is such a simple technique but when applied by someone who has mastered the technique, the hold can make the strongest of men weep, and such was the case with Thorne, who was not even the strongest of men to begin with.

"Speak!" Spence admonished.

Now realizing he had little choice, Thorne began to speak faster than a Hewlett Packard printer could convey information on the printed page.

"What dumb luck! This is the second time in six months that I have been set up! You guys don't know who you are dealing with!" Thorne said with the hopes of maybe, just maybe, pulling off one last bluff.

"We have you right now, and that we know for sure. You're just a small-time loser," Spence said.

"But Ernesto Cardeno is not!" Thorne said again, somewhat defiantly hoping to regain some leverage through reference and use of Cardeno's name.

"Go on," Spence encouraged as new pressure was applied to Thorne's finger, ear, and arms.

"I lost big time on a 'winning hand' in a game run by Cardeno. Of course, like tonight, I did not know that, when I lost, my marker was really being held by Cardeno. I couldn't even come close to paying off the marker to Cardeno. The only thing I had to bargain with, after having already lost the Dirty Turtle, was the knowledge of the details behind the Chicago bank job. Having some knowledge of Cardeno's criminal history, I suspected that the details of the unique and unsolved bank theft in Chicago, no matter how old, would be worth a lot to someone like Cardeno. And I was right!"

"Go on," Spence urged.

"I guessed my knowledge was valuable to someone like Cardeno, and it was. I traded the information for the gambling debt—information that I had promised my father I would never disclose. A family secret, if you will."

"Well, now you can make a similar trade," Thorne was advised by Spence.

"Deal or no deal, Mr. Thorne!" Spence said as he chuckled to himself and thought, *Deal or no deal sounds like the television show.*

He thought the phrase was a little corny, but if it got Thorne to fork up the information, then so be it.

With one last painful twist of encouragement, Thorne blurted out everything Spence and Ginger wanted to know and far more than they had expected. Spence turned in the dark and lightly squeezed Ginger's hand. They both knew they now had the information to break the case.

"Thank you, Mr. Tony Thorne; you have made a contingent payment in full of your debt," Spence said.

"What do you mean, *contingent*!"

"We bought this information from you. The information is now ours and ours alone. You are off the hook with us so long as you never give the information about the Chicago bank theft to another soul. And, by the way, no more gambling! If you ever do either, we will find you, and fish bait you will be! Trust me, there is nothing these two gentlemen would rather do than be entertained by feeding you to the fishes." At the moment Spence finished speaking, the two men added an exclamation point to Spence's words by applying a further painful twist to Thorne's arms.

"Agreed?" Spence challenged.

"Agreed," Thorne responded meekly.

Spence then handed a hotel key to Thorne.

"What's this for?" Thorne asked.

"It's late, and we don't want you wandering off and getting lost. We have a cab waiting for you outside the lobby. There is a reservation in your name at the Harbor Inn near the dock—the room has been prepaid. Catch the first ferry in the morning to St. Kitts and don't look back. We won't be here anyway!"

"Got it?!" Spence questioned, but the tone was more of a demand than of a question.

"Yeah, I got it."

"Okay, and one more thing," Spence added. "If you don't catch the first ferry, we will know. Just so you know, we do not work under the philosophy of second chances," Spence cautioned.

With Spence's last words, Thorne was escorted by three of the gentlemen from the organization out of the darkened room, through the casino, and through the hotel lobby to the waiting cab. When the three had returned and reported that Thorne was on his way, Spence turned to the assembled team and said, "Well done; thanks everyone. Safe travels."

CHAPTER 47

The operational plan provided for everyone on the team, except Spence and Ginger, to leave Nevis by private boats to Antigua and St. Maarten and then from there by air on to their respective home bases. Spence and Ginger were planning to spend two additional days in Nevis enjoying the sun and sand. More importantly, depending on the information obtained from Tony Thorne, Spence intended to develop the next steps in cracking the Pittsburgh bank case.

Jack Andrews was scheduled to fly into the Nevis Amory International Airport in two days to pick up Spence and Ginger for a flight to Key Largo, Florida, on his private plane. From Key Largo, Spence and Ginger would drive to Miami International and then take separate routes back to Burlington, Vermont.

It was now almost two in the morning, and the other members of the team from the organization had just left the casino. Ginger turned to Spence and spoke first. "Wow!"

"I would say so." Spence laughed.

"It's late, and I'm beat. Let's get some sleep and meet for lunch. We can try to sort out what all of this means then. Okay?' Spence asked.

"Sounds good. I am going to sleep in late, hopefully, and then head for the spa. How about lunch at the Pool Cabana around say 1:00 p.m.?" Ginger said in the form of a recommendation.

"Great." Spence concurred with a tired smile as his mind ran full speed processing the information that had been extracted from Tony Thorne.

Ginger hugged Spence firmly but only briefly. "Great job!" she said. They then walked through the still-noisy main floor of the casino and to the elevators that led to their respective rooms.

Spence and Ginger knew that the organization was in good hands with the regional leaders, and they knew that they would not be interrupted in Nevis unless the matters were of the greatest urgency. The mundane matters could wait to be addressed until they returned to Burlington.

For the next two days, Ginger and Spence enjoyed the offerings of the Four Seasons Resort with Ginger spending an inordinate amount of time frequenting the spa. Spence utilized some of his downtime to read and relax in the tree-shaded areas along the pool with an occasional frozen drink in hand. As was normally the case, Spence spent time working on plans to further develop and strengthen the organization. He also formulated the plan to deliver the promised results to Jill Winslow on the Pittsburgh bank case. He was looking forward to seeing the look on Jill's face when she learned that he and his team had performed what he knew she thought was the impossible.

The last evening in Nevis, Spence and Ginger met for dinner, after having spent most of the previous two days on their own, at the dining room of the Four Seasons. The main dining room was an open-air restaurant with a commanding view of the Caribbean Sea.

"Do we have to leave paradise so soon?" Ginger said as soon as she sat down at the candlelit table. Spence had arrived a few minutes earlier and had already ordered their favorite drinks.

"It's back to work tomorrow for both of us!" he answered with a smile.

"I know."

"How was your day?" he asked.

Ginger winked. "Not bad, not bad at all."

She paused as the waiter delivered their drinks and then with a more serious tone went on as the sun was in its final phase of setting for the evening. "Spence, do you know what I like about working with you?"

Spence smiled with the boyish grin. "My charm?"

"No! What I really like is never knowing what exotic location we will be visiting next. Not to mention that I trust you with my body and soul on these adventures!"

"Hmm," Spence said with a devilish smile.

"Stop that!" Ginger teased.

"I trust you, too. I can't imagine doing this without you," Ginger said softly.

Spence picked up the menu. "Let's order," he murmured, getting a little uncomfortable and wanting to change the direction of the conversation.

Just as Ginger placed her menu on the table as a sign she was ready to order, the waiter arrived. "I will have the Skookum oysters with the conch ceviche to begin and the seared diver scallops with the green papaya slaw," Ginger said as she politely provided her dinner wishes to the waiter. "I will have the citrus crusted soft shell crab with the mango chutney, and for the main course I will have the pan-seared line-caught barramundi with the roasted purple potatoes," Spence told the waiter.

"Excellent choices," the waiter acknowledged.

When the waiter had left, Spence turned to Ginger. "Well, now all we have to do is find Ernesto Cardeno and recover the $10 million for Ms. Winslow."

"Has the time on the beach resulted in any ideas?" Ginger asked.

"First, as soon as we get back to Burlington, let's canvass by telephone each of the regions and see if anyone has heard of this Ernesto Cardeno, and then we can map out our game plan."

Spence and Ginger finished the very enjoyable dinner and enjoyed the evening knowing that in the morning they would be meeting Jack Tracey for the first leg of their respective return trips to Burlington.

CHAPTER 48

Spence and Ginger had both arrived back in Burlington the prior evening by different routes through Miami from Nevis. They were now both in the office of Spence's secluded lakeside home on the shore of Lake Champlain. They had a busy day ahead since it was time again for the semimonthly briefing from the leaders of the organization's regions around the world. At one point or another during each of the regional updates, Spence had inquired about Ernesto Cardeno.

The conference calls had been relatively routine with the various status updates until the call with Rafael Posada—managing director of South America.

"Rafael, have you heard of an Ernesto Cardeno?" Spence asked.

"Spence, I knew you were good, but I would never have guessed you were a mind reader," Rafael said laughingly.

"What do you mean?" Spence questioned.

"Remember those forged US corporate bond rumors you asked us to look into?" Rafael said.

"Yes. Have you found something?" Spence responded wondering where this was leading.

"It's a fact. There is a guy named Ernesto Cardeno behind the forged bonds. We have tracked him to Puerto Costa Maya—a town on the Rivera Maya in Mexico."

"Huh," Spence said as he thought about the direction to take.

"I need to know everything you can find out about Ernesto Cardeno. Employ our full surveillance capabilities—electronic and on-site assets. Whatever organization resources you need, just let Ginger know, and she will make the arrangements," Spence instructed.

"Give me a week to ten days, and I will get a detailed dossier to you," Rafael said, challenging himself to the tight deadline.

"Okay, but a week is about all the time we have on this," Spence said as he encouraged Rafael to move quickly.

Less than a week later, Spence was sitting on the deck of his home in Burlington when Ginger came out of the house with a secure printout of a report from Rafael Posada entitled "Dossier on Ernesto Cardeno." The report was fifteen pages in length and provided an exhaustive background on Cardeno.

The key excerpts from the dossier included the following information:

1. Principal residence—Felipe Carrillo Puerto (Yucatan Peninsula of Mexico).
2. Hideaway—Seaside villa in Puerto Costa Maya (spends two weeks each month alone on "vacation" at the villa).
3. Colombian by birth. Moved to Mexico with his parents when he was ten.
4. Heads a group of criminals actively involved in forging corporate bonds and other negotiable financial instruments (principally US securities).
5. Long thought to be the mastermind behind a number of financial thefts in South America.
6. Operations are based in the city of Felipe Carrillo Puerto (the specific location of the counterfeiting operations has been identified—a layout of the facility is attached to the dossier as an exhibit).

7. Has long, relaxing lunches alone each Wednesday and Saturday at Bandido's restaurant when he is at his villa in Costa Maya.

After reading the report twice, Spence turned to Ginger. "Ginger, get Rafael on the telephone."

A few moments later, Ginger returned to the deck. "I have Rafael."

"Rafael, it's Spence."

"Get the report on Cardeno?" Rafael asked.

"Yes, thanks. I have another project for you," Spence said as he then explained in detail what he had in mind and outlined the services he needed from Rafael and the organization's South American team. After outlining the scope of the project, Spence provided one further instruction. "Make certain that you resource the project adequately, and let me know if you need assistance from any of the other regions from within the organization."

"Will do. There is always something that will arise that is unexpected, but this will be fun!" Rafael said as he and Spence finished the conversation.

CHAPTER 49

Beginning where the Mayan Rivera (Cancun, Playa del Carmen, and Tulum) on the eastern side of the Yucatan Peninsula of Mexico ends, the Costa Maya stretches along the Mexican coastline down to Belize. Nowhere near as much development has occurred along this part of the coastline as has occurred on the Mexican Rivera. The Costa Maya is the last remaining section of the eastern Yucatan Peninsula coastal properties yet to be exploited, and, as a result, there are miles of coastal land with no development. The odd fishing village spots the landscape but not much beyond that.

Driving south from Playa del Carmen along the Costa Maya on Mexico Highway 307, not much is encountered except butterflies until you reach the city of Felipe Carrillo Puerto, which is located approximately 230 kilometers (approximately 150 miles) south of Cancun. Unlike Playa del Carmen and Cancun, Carrillo Puerto is a Mayan city and is considered the most cosmopolitan city on the peninsula. Rich with history, Carrillo Puerto successfully blends traditional Mayan life with the advancements of modern culture and technologies.

What a traveler notices in Carrillo Puerto is that the residents are extremely proud and dignified. The atmosphere of Carillo Puerto is far different than that of Cancun or Cozumel. Carillo Puerto has a much stronger cultural ambiance. In fact, if you are a "gringo," the locals will pay you no mind whatsoever. With no beaches nearby, this city is not a major tourist destination, and you many go a full day in Carillo Puerto without seeing another tourist. This can be an interesting experience, as just when you thought you had found a place void of absolutely every other gringo, one walks around the corner.

Fifty kilometers or so to the east is the coastline and the coastal village of Puerto Costa Maya.

Puerto Costa Maya was carved out of the Mayan jungle to attract cruise ships in order for the Mexican authorities to develop this area of the Yucatan Peninsula. The Costa Mayan area of the Yucatan Peninsula is simply pure magic consisting of the ancient world of the Mayas, with their subterranean rivers and caves, the sugary beaches, and somewhat to the north near Playa del Carmen, the second-largest coral reef in the world, bathed by the crystalline waters of the Caribbean. The combination of the pristine nature found in the national park of Sian Ka'an, the oceanfront ruins of Tulum as well as other vestiges of Mayan civilization, and the sea are turning the Rivera into the fastest-growing area in Mexico. However, both Carrillo Puerto, which is inland, and Costa Maya, which although on the coast is difficult to access other than by cruise ship, remain relatively undiscovered. Because of its natural beauty and remote coastal location, the Mexican authorities, with a long-term desire to develop Costa Maya into a tourist destination similar to Cancun or Playa del Carmen, have financed the construction of a pier to accommodate the docking of cruise ships at Costa Maya. Costa Maya is the vision of undiscovered paradise.

The cruise ships dock at the end of a very long pier that juts out into the ocean from the coast. When you see the majestic expanse of the undeveloped Puerto Costa Maya tree-lined coastline from aboard a cruise ship, your first impression, or perhaps question, will be, "Where in the world are we?" From the ship, other than for the natural beauty of the sandy beaches running from the waters' edge to the jungle, only a large walled pavilion entryway can be seen. The second impression, most likely, is that you know you have arrived somewhere special in a land of mystery and intrigue. Planned with great attention to detail, Costa Maya resembles an ancient Mayan city. Three grand pavilions host local artisans, unique works of art and culture, as well as shops with souvenirs and the typical shops, such as Columbian Emeralds, that cater to cruise ship tourists. However, these shops are all within the confines of the pavilions. Beyond the pavilions, Costa Maya provides access to the natural resources that make this region of the Mexican Caribbean so completely unique, offering a window into new and undeveloped areas of the coast and the Mayan jungle.

Costa Maya provides an excellent exotic hideaway for someone who does not necessarily want to be bothered, as was the case with Ernesto Cardeno, and who wants to enjoy the fruits of his efforts in a remote tropical location.

Rafael and the communications/electronics expert together with a four-member support team (including two highly skilled women in order to establish the appearance that the team members were nothing more than travel adventure tourists) had been in the Costa Maya and Carrillo Puerto areas for the past ten days posing as adventure tourists. During the ten days, the team had maintained 24/7 visual and electronic surveillance of Ernesto Cardeno. The team had made a clandestine "visit" to Cardeno's seaside villa the second night after their arrival in Costa Maya. During the visit, electronic key stroke monitoring transmission devices were installed on each of the computers in the villa. In addition, highly sophisticated miniaturized cameras had been strategically placed throughout the villa; all of the telephones had been tapped, and disguised voice-activated transmission units (in the form of ballpoint pens, cans of beans, and other innocent-appearing items) had been placed out of sight in the villa. The team also had set up cellular telephone electronic interception equipment a short distance from the villa in a thick grove of trees. Prior to their arrival, the team had also been able to secure the frequencies of the cellular telephone numbers used by Cardeno and his limited but tight-knit group of thugs.

To the best of his knowledge, Cardeno had been successful in keeping the existence of his villa in Costa Maya a secret (a secret that he thought was known by only the most trusted members of his inner circle). As a result, he believed his villa was a safe haven and a place where activities and plans could be freely discussed and developed without fear of the Federales (Mexican federal police) gaining knowledge of his activities. He had let his guard down, and his complacency would provide Spence's team from the organization tremendous opportunities to gather information and to develop an understanding of the behavior and patterns of activity of Cardeno.

The team had anticipated that it would take two weeks, at a minimum, to gain an understanding of Cardeno's behavior patterns and tendencies. However, in less than a week, the surveillance had hit pay dirt on several occasions, and to such a degree that they had been able to construct a comprehensive detailed understanding of Cardeno's activities. They now had the information that Spence had set them on a mission to discover.

Chapter 50

"Hello," Ginger said as she answered the secure communication line. She could tell from the routing number on the digital readout that the call had been initiated in Mexico.

"Ginger, this is Rafael Posada. Is Spence available?"

Spence was listening. He paused a few moments in respect to Ginger and then picked up the call. "Rafael, my friend, what have you found?"

"We hit the mother lode!" Rafael said excitedly.

"This guy feels so safe in Costa Maya that he has gotten lazy with his communications. He must think that no one is aware of his identity in Costa Maya. The combination of his communications sloppiness and our highly sophisticated monitoring equipment coupled with our on-the-ground assets has yielded an unbelievable degree of interesting information on this guy."

"What did you find?" Spence asked with growing anticipation.

"This is your guy. No question. From the conversations Cardeno has had with his financial consigliore, we know he is printing forged US corporate bonds in Carrillo Puerto. We also learned that he has over twenty-five million US dollars in an account in Miami. We even know the bank account number and the customer access password," Rafael proudly explained.

Rafael then went on to explain Cardeno's daily patterns that the teams embedded in Costa Maya and Carrillo Puerto had observed.

Spence absorbed the information that Rafael was providing, and at the same time his mind was processing the information and how next to proceed. Spence was fully aware that the information provided by the team would have a short meaningful life span and that if he was going to act, he would have to act quickly before Cardeno changed his patterns. He would have to act on the excellent information that was now available. There might not be another opportunity.

"Rafael, Ginger and I will meet you in Cancun two days from today and then travel with you to Costa Maya. Ginger will call you tomorrow with the specific arrangements." Spence then went on to outline to Rafael what he had in mind once they arrived in Costa Maya. Spence thought, *With a little luck and the skill of the team, my plan just might work.*

As soon as Spence had outlined his plan and completed the telephone call, Ginger began to laugh. Spence looked at Ginger with his mischievous grin, as if to say, "Ingenious, *huh!*"

"Someday, I would love to be able to find out what's inside your head. How do you come up with this stuff?" Ginger said as she continued laughing.

"Not a lot in there. That's why I have room for these ideas." Spence chuckled.

"Let's get Jill Winslow on the phone," Spence said as he switched gears.

Chapter 51

"Jill, this is the Travelin' Man," Spence announced as Jill Winslow answered her telephone.

"Yes, I was wondering if I would hear from you again. It's been almost a month." She giggled and said, "Job too tough for you?"

"We need to meet," Spence said disregarding her spirited jab.

"Good news?"

"I think you will be pleased," Spence said pleasantly, knowing that revenge is better served either cold or in a very subtle fashion.

"Where and when?" Jill asked, now very serious and curious about the information that might be forthcoming from the Travelin' Man.

"Can you make a meeting tomorrow morning?" Spence asked.

"Probably but depends on the location."

"Good. Tomorrow morning, drive from Washington, DC, to Charlottesville, Virginia. Take Route 29 south from Washington. Follow Route 29 until you reach the turnoff for the Charlottesville airport, which is approximately five miles north of the city. Continue south on Route 29 past the airport turnoff another two to three miles until you reach the Hilton Heights Street intersection. Turn right on Hilton Heights, drive up the hill, and park in the Doubletree Hotel parking lot. Please arrive no later than 9:00 a.m. Place a tissue box on the inside dash of your car and then wait in your car for further instructions. Got it?" Spence asked.

"Yes. I look forward to seeing you," Jill said as she began reviewing her available wardrobe in her mind, sorting the images and searching for her most alluring outfit.

Charlottesville is nestled at the foothills of the Blue Ridge Mountains in western central Virginia. The city is home to approximately forty thousand residents and is rated as one of the most livable places in the country. Located some one hundred miles south of Washington, DC, Charlottesville is a city deep in historic value. The area has raised three presidents and is the home to the University of Virginia, which was founded by Thomas Jefferson in 1825. The city has earned a reputation as a writers' and readers' paradise, with more newspaper readers per capita than anywhere else in the nation. The city is also the home to many prominent writers including John Grisham, Rita Mae Brown, and past acclaimed authors such as Edgar Alan Poe and William Faulkner.

Charlottesville's close proximity to the Blue Ridge Mountains and the Atlantic Ocean provides a mild climate with four distinct seasons. The city and surrounding area, with its spectacular scenery of Central Virginia, is blessed with a rich historical legacy including Monticello (the home of Thomas Jefferson, which sits on a nearby mountain overlooking Charlottesville), the Ash Lawn-Highland home of James Monroe, and Montpelier (the home of James and Dolly Madison).

From the window of his room facing east on the third floor of the Doubletree Hotel, Spence could easily see the cars in the hotel parking lot. His challenge was not to become distracted with the beauty of the grounds of the Doubletree and the view of the mountains to the east. Shortly before 9:00 a.m., Spence saw the gray Toyota Camry pull into the parking lot, and he saw the driver, a woman, place a tissue box on the dash of the car. Spence had prearranged for one of the valets to escort Winslow, once identified, to the lobby of the hotel and then to the first-floor elevator. As soon as Spence saw the tissue box placed on the dash, he telephoned to the valet desk just outside the entrance to the hotel and provided the description of Winslow's car to the valet.

As soon as Jill and the valet reached the elevator and began to enter the elevator, the valet quickly stepped out of the elevator and Spence stepped into the elevator. Just as Spence entered the elevator, the door closed, leaving just Spence and Winslow alone in the elevator.

"We meet in the strangest places," Jill said as she smiled at Spence.

With a smile but with a look of strictly business, Spence opened his jacket and pulled out two strange-looking foot-long instruments. Jill suspected what was coming next.

"I apologize, but I suspect you knew this was coming. Please raise your arms," Spence said firmly but politely. Jill did as instructed. With her arms raised, Spence ran each of the instruments closely along the many curves of her body as he listened for any electronic warning signals from the instruments that would indicate Winslow had any tracking or transmission devices on her body.

Jill smiled as she attempted to engage Spence in conversation. "Would you like for me to take something off? Would that help with the search?" she said in her best innocent voice. She was pleased that she had worn a bra and a blouse that further enhanced her figure and that she had applied her most seductive perfume.

"Depends." Spence laughed.

"That's what I thought!" Jill giggled as she feigned embarrassment.

"Okay. Off to my room," Spence said as the elevator door opened at the third floor.

"My dream's come true!" Jill laughed, as much as she also hoped.

Jill followed closely behind Spence until he reached room 324. Spence stopped, placed the electronic key in the slot and opened the door. They both quickly entered the room. Jill could see that the room appeared not to have previously been occupied; the bed was still made. However, there was a pot of coffee, a carafe of juice, and a tray of fruit and danish pastries.

"Would you like some coffee?" Spence asked as he stepped toward the tray with the coffee and juice.

"Black with a little sugar and maybe also a small danish," Jill said as she settled into one of the two large overstuffed chairs next to a coffee table. Spence placed the coffee and the tray with the fruit and pastries on the coffee table, poured two cups of coffee and sat in the chair facing Jill across from the coffee table.

"Well is this business, or do you just like to frisk government agents?" Jill said with a smile as she savored the first sip of coffee.

"Is that a complaint?" Spence said with his devilish grin.

Jill thought, *Actually, it felt quite good*, but she did not respond other than to provide her most seductive yet reserved smile. A smile that she hoped said, "I am available but not easy to get—but the reward is well worth the effort." She let her smile linger as she locked her soft brown eyes on Spence's steely eyes. She had not been able to forget their first meeting at Quigley's in Naperville. She had been yearning to come in contact again with this mysterious, seductive man. She had abandoned her safeguards and had been drawn to the sexual attractiveness of this man of intrigue.

Spence was immediately reminded, *Never mix business with pleasure*. He had violated this rule once—in Australia, and his heart was still there, those many thousands of miles away. He knew he would never betray Piper no matter how great the temptation that might be placed in his way, and clearly Jill represented a temptation that might, otherwise, be very appealing.

"We got your guy," Spence informed Jill without any fanfare.

"How? Who? Where? How did you do it?" Jill believed what she was hearing but was stunned. How could this stranger deliver so quickly on a case that had provided no apparent clues and that seemed so impossible to solve—at least it had continued to seem impossible to her team of highly skilled and experienced Treasury agents.

"There is always a little luck involved in any case. Well, sometimes a lot of luck," Spence said in response to Jill's series of quick rambling questions.

"My guess is that there was a lot more than luck involved!" Jill countered as she regained her composure. She was now deeply engaged in thinking of the case, and her thoughts of moving forward a relationship with Spence or perhaps "getting lucky" had taken a back seat. Perhaps another day.

"In any event, we got your guy and will have the bank's funds safely returned soon."

"You mean the $10 million, all of the ten million!" Jill said with further surprise.

"Yes, and there is one other thing that you may find of interest," Spence said and then paused to build anticipation and to underscore the importance of his words that were to follow. "How would you like to grab the group that is forging US corporate bonds and other securities?"

Jill looked at Spence in disbelief. "How do you know about that?!"

"Do you want the guy or not?" Spence said as he flashed his mischievous grin.

"Of course. Of course, we do. But how did you find out about the forgeries? This matter has been kept extremely confidential, and only the highest levels of the Treasury Department are aware of the problem, and, even then, we do not know the extent of the problem, but we think it is very serious."

"Well, it's your lucky day. You are going to get two for one. Two world-class criminals for the price of one!" Spence said as he laughed and then took a bite of a danish and reached for his coffee cup.

Jill looked puzzled. "What do you mean?" she asked.

"The same guy who was the mastermind behind the Pittsburgh bank theft is also the mastermind and leader of the US corporate bond forging operation. I must tell you, the quality of the forgeries is excellent—world class."

"Yeah, we know about the quality. Are you sure it's the same guy?" Jill questioned.

"Oh yeah. Same guy. We located him and have more than sufficient evidence. For your information, he is not a resident of the United States," Spence explained while careful not to provide any more information than necessary.

"Where is he? I need to know so we can contact the appropriate local officials and arrange for the arrest and then start the extradition procedures to get this guy back to the United States for prosecution."

"Oh, don't worry about those time-consuming and troublesome procedures; extradition is just part of the services we provide. We like to deliver the bad guys right to your doorstep. Much less trouble for you!" Spence said laughing.

Jill glared at Spence for a few moments with a stern glaze and thought again, *Who is this mystery man, and how is it that he can be so much more effective than some of the world's best-equipped and experienced criminal justice organizations?* "And what's in this for you?" she asked.

Spence grinned. "Well, beyond our fee, just the pleasure of taking one more world-class criminal out of circulation and the pleasure of being of assistance to a lady in need!" He paused and then explained the fee comment. "Regarding our fee, we will just take our charges out of a portion of the cash we recover. Assuming everything goes well, we plan to deliver ten million to the Pittsburgh bank and at least twenty million to the Treasury Department to cover the losses arising from the forgeries."

Jill was stunned and at a loss for words other than to say, "But how?"

"We take care of the details. All you need to do is just wait for our call with further instructions. You will be contacted with the instructions on where to pick up your query—hopefully within the next two weeks."

With that, Spence rose and stepped next to Jill and kissed her lightly on the cheek and said, "Nice working with you. Most likely we will never meet again, but if you ever need anything, call the confidential telephone number and ask for the Travelin' Man. I've got to run." Jill rose and began to say something, but Spence placed his index finger on his lips indicating nothing more need be said between the two of them. His last comment was, "Wait ten minutes or so before you leave." He walked to the door, opened it, and then turned toward Jill, who was standing near the other side of the room still in somewhat a state of confusion and disbelief. Spence winked, closed the door, and left Jill Winslow alone in the room pondering what was coming next.

Chapter 52

Bandito's Bar and Restaurant is a quaint, sometimes lively—especially when the cruise ship is at the dock—cozy, laid-back, beach restaurant snuggled on the beach in Costa Maya. The restaurant faces the beach and the sparkling blue waters of the Caribbean on one side and is surrounded on the other three sides by beautiful tall green palm trees with their upper branches waving in the ocean breezes. The menu describes Bandito's as "a taste of the Caribbean and a taste of civilization deep in the Mayan Jungle." A sign prominently displayed inside the restaurant and a similar message on the menu attempts to assure the patrons (most likely intended for gringos and any Europeans that might venture into the restaurant) not to worry essentially about Montezuma's revenge. The message reads, "Don't worry—all food, drinks, and ice are prepared with purified water from our reverse osmosis system."

Spence sat at a corner table with Rafael Posada and Ginger. Although he appreciated the thoughtfulness of the messages and the reassurances of Bandito's, he thought it best, especially given the need to be at the top of his game over the next few days, to not take Bandito's entirely at their word. No sense taking an unnecessary risk. The cute young waitress stood waiting to take drink orders. As he kept the possibility of severe stomach pains, not to mention the many other unpleasant side effects from Montezuma's revenge in mind, Spence placed his drink order. "I'll have an ice-cold *cerveza,* but hold the ice! Make it a Pacifico." The waitress turned to Rafael and asked if he would like a *cerveza,* perhaps a Corona.

"No way; no burro pee for me!" Rafael said.

After feigning seriousness and withholding their laughter, Rafael and Ginger then followed suit and ordered two beers; both ordered Dos Equis XX Special Lagers.

"Gracias," the waitress said laughing as she turned and headed toward the bar.

It was now shortly after three o'clock Monday afternoon. Rafael had met Spence and Ginger in Cancun early that morning, and they had driven together from Cancun to Costa Maya. The plan was to have lunch at Bandito's posing as tourists and for Spence and Ginger to see the place and to get the "lay of the land" and then meet with the Costa Maya team at the safe house that Rafael had established on the outskirts of town. The following day, Tuesday, would be a day of reviewing and fine-tuning the plans with Rafael and the "incursion team" and finalizing the timing with the second team, which was already in place in Puerto Carrillo. The incursion team had been in place in Costa Maya for three days; they were posing as divers and adventure-seeking tourists.

The waitress returned carrying a tray with three cold beers. Ginger could not help but notice that when the waitress placed the beer in front of Spence, the waitress bent slightly at the waist. Just enough that her loose and low-cut blouse faced Spence and invited a view of her cleavage. Ginger thought, *On the prowl for a good tip! Flashing some flesh will not get you anywhere with this gringo! I know; I have tried!* Spence lifted his beer toward Rafael and Ginger and, as soon as the waitress had departed, said, "To a fun time, compadres." In the background, Spence could hear one of his favorite tunes from the sixties, "Suspicion," and he lingered on the haunting melodies of the song.

As is the accepted practice in most of the resorts and bars in Mexico, beer is served, especially for gringos, with a slice of lime stuffed in the neck of the bottle. Most tourists expect to see the lime in the bottle. However, most locals won't have it and claim the lime is a gimmick for *los turistas.*

Spence was fully aware of the tradition and how the practice was disavowed in many areas outside of the United States. He recalled that one story has it that in the not so distant past, a beer marketer came up with the idea to place a lime in each bottle as the beer was being served. So far, no one has stepped forward to claim credit for the idea. Another story says the lime's acidity helps cut the slightly sweet corn flavor of the beers. Another story says that cans of beer would be stored in dusty conditions. Drinkers naturally wanted to clean up the mouth of the can, and they found a wedge of lime to be a perfect solution. This explanation may make some sense since limes may have already been on the table for serving with shots of Tequila. Still another account says the wedge of lime could be laid on top of the opening to keep flies from getting into the beer. Then again, perhaps the more plausible explanation might be that early bottles of Mexican beer were said to be sealed with linerless caps, resulting in a ring of rust on the bottle rim. A swipe of lime, and the bottle came clean. In any event, the lime in the bottle was clearly now a marketing ploy directed toward the fun-loving tourists.

As the waitress placed the beer on the table in front of Spence, he smiled and turned toward Rafael and with the scene from *Treasure of the Sierra Madre* in mind loudly said, "Limones, we don't need no stinking limones!" The waitress left the table, again in laughter.

After a somewhat reasonable passage of time, the perky, young, dark-haired, well-tanned Mexican waitress returned and asked in broken but endearing English, "What would you like?" She smiled at Spence as she asked the question. She seemed like a lively type who was quite accustomed to flirting with the more attractive members of the opposite sex—especially the ones who she pegged as most likely to be the one picking up the check. Spence returned the smile as Ginger, in perfect Spanish, ordered a grouper sandwich. Spence and Rafael, both in Spanish—although clearly Rafael's Spanish was much better than that of Spence—both selected the Caribbean jerk beef sandwiches, cooked sweet peppers to be shared by all three, and another round of beer. Spence told the waitress to tell the kitchen to wait thirty minutes or so before delivering their lunch but not to wait on the beer!

It was important that they played the part of free-spirited tourists with no discussion of the mission, at least while at Bandito's. Spence, Rafael, and Ginger spent the next couple of hours enjoying lunch and watching the coming and going of the Bandito patrons and pretending to be enamored with the laid-back activities on the beach. As soon as the waitress had taken their order for lunch, Ginger stood and removed her shorts and blouse, revealing a very attractive blue and white two-piece swimsuit. When Spence saw Ginger's swimsuit, his mind immediately brought into focus a vision of Piper Morgan in her swimsuit on the beach off the coast of Australia, and he was reminded of the wonderful time he and Piper had shared. He was reminded how much he yearned to see her again.

"Join me!" Ginger urged Spence and Rafael.

"You go ahead," Rafael said to Spence. "I will stay here and watch the beer!" Spence knew what Rafael really meant and was saying was that Spence should go ahead and play the part of a fun-loving tourist and that Rafael would stay in the restaurant and watch the general activities within the restaurant. For the next half an hour or so, Ginger and Spence enjoyed the refreshing waters of the Caribbean as the bright rays of the afternoon sun warmed their bodies. Just as they returned to their table after having toweled themselves dry, the waitress returned with their lunch, careful to ensure that Spence saw her wink with her approval as she gave his lean body a quick inspection.

After lunch, the three jumped into Rafael's Land Rover and drove to the safe house, reversing directions on a few occasions to ensure they were not being followed. By the time they arrived at the safe house, it was around six in the evening. When they arrived at the safe house, Rafael introduced Spence as "Greg Winston" and Ginger as "Heather Monroe." As far as the assembled team was concerned, there was no need for them to know the true identities of Spence and Ginger. Rafael told the team that they would all meet at nine o'clock in the morning for a final review of the operational plan and to ensure that everyone understood their individual assignments. After dinner, prepared by Rafael and one of the team members, the group of eight, including Spence, Ginger, and Rafael, spent a couple of hours playing cards and just relaxing in general. Spence was impressed with the high quality of the five other team members that Rafael had recruited on behalf of the organization's efforts in South and Central America and the Caribbean.

At nine the next morning, after Rafael had prepared a light breakfast, the team members assembled for the final briefing and mission review. Spence, Rafael, and Ginger had carefully reviewed and discussed the mission plan during the car trip from Cancun to Puerto Costa Maya. The plan consisted of the following three tactical components:

1. The grab (Puerto Costa Maya)
2. The funds transfer (Carillo Costa Maya)
3. The delivery (Vero Beach, Florida)

The team members were privy to only the portions of the plan necessary for them to complete their respective assigned tasks. Even Rafael was not aware of the location (Vero Beach) for the delivery. The strategic plan that Spence had created and the tactical actions that had been identified with the assistance of Ginger and Rafael provided for the team in Costa Maya to snatch

Ernesto Cardeno and "escort" him to a pickup zone where he would be transported to a location in the United States and then held until the US Treasury officials could place Cardeno under arrest.

The second part of the plan called for the team members, with high levels of electronic computerized experience and expertise, to initiate bank wire transfers against Cardeno's bank accounts, to essentially wipe out his ill-gained account balances. Without the accumulated cash and without Cardeno, Cardeno's group would cease to be effective. Cardeno's bank balances would be routed in such a way that the funds transfers would be almost impossible to trace, with the funds ultimately landing in three accounts. Ten million five hundred thousand dollars would be directed to an account at the Pittsburgh bank (the original ten million dollars that Cardeno had stolen together with interest!); $5 million would be directed to a numbered account in Zurich, Switzerland (for the account of Spence Harrington as the fee for the project), and the balance, in the range of $20 million, would be directed to an existing account at the Bank of New York held in the name of the US Treasury. The $20 million would be available to apply to losses caused by Cardeno's forging activities.

The "snatch" of Cardeno was scheduled to occur the following day after Cardeno finished his normal Wednesday lunch and early afternoon of drinking at Bandito's.

CHAPTER 53

It was another beautiful morning along the coast in Puerto Costa Maya. The team led by Rafael Posada had just completed the final walk-through of the Costa Maya phase of the plan, which was the "grab" of Ernesto Cardeno. For the next couple of hours, before heading for their respective preassigned positions, the team members were to spend their time ensuring that all of the items they had brought with them had been packed and that the safe house had been carefully sanitized.

After briefing the team and walking through the plan with the Costa Maya team one last time, Spence, Ginger, and Rafael placed a secure telephone call to the leader of the electronics team in Puerto Carillo to review the coordination of the timing of the "funds transfer" phase also one last time. The plan called for the grab of Cardeno in Costa Maya and the wiping out and transferring of his bank accounts in Puerto Carrillo at approximately the same time. The intent was to have Cardeno and his ill-gained cash disappear at the same time and to leave Cardeno's organization befuddled and in disarray.

It was now shortly after noon, and Rafael, Ginger, and Spence were sitting at one of the tables in Bandito's with a strategic view of the table where Ernesto Cardeno was sitting alone having lunch. The waitress, the same waitress from two days earlier, was flirting again with Spence with the hopes, most likely, of perhaps enhancing her opportunity for an even larger gratuity. The three ordered drinks and then lunch. As they watched Cardeno during lunch, it very much appeared, by his relaxed behavior, that he was intending, as usual, to turn lunch into an activity of leisure. It appeared that he had no intention of leaving Bandito's anytime soon.

However, thirty minutes or so later, Spence watched as Cardeno reached into his pants pocket and opened a clamshell cellular telephone. Cardeno seemed to be listening intently. As soon as Cardeno appeared to have finished the telephone call, he caught the attention of a waitress and motioned for his check. Shortly after the waitress left the small tray with the check on the table, Spence saw Cardeno toss some peso currency on top of the check and then begin to quickly push his chair back from the table. Cardeno walked briskly toward the door of Bandito's.

Although Rafael and Ginger had intentionally not been watching Cardeno, Spence had whispered to them that something was changing from Cardeno's normal routine. As soon as Cardeno turned his back to their table and began to walk toward the door, Spence caught the eye of the admiring waitress and motioned her to their table. She was quick to respond, particularly since this was the first time that Spence had shown any real interest in her. When she reached the table, Spence asked the amount of the check. She started to turn, presumably to get the check, but Spence stopped her.

"Senorita, your service has been exquisite." Spence smiled. "Please accept this in payment of our bill with our most gracious appreciation." He placed in her hand enough pesos to settle their bill and still leave a very nice tip. The waitress scanned the wad of pesos and quickly realized the amount that was to be hers after deducting the amount she would need to remit to the house. "Gracias. Gracias, senor," the waitress said in her most sexy voice hoping that he would return again.

Spence, Rafael, and Ginger quickly, but without causing attention, left the table and walked to the door of Bandito's. The plan had been to "snatch" Cardeno two blocks from Bandito's, along a tree-lined path, as he took his normal leisurely walk back to his seaside villa. However, Spence, Rafael, and Ginger were shocked as they walked out of Bandito's to see Cardeno on the other side of the street. He was getting on an ATV (all-terrain vehicle). This, they had not planned for, and they had no contingency plan. Cardeno had always walked.

Rafael looked at Ginger and Spence. It was clear that his thought was, *What do we do now?*

Spence was not happy, not happy at all. It was highly unusual for the organization to have overlooked such a possibility. However, he was, if nothing else, pragmatic, and there was no value at this moment in wasting time on what could have or should have been done, but rather their energy needed to be focused on what could now be done. What resources were available? At this point, without transportation, the chances of snatching Cardeno seemed slim to none, if Cardeno was allowed to ride off into the distance. His mind was racing as he quickly considered and dismissed alternatives. As he evaluated the possibilities, all of a sudden his vision locked in on movement a block or so away coming in their direction.

It was amazing. Spence's first thought as soon as he realized what was coming in their direction was, *Better lucky than good*—although a little of both always seemed to be the best formula. Now just to their right was a string of all-terrain vehicles coming down the dusty street in their direction. Spence could see that Cardeno had incurred some difficulty in starting his ATV, but Spence could now see sand being blown from the exhaust of Cardeno's ATV that he was about ready to ride. Cardeno pulled out onto the street and was heading in an opposite direction from the string of ATVs.

Spence shouted to Rafael, "Follow me!" as he stepped out into the street and in front of the approaching string of all-terrain vehicles. It was clear to Spence that the loose string of ATVs was a shore excursion for tourists from the cruise ship. Spence waited for the first couple of ATVs to speed past, knowing that the lead ATV would be the tour leader. After the third ATV passed, Spence immediately flagged the next three to a stop and flashed a badge. To a tourist, who most likely would never have seen a Mexican police badge before, the Federales badge that Spence flashed sure looked authentic.

In his best possible broken and intentionally excited Spanish, Spence turned to the three ATV drivers and said, "This is official police business; we must have your ATVs." He then smiled as he, Rafael, and Ginger began to get on the ATVs. "Where are you from?" All three answered almost at the same time, "From southern Indiana. We are from the cruise ship. There are a couple more with our group," as they pointed to the next two ATVs, whose riders seemed puzzled and increasingly concerned about what was happening.

Spence hesitated for a moment. He would have loved to be able to visit and to know if these pleasant three were familiar with the area where he had grown up in Indiana, but his need for security would not have allowed it, and, as importantly, they had no time. These folks seemed to be nice people and seemed to be excited to be part of the excitement, now that it was clear they were not being placed in danger. Spence quickly reached into his pocket and pulled out the rest of his pesos, the equivalent of slightly more than a thousand US dollars and distributed the currency in rapid fashion among the three.

"Gracias, my friends. Have a wonderful time on the rest of your vacation. Adios!" Spence yelled as he, Rafael, and Ginger began to speed away in pursuit of Cardeno. The group of Hoosiers waved as they shared the excitement of what had just happened.

Spence could see that Cardeno was now two blocks or so away and the distance was growing. Fortunately, Cardeno was not aware that he was being tracked, and he was driving at a leisurely pace down the street. In his mind, Spence measured the distance and the speed of Cardeno against the speed his group was now traveling and knew at these speeds that within a few blocks they would overtake Cardeno. They were fortunate. He was traveling alone. Spence also knew that Cardeno was not armed since Cardeno believed he was completely safe in his Costa Maya hideaway, and it was known, or at least believed, that he did not carry a gun. However, Spence, Rafael, and Ginger were well armed with the latest lightweight, high-performance, fully silenced, semiautomatic handguns.

After traveling another three blocks or so at high speed, and as they neared the outskirts of the small village, Spence and Rafael began to pull alongside Cardeno's ATV. Cardeno looked to one side and then to the other. As he looked to his left, he saw Spence flash the Federales badge. Cardeno was surprised and frightened. This could not be good, and he realized he was being pursued. It did not matter what the grievance, he knew there could be numerous reasons for the pursuit. Cardeno knew that he must not be detained and that he must not allow his ATV to be stopped. He momentarily smiled and issued a friendly wave to his pursuers and nodded his head as if to indicate that he would come to a stop. But just as quickly, he hit the accelerator and sped ahead, leaving his pursuers twenty feet or so behind.

Spence immediately pushed the accelerator on his ATV to the limit and raced to stay up with Cardeno. Rafael and Ginger fell in line behind Spence.

They were now all four racing down a paved, single lane, dusty, pothole dotted road outside of the village heading into a more and more remote-appearing area. The performance of the four ATVs seemed relatively equal, and while Cardeno had not been able to pull ahead measurably, his three pursuers had not been able to shorten his lead.

After another ten minutes or so of high pursuit, Cardeno suddenly slid his ATV sideways on the paved road and then sped down a slight embankment and onto a trail that led toward the jungle. Spence, Rafael, and Ginger followed in close pursuit with ATVs noisily throwing dust and dirt and scaring the birds and nearby wildlife. As the trail entered the jungle, Spence realized that they must be traveling on a trail cut for the ATV shore tour excursions. The trail—and it was a trail not any type of formal road—was rough and narrow and was taking them over many rocky areas and through low water-filled areas. Spence knew it was very unlikely that they could overtake Cardeno as long as they were on the jungle trail since the trail was so narrow. They just needed to maintain pursuit and wait for the next best opportunity.

Another fifteen minutes or so had passed. Spence's arms and backside were beginning to become weary from the continuous jolts and hard bounces. He could only imagine how Ginger was feeling from the continuous pounding as the large tires of the ATVs bounced the riders from one rock to another along the trail. Just as the pain was reaching the point where his mind was beginning to question how much longer he could endure, he saw ahead that there appeared to be more sunlight and saw that Cardeno had made a hard turn to his left and had momentarily disappeared. Moments later, when Spence reached the area, he found that the jungle trail had terminated at a paved road that seemed to lead back in the general direction of the town. Spence, still followed by Rafael and Ginger, made a hard left turn and, reaching full speed, continued in pursuit of Cardeno, who Spence could now again see was the equivalent of perhaps two blocks ahead. It was a relief to be racing on a paved road as opposed to the very rough jungle trail. It was now almost fun. Well, that might be somewhat of a stretch since they did not know what lay ahead, and they had no assurance that Cardeno's capture was assured.

They were now on the open road, and Spence was doing everything possible to coax the maximum speed from his ATV. He was slowly cutting into the distance between him and his prey. He was now less than fifty feet behind and closing. Cardeno turned to check on his lead. Spence could see by the surprised look on

Cardeno's face that Cardeno was becoming desperate knowing that the pursuers were committed and relentless in their pursuit. They were nearing the outskirts of the village, and the road was now running along the beach with the ocean to the right. Cardeno was racing at full speed and swerving from one side to the other on the road in an attempt to keep Spence and the two other pursuers from pulling alongside. However, Spence was now right on Cardeno's tail. That was the good news. The not so good news was that Spence was so close that he was being pummeled by the dust and sand being thrown by Cardeno's ATV. Spence knew, or suspected, that Rafael and Ginger were experiencing the same difficulties. Just then, both Cardeno and Spence swerved almost in unison to miss a dog that was wandering across the road and oblivious to the racing ATVs.

Cardeno made a desperate turn to his right. He sped over a small sand dune, past a small beach sandwich and beer shack, and then onto the beach. Spence followed, but Rafael and Ginger wisely sped ahead on the road watching for the best opportunity to exit onto the beach at a point ahead of Cardeno. A few minutes later, Rafael saw what appeared to be a path between two sand dunes and wheeled his ATV to the right and onto the beach followed closely by Ginger. The beach was relatively remote, and no one was on the beach along this stretch. Rafael and Ginger were now racing toward Cardeno, who was being pursued by Spence. As Cardeno neared Rafael and Ginger at full speed, he panicked. Rather than playing a game of chicken or perhaps attempting to fake them one way and then going the other way passing them, he turned away from the ocean toward the sand dunes. Within moments, the tires of Cardeno's ATV began to slow from the loose sand, and his ATV became mired in the sand. Spence, Rafael, and Ginger circled Cardeno with their ATVs. They were exhausted but no more so than Cardeno.

"Who are you, and what do you want!?" Cardeno screamed in an exhausted and frightened voice in Spanish.

"Well, sir, the answer to that question may take a bit of time to explain. Time that we do not have at this moment!" Spence responded quickly.

"You're gringos!"

Cardeno shouted with concern in his voice. He knew that he could, most likely, bribe his way out of trouble with the local police. But this was different. This was serious. He could tell from the chase and from their demeanor that these folks were professionals. Professionals!

"I am just a tourist from Mexico City. I thought you were bandits," Cardeno said, hoping that he might persuade these gringos that they had misidentified their objective.

"Now, now Ernesto. Shame on you. We know you are Ernesto Cardeno! We also know that you have been busy enriching yourself at the expense of the US taxpayers," Spence said as he admonished Cardeno.

"Good luck getting me back to the United States!" Cardeno growled and laughed.

"Oh, I don't think luck will come into play. Do you?" Spence chuckled. At that moment, Cardeno lurched slightly backward as he was hit in the shoulder by a small syringe fired from an injector held by Rafael. Cardeno turned toward Spence and began to form a word before his head nodded forward, his eyes closed, and he collapsed onto the steering wheel of his ATV. Cardeno had been injected with a strong sedative that would keep him peacefully asleep for the next several hours.

CHAPTER 54

The private plane piloted by Jack Andrews was now gaining speed on takeoff from the Cancun International Airport on a route that would take the flight to an unregistered abandoned landing strip near Miami and then from there to a landing strip maintained by the Piper Aircraft Company near Vero Beach, Florida. In addition to Andrews, the passengers on the plane were Ernesto Cardeno and three guards from the organization. The mission was to deliver the still-drugged Cardeno to the location where Cardeno was to be delivered to the US Treasury officials. After being apprehended in Puerto Costa Maya, Cardeno had been kept sedated and had been driven to Cancun by Rafael, Spence, and Ginger. To this point, the mission had been a complete success, except for the ATV adventure. Not only had Cardeno been captured, but all of the Cardeno's bank accounts had been cleaned out, and the funds had been wired to the accounts designated by Spence in the United States.

Rafael had stayed behind in Mexico. Spence and Ginger had taken separate flights to Orlando, where they had rented a car and driven south on I-95 to the Vero Beach area.

Vero Beach is located on the Atlantic side of Florida some 135 miles north of Miami in Indian River County. Vero Beach is a community with a population of slightly less than twenty thousand and is the home of Dodgertown—where the Los Angeles Dodgers have held their spring training since 1948—tourism, and citrus fruit packing. Vero Beach is known for its outstanding beaches and pirate lore. As part of Florida's Treasure Coast, Vero is situated north of South Florida's Gold Coast and just south of Sebastian Inlet, the surf capital of the East Coast. The downtown community of Vero Beach is separated from the beach by the Intracoastal Waterway. However, along the ocean, across the causeway to the east, is the central beach business district, and to the north along Highway A1A, for several miles, are numerous world-recognized exclusive and very expensive residential areas occupied, for the most part, during the winter months by "snowbirds" from the north. Also, a few miles to the north is the Walt Disney Vero Beach resort—a beautiful, peaceful, beachside resort that is much less well known than the Disney resorts in the Orlando area but with views and amenities that rival the Orlando locations.

Spence and Ginger were now in Vero Beach and were having dinner on the beach at the renowned Ocean Grill. The Ocean Grill was built over sixty years ago by an eccentric entrepreneur on a sand dune overlooking the rolling Atlantic. The restaurant was built with pecky cypress, mahogany, and wrought iron and was furnished with Spanish nautical antiques. Over the years, given the location, atmosphere, and excellent food and service, the Ocean Grill has become a landmark and a highly desired location to enjoy lunch or dinner.

They had just ordered dinner. Ginger had ordered the baked brie with sweet chili drizzle as an appetizer and the Indian River crab cakes—fresh backfin claw meat combined with spices and covered with cracker meal and deep-fried. Spence ordered the "wedge"—a wedge of iceberg lettuce with chopped tomatoes, bacon, and sweet blue cheese dressing. For the main course, Spence ordered the legendary stone crab claws. He had read that the stone crab claws were harvested (legally) from October 15 through May 15. The crabs are caught and claws removed, and then the animals are released back to the ocean to regenerate new claws. The Ocean Grill stone crab claws are served, much to the delight of Spence and Ginger—who shared some of Spence's claws—chilled with creamy mustard sauce on the side.

Spence and Ginger had arrived in the Vero Beach area early that afternoon and had checked into the Disney Resort. Spence had stayed at the resort a few years earlier, not long after the beach resort had opened, and had found the resort to be a wonderful place secluded away from other intrusive development that plagues most other resorts. As Ginger explored the Disney resort, she quickly understood why Spence had recommended that they spend the next two days at this wonderful location. Their plan called for them to stay in the area until Winslow and her team had been alerted and until Winslow arrived and arrested Cardeno, who was to be held at another location just off Highway A1A.

Just as Spence and Ginger were finishing dessert, a piece of key lime pie that they were sharing, Spence's cellular telephone silently vibrated. Spence opened the clamshell telephone, quietly listened, and then said, "I understand. Two o'clock tomorrow afternoon."

Spence turned to Ginger, "Our friend is tucked away safely. All we have to do now is contact Winslow and arrange delivery."

Ginger nodded her understanding and pleasure. "Want me to reach Winslow?" Spence nodded yes.

The call to Winslow was a call that Spence had been looking forward to for some time. The race through the jungle and the dirt and sweat would be but a small price in return for the satisfaction of hearing the disbelief in Jill Winslow's voice that the organization had really delivered the virtually impossible.

"Hello," Jill Winslow answered as Ginger handed the telephone to Spence.

"Jill, this is—" Spence was cut off by Jill before he could continue.

"Well, hello, mysterious Travelin' Man. What is your intent bothering a young lady this late in the evening? Could be you're interrupting something important or quite special at the moment." Winslow chuckled.

"Really?" Spence countered.

"No, not really," Jill responded somewhat dejectedly.

"We have your package. All tidy and ready for pickup," Spence announced.

"And to what interesting locale do I travel to this time?" she asked.

"Fly to Vero Beach, Florida, the day after tomorrow. You will need to arrive at the following destination at 2:00 p.m. Mr. Ernesto Cardeno will be asleep and awaiting your pickup, at bungalow number 12 at the Driftwood Inn north of Vero Beach. He will be alone."

"That's it?!" Winslow challenged.

"Is there something more you need? You know we can't deliver him to your doorstep!" Spence laughed.

"Oh, I don't know. Maybe some solid evidence. I'm just guessing, but I may have a hard time getting a conviction by just testifying that Ernesto Cardeno is responsible for the crimes based on the word of some unidentified mysterious man."

"Oh, that!" Spence laughed. "I guess I have left out a few important things. First, the $10 million plus interest has been wired to the Pittsburgh bank from Mr. Cardeno's accounts. In addition, his remaining ill-gained funds from the forgery activities, after deducting our fee, have been wired to the US Treasury. I would imagine you should be getting an excited thank-you call from the Pittsburgh bank officials early tomorrow morning. Oh, and one last thing. You will be receiving a Federal Express delivery at your office tomorrow morning with all the evidence you need to convict Cardeno for the Pittsburgh bank case and for a conviction on several counts of forging US corporate and Treasury bonds."

"You've got to be kidding!" Jill said in disbelief.

"What about extradition?!" Jill went on to ask.

"The documents included in the Federal Express package will clearly show, no matter what Cardeno claims to the contrary, that he came to the United States voluntarily and that he has been in the United States for at least the past week," Spence assured Jill. "Among other supporting evidence of his stay in the United States, the package will include hotel receipts, restaurant receipts, and a car rental receipt all in Cardeno's name. Even a ticket for having been stopped for speeding on I-95."

"Just part of the full service we provide. Glad to be able to be of help and to be able to be a part of cleaning up the environment!" Spence chuckled.

"Will I see you when I arrive in Florida?" Winslow said, hoping but knowing the answer.

"No. He is all yours. Gotta go. Take care," Spence said as he closed the clamshell face of the telephone.

"You too!" Jill whispered as she heard the dial tone begin signaling that Spence was no longer on the line.

CHAPTER 55

Spence and Ginger were safely back in Burlington. What a change from the warm, sunny climates of Costa Maya and southern Florida. Spence was sitting at his desk with a view looking out the large window of his den toward Lake Champlain through the now leaf-barren trees. The fireplace was crackling on the other side of the room. It was a gray day with low-hanging clouds and lightly falling snow as is normally the case in early December. It was a nice day to be inside with a good book or curled up reviewing and catching up on various documents and reports.

Spence and Ginger had returned to Burlington late the night before after having watched, unnoticed from a bungalow across the street in Florida, as Jill Winslow accompanied by numerous Treasury agents raided bungalow 12 and arrested the sleeping Cardeno. The organization personnel had continued to keep Cardeno in a light drug-induced sleep during the past two days. Local ABC, NBC, and CBS as well as CNN television film crews had been alerted, apparently by Winslow, and were stationed a block or so from the bungalow waiting to film the activities and the arrest of a major criminal. A few representatives from the television crews had been allowed to accompany the Treasury agents when they made the arrest, although the crews were kept at a safe distance until the arrest was made.

One of the personnel from the organization was posing as a television crew member and was able to observe the arrest. He reported back to Spence and Ginger, that, as anticipated, when Cardeno was awakened by the Treasury agents and informed that he was being arrested by agents from the US Treasury, Cardeno's first words were, "You have no jurisdiction here! You cannot arrest me in Mexico!" He was immediately reminded by Winslow, as the cameras rolled, that he was in Florida, to stop the foolishness, and that he was under arrest. The television films showed Cardeno looking dumfounded.

Spence and Ginger had laughed when they heard the firsthand report from the organization's observer about Cardeno's claim that he was not in the United States, knowing that the Federal Express package delivered to Jill Winslow the previous day had included falsified airline ticket stubs showing Cardeno had flown several days earlier into Miami from Mexico City, a car rental receipt in Cardeno's name, and various credit card receipts for meals and various purchases that Cardeno had supposedly incurred while in the United States during the past several days. Ginger and Spence had looked at each other and smiled as if to say, "Amateur. He's up against players from a different league now!"

As Spence sat gazing out the window appreciating the beauty and peacefulness of the gently falling snow on this early-winter day in northern Vermont, he was awakened from his meandering thoughts by the sound of footsteps as Ginger entered the room.

"I've made some fine caramel coffee with whipped cream!" Ginger cheerfully announced.

"Terrific! Your caramel coffee house specialty is just the right thing for this chilly postcard Vermont winter morning," Spence said as he vigorously rubbed both of his shoulders, feigned shivering, and then flashed his devilish grin.

Ginger was carrying a tray with two mugs of coffee and a couple of iced muffins. She sat the tray on the right side of Spence's desk and then left the room for a few moments. She returned with several morning newspapers, which she also placed on one of the few open spaces on Spence's desk.

"Thought you might find the headlines interesting!" Ginger said as she handed a mug of steaming coffee to Spence.

"Great stuff!" Spence said as he savored the first taste of the caramel coffee. "Thanks."

Spence then took the first newspaper from the top of the stack of newspapers. It was the *New York Times*, his favorite morning reading. He held up the front page and immediately noticed the major headline:

> "US Treasury Agent Nabs Big Fish in Florida"
>
> Washington, DC—Jill Winslow, deputy director of the US Treasury Department and director of the department's Special Investigations Branch was instrumental in solving the $10 million theft at the First Metropolitan Bank of Pittsburgh. The US Department of the Treasury in an announcement released late yesterday disclosed that Ernesto Cardeno, a citizen of Colombia, who prior to his recent ill-advised trip to the United States had been residing in one of the coastal villages of Mexico, was arrested yesterday in Florida by deputy director Winslow and a team of agents under her direction. In addition to having been identified as the mastermind behind the theft at the First Metropolitan Bank of Pittsburgh, a crime which many banking and law enforcement officials had described as perhaps unsolvable and perhaps the "perfect crime," Cardeno has been identified as also the mastermind behind an operation that has been forging and laundering US corporate and US Treasury bonds.
>
> In an interview late yesterday, Winslow stated that the existence of the forging operation had been closely guarded within the Treasury Department and had been of the utmost concern at the highest levels of the department. She went on to state that not only is the mastermind behind the bank theft and the forging operation now in federal

custody, but also all of the stolen bank funds have been recovered together with millions of dollars of cash believed to have been generated from the forging operations.

When contacted, the director of the US Treasury released the following additional statement: "We are very proud of the work of Jill Winslow and her team and extremely pleased that these two very challenging and troublesome cases have been resolved."

Spence handed the newspaper to Ginger and just smiled. "What's next?" he asked.

"Based on the latest recommendations from our regions, there are a couple of projects of growing potential interest, one in Europe and one in the Far East but nothing that can't wait for a couple of weeks," Ginger replied knowing what was tugging at Spence's heart.

Holding the mug of still-warm coffee in his hand and gazing again out the window at the swirling snow, Spence said without looking at Ginger, "You know, I was thinking of perhaps getting to Australia to see how Piper Morgan is coming along in her new role."

"The telephone doesn't work?!" Ginger said grinning, knowing her comment would go unanswered.

Epilogue

The Falcon 900 EX taxied to a stop in the executive jet arrival area of the Sydney International Airport. Shortly after the jet came to a stop, the jet's stairway was lowered, and the red welcome mat was placed at the foot of the stairway by the ground service crew. As soon as the stairway had been lowered, a black Audi A8 pulled up alongside the jet and stopped adjacent to the stairway.

It was a beautiful spring day in Sydney, and the air was refreshing. Spence grabbed his leather duffle bag from inside the aircraft cabin and walked to the top of the open stairway. He paused just inside the aircraft, at the top of the stairway, for a few moments and was invigorated by the fresh air and sunshine. He looked down at the Audi with growing anticipation on one hand and apprehension at the same time. It was at this moment, as he stood at the top of the stairs, when he was about to embark on hopefully a life-changing relationship, and a moment when his feelings were telling him something that he already knew—that he was still at heart just that same little boy from southern Indiana—it was then that one of his favorite guiding principles came to mind.

He was reminded of the quotation from an unknown author. "What I do today is important because I am paying a day of my life for it. What I accomplish must be worthwhile because the price is high." It was a saying that had tended to keep him grounded and his life in perspective over the years.

He gazed down at Piper Morgan, who was now standing along the driver's side of the Audi. She was looking up at him, her golden hair blowing gently in the breeze, with a warm, free-spirited, and yet not so innocent inviting smile. As he stood looking down in those few moments, he knew that the reward of having Piper's love was far, far greater than the price—the commitment of his life and love. His love for Piper and her love for him was again confirmed by the warmth of her loving embrace when he reached the foot of the stairs.

But, as he held Piper tightly in his arms in the warm Australian morning sun, he knew that his search for adventure would never end.

ACKNOWLEDGMENTS AND APPRECIATION

<u>Appreciation</u>

To the readers throughout the world who have gained great enjoyment in following the adventures of Spence Harrington and Ginger Martin and to the many readers who have encountered Spence and Ginger for the first time in ***Travelin' Man***, thank you for sharing your time as the two have again unraveled another unique and fascinating mystery. If you enjoyed their exploits in ***Travelin' Man*** and their previous adventures in ***Treasure of the Sea Oats*** and would like to engage with them in their future international intrigue and crime-solving endeavors, please watch for the release of ***The Lucky Find***, a novel in which they encounter deception, danger and excitement in solving a most unusual case.

The setting for ***Travelin' Man*** was inspired by an unsolved and hard to fathom crime that occurred decades ago and is surrounded by the recollections of exotic locations once visited and dreams of places yet to be experienced.

I may wander far and wide in search of the next story but throughout every quest, I've been blessed to have the love, support and understanding of my family, friends and associates who know enough about me to leave me alone when necessary but to reel me back to reality at the right times. For this, I am extremely thankful.

I will also be eternally grateful for the many forms and expressions of praise, encouragement and kind words that were sent my way related to my first novel, ***Treasure of the Sea Oats***. Thank you so much! To know that the novel was so well received and enjoyed by so many has been of enduring pleasure and further tangible encouragement.

To the readers of my novels, you are always in my thoughts. When you choose to read any of my novels, I want you to feel as though you have not only spent your time well but that you have had a wonderful and though-provoking time and found great enjoyment as you travel vicariously by the side of the main characters while they navigate through the dangers and exploits of experiencing exotic lifestyles and solve intriguing mysteries.

Acknowledgements

Much like ***Treasure of the Sea Oats, Travelin' Man*** was a true pleasure to write as the characters responded to new challenges and experienced the thrills and excitement of enticing exotic locations as they again creatively went about surfacing the clues to solve, in this case, what was a long-unsolved crime. I found great joy in watching the tale unfold and hope you find similar enjoyment. However, as was the case with ***Treasure of the Sea Oats, Travelin' Man*** would not have been written or have been published without the enduring support and encouragement that I received and relied upon.

I am deeply grateful to my wife, Carolyn, for her loving support and for her encouragement that allows me to continue to create and be part of the adventures of two great, smart, clever, and adventuresome partners –Spence Harrington and Ginger Martin.

I can tell you more exciting and intriguing adventures are in store for these two.

I would certainly be remiss if I did not acknowledge and extend my deepest appreciation for my friend and associate Becky Spooner. Her proofreading, insights and suggestions were, as always, invaluable as the characters evolved and the story unfolded. Her enthusiastic, unquenched curiosity as to what the characters might be facing next contributed even greater enjoyment to the writing and creative process.

I am also extremely thankful for the support and encouragement of our two daughters, Holly and Heather, and their families and for the true excitement they shared upon reading both Travelin' Man and Treasure of the Sea Oats.

As the further exploits of Spence and Ginger evolved, much of my writing continued to be on extended airline flights and during cherished periods of late-evening solitude. My constant companion during those quiet periods at my writing desk, while envisioning how the adventure would next unfold, was our dog Minnie who I sincerely believe shares my love for adventure. I look forward to many more years of her quiet, peaceful support as a steadfast companion.

Travelin' Man is dedicated to our three grandchildren, Tucker, Jack and Audrey with whom we have shared wonderful adventures. May your lives always be filled with adventures that bring joy and enrichment!

About the Author

In addition to Travelin' Man, Louhon Tucker is the author of the highly acclaimed novel "Treasure of the Sea Oats."

A wide-ranging and distinguished career in international business has provided Mr. Tucker the opportunity to travel extensively to various distant world capitals and to many interesting, exotic and unusual locations around the world. His travels and adventures not only have presented him with many memorable and unique experiences, but also have brought him into contact with unique individuals, some of whom have been extremely clever and engaged in highly creative mischief.

Mr. Tucker was born and raised in South-central Indiana. He has spent the majority of his business career based in Chicago focused on international clients and on managing global business.

His small-town Indiana values, life experiences, and keen observations of people and places on an international scale, as well as his extensive knowledge and experience gained from an understanding of highly creative financial mischief provides the background for the locales and the interesting characters within his books. These characters and experiences, coupled with his ability to tell an intriguing and entertaining story, all come together again in the suspenseful and thrilling mystery adventure of Travelin' Man.

Mr. Tucker and his wife, Carolyn, reside in the Chicago area with their lovable canine friend and rascal, Minnie.